The LAST BOYFRIENDS Rules For REVENGE

The LAST BOYFRIENDS Rules For REVENGE

MATTHEW HUBBARD

DELACORTE PRESS

Text copyright © 2024 by Matthew Hubbard
Jacket art copyright © 2024 by Jess Vosseteig

All rights reserved. Published in the United States by Delacorte Press,
an imprint of Random House Children's Books, a division of
Penguin Random House LLC, New York.

Delacorte Press is a registered trademark and the colophon
is a trademark of Penguin Random House LLC.

GetUnderlined.com

Educators and librarians, for a variety of teaching tools,
visit us at RHTeachersLibrarians.com

Library of Congress Cataloging-in-Publication Data is available upon request.
ISBN 978-0-593-70717-3 (trade) — ISBN 978-0-593-70718-0 (lib. bdg.) —
ISBN 978-0-593-70719-7 (ebook)

The text of this book is set in 11.5-point Adobe Garamond Pro.
Interior design by Megan Shortt

Printed in the United States of America
10 9 8 7 6 5 4 3 2 1
First Edition

FOR EVERY QUEER PERSON
WHO HAS FOUGHT TO EXIST

AND FOR MY HUSBAND, CHRIS,
WHO NEVER STOPPED BELIEVING IN ME

THE BEST REVENGE IS BELIEVING IN YOURSELF.

–*My Dad*

One

Hiding spots were easy to find if you knew where to look.

Growing up on my grandparents' farm, I always found somewhere to disappear to when life got to be too much. Between bales of hay in the barn loft, in the old tractor shed, even in the root cellar used for tornado season. Wherever I ended up, nothing could hurt me until I decided it was time to stop hiding.

High school wasn't so simple for queer students, though, especially in Harper Valley, Alabama.

Harper Valley High School was a rectangle of a building with only one long hallway. Between the Agriculture Shop on the south end and the Media Center on the north end, there was nowhere to hide. Instead, my friends and I learned how to disappear in plain sight—stick together and do our best not to be noticed in small-town Alabama.

It had worked well for the last two years, an easy navigation around Acheron County's strict family values and obsession with HVHS's five-time state champion football team, the Mighty Lions. Until Lucas started dating Cass the Ass. Until Finley got

1

swept into the drama that was Logan James Michael the Third. Until they'd left me on the sidelines to fend for myself, a third wheel to their respective love lives.

The old, cheesy rom-coms I'd grown up watching with my grandma taught me everything I needed to know about third wheels. They were destined to be stuck in the background. And I refused to be a bystander while my friends got what I wanted.

If only they knew, I thought, gripping my backpack straps.

I pushed through the crowd and stole a glance at a group of Mighty Lions. They were gathered at the North Hall exit, waiting for the team's athletic training. And he was there like always. I told myself not to look, but Presley "Golden Boy" Daniels had just gotten a new haircut.

My eyes raked over his six-foot-two frame. Following the dip at his waist and the climb into the letter V, higher to where his neck and shoulders meet. Even higher to that golden mane of hair he'd shaved on the sides but kept long on top. The need to touch it flared through my fingertips as I followed a cascading tousle down to the most perfect lips—

"Yo, Daniels," one of the dude-bros said, nudging him. "Who's this chubbster eye-fucking you?"

Shit! I panicked, unable to move. I'd forgotten to be non-existent.

Heads swiveled toward me, including Presley's. His blue-eyed gaze pierced me before he looked away, and his varsity jacket stretched taut against his broad shoulders as he crossed his arms. "Me?" He played it off with a laugh, turning instead to his annoying best friend. "More like he's got a thing for Jackson here."

Crimson bloomed across Jackson F'ing Darcy's pale face. He shuffled his feet, scratching at his flop of brown hair. I'd worked with Jackson long enough at Magnolia Bookstore and Café to know when he was embarrassed. "Stop, dude," his deep voice grumbled as I took a step backward. "You're being an asshat."

"Who cares?" Presley retorted. "He's just a fat-ass nobody."

It took a second to realize he'd aimed those words at me. My heart tripped over itself as my thoughts raced: *Huh?* and *What did he just say?* and *Why did he call me that?* His laughter was a sucker punch to the gut, and my eyes began to water involuntarily.

Hyena cackles and the look of pity on Jackson's face chased me into the bathroom. The heavy artificial-cherry air freshener burned my nose as I breathed through the ache in my chest. As doubt tangled my thoughts. Everything I wanted to be true—needed to be true—was being called into question yet again.

Nausea forced me to the sink, my boot heels echoing across the tiled floor. I splashed water on my face and searched the mirror for a reason why he'd deliberately hurt me. Again. Instead, I found too many reminders of a background character: more than enough nose, a stress zit on my forehead too big to be hidden with concealer, my bulky body that refused to drop pounds no matter how hard I exercised.

Disgusted with myself, I dried off with a paper towel. The sound of the door creaking open snapped my attention to the mirror again. In the reflection, I watched Golden Boy Daniels step into the bathroom. He twisted the lock on the door, twisted the knot of doubt inside me.

"P-Presley," I stammered, turning around.

"Ezra," he said quietly.

I braced for another stinging insult, but his calculating glare turned toward the stalls instead, checking under the doors. A smirk tugged at his mouth when he realized we were alone. He crossed to me in three long strides and grabbed the front of my hoodie.

"S-sorry," I tried to say, but he jerked me forward. The apology died on my tongue as his lips found mine. I sighed into the kiss, clinging to him. Clinging to the reassurance he was still my boyfriend despite what'd just happened in the hallway.

If only my friends knew I wasn't a third wheel after all.

The lines of his body—the same lines my fingers had traced every time we'd been naked over the last five months—intersected with mine and unraveled my worry. His hands groped me, pulling at the waistband of the flannel pants I'd worn for Pajama Friday. "We have to hurry," he urged, mouth hot against my throat. "Gotta warm up before the game."

His fingers slipped into my boxer briefs, and I wanted to enjoy his touch. Enjoy this moment of him wanting me and ride the high before he changed his mind. In between his heavy breathing, all I could hear was laughter, though. All I could feel was his lingering touch on every part of my body I'd deemed imperfect.

"N-no," I managed to say, my voice strangled as I pushed him away. His eyes narrowed, becoming a darker shade of blue that I hadn't seen before. "Not like this."

"What's wrong?" He reached to hold me again, and I stepped back. "You never had a problem with a quick get-off before."

"Youmadefunofme," I said in a rush before I lost my nerve.

He laughed incredulously and punctuated it with an eye roll. It was another sucker punch. "Are you *actually* serious right now?"

"You called me a fat-ass nobody," I pressed, already regretting that I was wasting another stolen moment with a fight. "I thought we were . . ." I picked at my nail polish, watching flakes of gold and black drift to the floor.

"We were great until you creeped on me at school. You know I have to keep this hidden."

"S-sorr—"

"Thought I could trust you with my secret."

A breath rushed from my lungs as I looked up at him. "You can!"

"Then why are you fighting with me?" He held his hands up like he was trying to calm me down. "You know I can't come out. If my parents knew, they'd disown me. They'd kick me out of the house. Is that what you want?"

"No," I said weakly, shame flooding me as fourth block's warning bell sounded. "I would never want that."

"Definitely not horned up now. Way to ruin my big night." He turned to leave but hesitated. His face softened into a pout. "I forgive you, okay? Just don't do anything stupid again. Seriously. No one can find out I'm with you."

"I'm sorry." My words came out strangled with emotion, and I blinked away the tears.

"Don't come to the Homecoming game tonight," he added, unlocking the door. "My parents will be there, and the team'll be suspicious after that stunt you just pulled. It'd be embarrassing if you cheered me on."

I nodded once, picking at the last bits of my polish.

"Give me a head start." He left without kissing me goodbye.

I counted to twenty, forty, sixty before slipping out into the hallway. Disappearing into the background.

Lucas Rivera had been my best friend since we fought over My Little Pony dolls in pre-K (he won but let me play with him). We were like brothers now—unidentical twins, he'd say. We lived next door to one another, and for a long time it'd been just the two of us. Then Finley Lewis moved into our Middlebury subdivision the summer before eighth grade. While his father was busy opening the first Black-owned car dealership in town, he kept riding his scooter around our block until Lucas marched out to introduce himself. We all bonded over country era Taylor Swift and immediately created a besties group chat. Nothing had changed since.

Except we all got boyfriends.

I dropped my heavy backpack on the floor and fell into the creaky chair. Lucas startled, looking up from his phone. One of his immaculate eyebrows arched.

"Nothing's wrong," I lied before he could ask.

The slanting October sun winked off the sequined robe he'd bought for Pajama Friday. He sat forward to hold my gaze, but

I focused my attention on the shimmer instead. Rainbow light danced across his golden-brown skin, highlighting his enviable bone structure while he waited for me to look at him. I couldn't, though. His brown eyes had a habit of making me vomit the truth, and he wouldn't understand why I was being kept a secret. Why I so desperately wanted to be like him, like Finley. They were both . . . the opposite of me. They carried themselves with the confidence of main-character-love-interests who got all the attention.

"Wanna cut class and talk about whatever's bothering you?" he asked, resting a hand on my shoulder. "We could all get high and watch videos of Maeve Kimball putting assholes on blast."

"*Nothing* is bothering me," I emphasized.

"Fin, something's bothering him."

"What's bothering who?" Finley asked, tearing his attention away from TikTok scrolling.

"I swear to god, Fin, focus," Lucas said, snatching his phone away. Then he scowled down at it. "Why is your screen cracked again?"

"Logan knocked it out of my hands after lunch," Finley explained with a defeated groan.

"Why is LJM3 *still* being a petty spaghetti?" Lucas shook his head. "He was the dumbass who broke up with *you*."

"And why is he *still* holding a grudge?" I tacked on, attempting to steer the conversation away from my own problems and back to Finley's ex drama. "He has some deeply rooted fears that you've been lying about your feelings for him. . . ."

"I literally can't anymore with his insecurities over my bisexuality." Finley rolled his eyes, the overhead fluorescents catching the honey in them, and turned toward me. "But for real, what's bothering you, dude?"

Damn it.

"Can we not do this right now?" Avoiding their skeptical glares, I shifted my gaze to the window and tried to wrap my head around what'd happened with Presley. "It's time for our favorite show anyway."

"That's fair, booboo," Lucas began as he intently stared out the window, "because *One-Thirsty PM* never disappoints."

Outside, the door to the athletic building opened. The Mighty Lions marched out, led by the Lion King himself, Golden Boy Daniels. He squinted in the afternoon sunlight with his mane tousling in the wind. My heart lurched as he horsed around with Jackson F'ing Darcy. They raced full speed toward the field to unlock the gate. I wasn't allowed to do that. To touch him or notice him or be anything other than a *nobody*.

"Jock butt is definitely a mood lifter," Lucas whispered in awe. "Just think, Fin, you could have been out there double-cheeked up with the best of 'em."

A sardonic grimace twisted the rich brown of Finley's cheeks. "If my pop had his way, I would have made tryouts. At least Coach Carter's homophobia worked in my favor."

"I know it's toxic masculinity at its finest, but damn." Lucas fanned himself as he intently watched the butt parade. "I'd love to be in the middle of *that*."

"Does Cass know you like to objectify the dude-bros?" I asked.

"Let me live." He pushed back a lock of silver-dyed hair, muttering, "He can suck my ass for all I care."

"What happened?" I asked, turning away from the window.

"He's upset I wore a 'girl' robe today. Pulled gender-role bullshit and asked why I had to be 'so gay' all the time." His eyes raked over my body, making me cross my arms self-consciously. "Maybe I should've worn something like this boring hockey fan ensemble you call pajamas."

"Two things," I started. "One, how dare you come for Rolf 'The Iceberg' Nyberg? He's an iconic defenseman for the Bama Slammers, *and* he's openly queer."

"And two," Finley concluded for me, "why is Cass acting like my pop with the macho bullshit?"

"Bet we'll fight about it later." Lucas adjusted the robe on his shoulders, not looking at us. We both knew they had an illustrious history of breakup-makeup drama. "Can we pull an Ezra and not talk about it right now?"

I gave him a pointed look as Ms. Dion came out of the Media Center office. Lucas was having a shit day like Finley. Like me. Maybe some planetary misalignment was to blame, or maybe relationships were just shitty no matter who you were. Either way, the boyfriend theatrics were wilding out today.

If only I could tell them about Presley so we could commiserate; then I wouldn't be alone in all this.

Tightness weaved through my ribs as I tried to breathe. As

I tried to shake it off and go through all the Spirit Day photos I'd taken for the yearbook this week. As I clicked through photo after photo of my boyfriend pretending that I didn't exist.

"So . . ." Lucas leaned around his monitor. "Any chance you could mediate between Cass and me at Homecoming? Gotta feeling I'll need it."

"Uh," I started, flinching at the memory of Presley telling me not to come tonight, "I'd rather sit at home and do nothing than subject myself to that nightmare."

"Fine," he huffed as Finley chuckled under his breath. "But you'll at least help me get ready for the dance?"

"Sure, I have nothing better to do tonight."

"Oh?" Finley asked, interest piqued. "Maybe you could do me a solid, too, then."

"The last time I did you a favor, it involved waiting in line for five hours so you could finally get a PS5."

"This is neither life-changing nor drastic." He anxiously ran a hand through his curly top fade. "Lewis Auto Sales is sponsoring the classic movie night at Twinkle Lights . . . and Pop is making me go represent instead of him. Wanna keep me company?" I started to decline, but he continued. "Please? I'd rather die than sit through some rom-com by myself."

Rom-com?

A montage of scenes flickered through my mind. Heath Ledger belting out a song in *10 Things I Hate About You,* Queen Latifah refusing to be plan B in *Just Wright,* Reese Witherspoon yelling to kiss her man anytime she wants in *Sweet Home Alabama*—all of them had taught me the most important lesson in romance. Capital M Moments make or break every love story. What I needed was a grand declaration, something to show Presley that I was a *somebody*.

"Okay," I agreed, hoping the movie night would help me figure out what my own capital M Moment might be.

Two

The midnight walls of Lucas's room were calming. While he got ready, I lay back on the fluffy duvet and blew on my fresh coat of nail polish. Each time my lungs emptied, I focused on the glittery gold stars we'd painted on the ceiling above his bed.

We had a tradition of confiding our deepest secrets underneath them, glitter-bombing our truths. It'd all started in fifth grade when Lucas admitted he'd kissed Bobby Tucker under the bleachers. Those same stars had watched over us when Finley came out as bisexual, when I was dying from embarrassment after my dad walked in on me jerking it, and now . . .

My nails were nearly dry, and I blew on them again. Those glitzy stars watched me between each exhale. Their shine lassoed the truth I'd kept buried and pulled. Five months of worry had exhausted my defenses, and today had filled me with even more doubt. I was too tired of being alone with my thoughts and wanted someone to know. . . .

"Presley Daniels is my boyfriend," I admitted aloud.

"Huh?" Lucas called from the bathroom.

"Last May, he came into the bookstore when I was closing, and it was a total meet-cute."

"What?"

"I know. I can't believe he's gay either. But he kept coming back, staying late and talking to me. *Me* of all people. Then he asked if I wanted to go for a ride in his truck, and . . ." I inhaled deeply as I relived the memory of my first time. "Everything was perfect, but I keep fucking it up."

Silence thrummed for a moment, and then the rattling of the doorknob made me tense. "You say something?" Lucas asked, opening the door.

"Nope," I lied, knowing I'd be unable to defend myself if I actually told him. Lucas would never get why I'd let myself fall this deep in my feels over Presley.

He sauntered into the bedroom, oblivious to my turmoil, and slowly spun to give me the full effect. "What do we think about this bold color choice?" he asked. His fuchsia tux was bright against his bare chest and boasted black accents that were much too stylish for HVHS.

"Okay, *Euphoria*."

He shot me a smirk in the full-length mirror, and then he frowned as he looked at his forehead. "Too bad this zit is all anyone will see."

"Shut up," I said, locking my secret further down. "We both know you're gorgeous."

"Cass might get upset. . . ."

"If a giant zit—" Lucas's face blanched in a pained expression. "I mean, it's *tiny*. Barely even visible. If that bothers him, then he can fuck right off."

"It's just that tonight has to be perfect. His after-party has to be perfect. Everyone has to think it's perfect."

"Yeah, yeah. He's an egotistical narcissist, I get it." I patted the space next to me on the bed. "Grab the concealer, and I'll disguise that planet on your—"

"So it *is* huge!" He pouted and grabbed the makeup bag from his vanity. "Make me look perfect."

"I'm uncomfortable with how many times you've used the word *perfect*," I said as he sat down. "Besides, you already know *you're* perfect."

He gave me major side-eye, and I returned it with a tight-lipped smile. "He thinks I'm wearing a 'normal' tux," Lucas admitted, using air quotes.

"Nothing about what you're wearing says normal."

"Exactly!" He snapped his head up in emphasis, and I held his chin to keep him still. "Normal is boring. This is the perfect shade to match the smoky gray of his suit. Think how great our pictures will look—don't roll your eyes."

"At least *you'll* look good." I finished blending the makeup and inspected my work. "You're done."

He sprang up from the bed to inspect his reflection yet again. I fell back across the duvet and checked my phone. Presley had posted a new story to Snapchat. My thumb hovered over it for a beat before I gave in. An image loaded of him with one of

14

the Mighty Lion cheerleaders, and my stomach dropped. He'd be dancing with her after the game like I didn't exist.

I had to remind him I was here. Reassure myself and get his attention. Checking to make sure Lucas wasn't looking, I quickly opened our message thread and began to type.

hockeyhayes9:
Sorry about earlier.

hockeyhayes9:
You were right.

hockeyhayes9:
Good luck tonight! 😌

A notification popped up that elvislion0007 was typing. My heart swelled with hope but quickly deflated when a reply never came. I groaned, slumping against way too many accent pillows.

"Excuse me?" Lucas asked, and I held my phone closer to my chest. He wagged his brows. "Why so secretive? Someone sending you nudes?"

"What? N-no!" I forced the hysteria back and tried to emulate one of Finley's easy-going grins. "I was just . . . waiting to take a pic. Of you. Because that fit is fire."

"By all means." He posed in his tux, hands on his hips as I snapped. "How does it look?"

"Like Cass the Ass will be counting down the minutes until he can rip it off."

"Then tonight will have been a success."

He smirked again (and I inwardly grimaced) as I posted it to my Snap story with fire emojis. I watched while he orbited around his reflection, touching up his mascara. Soothing down the strip of silver hair he'd styled. When his phone lit up on the vanity, his satisfied smile fell.

"Everything okay?" I asked.

He gave a curt shake of his head, and both thumbs tapped at the screen furiously. Then he held the phone up to his ear as a muffled ringing tone sounded before cutting off. "You did *not* just send me to voice mail," he snapped. "Don't pull this shit on Homecoming."

His chin jutted out, his eyes blinking rapidly to keep away the welling tears. There was only one thing that made him cry like that. Cass had pulled another breakup fight to feed his ego.

"Are you okay?" I asked softly, and he handed me his phone without a word. A text thread was open with a screenshot of the Snap I'd just posted.

Cass: u fuckin fr w tht stupid tux?

Lucas: Don't worry babe!
Trust it'll look good!

Cass: trusted u 2 not be so damn gay

16

> **Lucas:** You're seriously doing this right now?

> **Cass:** im done. we're over

I gripped the phone, wishing I didn't feel relieved they were breaking up again. Wishing I wasn't happy that all of us were dealing with boyfriend drama. Wishing he'd heard my Glitter Bomb so we could talk and neither of us would feel alone.

A sniffle turned my attention to Lucas. "I'm so sorry," I said, holding my arms out to him. "I shouldn't have posted that story."

"Not your fault." He let out a sob as I hugged him. "He knows how much I've been looking forward to this . . . after the hell we went through with Principal York enforcing the Watch What You Say initiative and fighting to get a couple's ticket . . . and now I can't go to Homecoming in this *stupid* tux by myself."

"First off," I started, pulling back to look down at him, "that tux isn't stupid, because it makes you look phe-nom-e-nal. Second, come with me and Fin to watch that movie. We can, like, sit in the dark and not think."

I really hated thinking.

He rolled his smudged eyes to stop the tears, brows pinching in thought. "Can we eat our weight in extra-buttery popcorn and Sour Patch Kids?"

"I'll even pick out all the red ones for you."

"Maybe we can get waffle fries at Linda Sue's after?"

"With cheesy sauce."

"Maybe help me throw out his shit when we get back?" he added, glancing around his room. "Do that new TikTok challenge that Maeve Kimball started?"

"I haven't seen that one yet, but I'm *so* here for it."

He wiped at the running mascara and took a steadying breath. Then he powered off his phone. Tossing it on the bed, he nodded as though he was reassuring himself. "Let's get out of here."

Soft twinkling lights danced in the night. I followed the glow up to the theater's marquee. Past the large red letters yelling THE FIRST WIVES CLUB. Even farther, past the end of Main Street to where the HVHS stadium glowed. Homecoming King had been crowned, and the Mighty Lions were one step closer to a sixth state championship.

"Fin, *what the hell* did you just make us watch?" Lucas asked, and my attention snapped away from Linda Sue's window and back to my friends. Lucas's fuchsia tux shined in the diner's fluorescent lights as he read from the movie's Wikipedia page on Finley's phone. "Don't get me wrong. Diane Keaton, Goldie Hawn, and Bette Midler ate that. It was definitely not a rom-com, though . . . and *what* was up with that random song-and-dance routine?"

"No clue," Finley said, his words edging on bitter. "If Pop thought that was a romance, I'm not surprised my mom divorced him and moved across the country."

The First Wives Club was nothing like the romance I'd been hoping for. It'd been near two hours of ex-wives seeking revenge on their asshole ex-husbands, and none of us had been prepared for how hard it went. The main characters didn't even have love interests—they were just fighting to make a place for themselves. Everything they went through had weighed me down in that theater chair, an uneasiness sinking in the pit of my stomach.

I hated how much I related to them.

Lucas laid his head on my shoulder, and I put my arm around him. "How're you holding up?" I asked, ignoring the nagging tug of my thoughts.

"Pissed after everything I've done for him." He held a hand up, raising a finger as he counted. "Who leveled up his style? Wrote his scholarship essays? Did all the planning for his stupid HalloWeird party at the pretentious Longleaf Farm country club? And *this* is how he repays me? Because I'm *too gay*? What does that even mean?"

"You deserve so much better than that," Finley said, reaching for his hand.

"His internalized misogyny over me being femme makes me want to punch him in the dick." The way he said *femme,* like he'd hocked Cass's word up and spat it out, made his brow furrow in anger. "I've heard that machismo shit all my life, and I don't need it from my boyfriend."

"You don't need us to remind you that you're perfect," I pointed out, wishing I was too.

"If that ass wipe doesn't think you're good enough, then that's on him, dude."

Lucas nodded, reassuring himself. "I was sad, but now . . . I'm one hundred percent done. With him. And his below-average dick game."

"I *obviously* have follow-up questions," I said with a snort. "But most importantly, good for you."

"Thanks, booboo. I know you don't like him."

"That's an understatement," I muttered as he sat upright. At least now both my best friends were single, and I wouldn't be forced into the role of third wheel.

But why does it feel like I still am?

Uneasiness pulled harder as I watched Finley shovel a waffle fry into his mouth. The smell of deep-fried grease sent a rumble through my stomach, and he pushed the plate toward me. "This is our second plate of cheesy fries," he said around a mouthful, "and you haven't eaten any."

"I'm good," I lied, too aware of my body, and crossed my arms. "Not that hungry."

"You didn't eat lunch today," Lucas pointed out, swirling a fry in cheese sauce. "You didn't eat any of the popcorn. You didn't even eat any of the blue Sour Patch Kids, and don't 'at me' because I know for a fact those are your favorite." He tilted his head and studied me for a beat. "You okay? Like for real?"

"God, you're like my dad," I joked, plastering on a smile. "I'm fine." But it was another lie. I wasn't okay, not after everything that'd happened today.

"You say you're fine when you aren't. You're not eating, and you're punishing yourself with those morning jogs. What's going on with you?"

Presley's laughter lived in between my heartbeats as Lucas and Finley stared at me. Because he was at the dance with a cheerleader. Not thinking about me. Not replying to my message. Not acting like my boyfriend. I closed my eyes, breathing evenly as my mind replayed scenes from the movie. As five months of worry and doubt ate away at me. Then I saw them, the glittering gold stars I'd stared at from Lucas's bed. *If only they knew . . .*

And I *needed* them to know.

"Glitter Bomb," I heard myself say aloud.

"This better not be about another rub burn from reading smutty hockey fanfic," Lucas said.

"No." I swallowed nervously. "Ihaveaboyfriend." The admission came out jumbled, escaping in one breath. It was the same way I'd tried to stand up to Presley earlier. I needed to get the words out before I lost my nerve.

Heat flashed across my face as they processed what I'd said.

"And you haven't told us?!" Lucas yelled simultaneously with Finley questioning, "The fuck, dude?"

The surprise on both of their faces was a double-edged sword. Part of me was hurt they were so shocked, and part of me was satisfied they were. "He isn't out," I backtracked carefully. "That's why I couldn't tell y'all."

"You don't seem happy about having a secret boyfriend," Finley said.

"It's fine," I said as Lucas waved a warning finger at me. "Okay. It's not fine. I don't know what I keep doing wrong."

"Here." Finley pushed the fries toward me. "Don't make that face. Eat and give us the rundown."

With a deep breath (and a handful of fries), I launched into the hows—how everything started, how it had to be a secret, how I couldn't seem to get it right no matter what I did. Saying it aloud made me feel stupid, and my head spun into more over-thought. Romance shouldn't be *this* hard.

"I'm so so so sorry," Lucas said once I'd finished, rubbing my arm. "I wish you would've told us sooner so we could help."

How could they help? How could I make them understand how it felt to be wanted by someone for a change? How could I explain that some people lived like a punchline, always "the fat friend," while everyone else laughed at them? How could I make them realize people like me had to tread carefully so we wouldn't fall through the floor?

"Are you . . ." Finley trailed off with a conspiratorial glance around the diner, and then he lowered his voice. "You're not hooking up with Presley Daniels, are you?"

My mouth fell open before I could stop it.

"Oh. My. God. He is!" Lucas slapped the table, his grin shifting into more sharp surprise. "He's gay and you're dicking him down!"

Everything he'd just said echoed through the diner, and Finley scooted down in the seat as heads turned our way. "Do you mind?" he hissed, his voice edged with apprehension. "What if Logan comes in? The last thing I need is to be the center of attention *again*."

"Sorry, Fin, but this sends me. I'm sent. Levitating. I need every hot and sweaty detail of—"

"Are you, Ezra?" Finley pressed in all seriousness. I sat there dumbfounded, unable to lie or tell the truth. "I get that you don't want to out him—respect—but that's bad news."

A heavy breath tightened my chest, a deep inhale threatening to burst it open and expose trembling heartbeats. I already knew I wasn't good enough for Presley, but my *best friend* didn't have to rub it in. "Why is it bad for him to be dating *me*?"

"What? *He's* the bad news," Fin corrected with a pitiful slant of his brow. "Let me guess, he said you had to keep it a secret so his parents wouldn't kick him out?"

I screwed my face up in confusion and tried to make sense of what he was saying. "How . . . how do you know that?"

"How do you *not* know about him? I thought literally every gay person within a fifty-mile radius knew he wasn't out. That's the point. He tells guys to keep it on the DL, using his parents as an excuse so he can hook up with whoever he wants. He's a player."

Player.

The word slapped me so hard that I flinched. Scooted down in the booth seat. Willed myself to disappear between the cushions. However, there was no hiding from the clarity it brought. An answer to the question I kept asking myself in disbelief: Why was Presley Daniels with *me*?

And it hurt.

I didn't want to believe *my Presley* would do that. Didn't want to believe the last five months meant nothing. How someone finally noticed me, him confessing how much he liked me in the back of his truck on Country Road 233, me falling in love with him. But the constant fight to get his attention, the way I kept doing it wrong no matter how hard I tried—all of it made more sense in light of Finley's intel.

The sting of tears choked me as I looked from Lucas to Finley. Both of them were watching me intently, understanding creasing their brows. Lucas pulled me into a hug while Finley grasped my hand on the counter. They were my best friends, and I felt ashamed I hadn't given them enough credit.

"What am I supposed to do about it?" I asked softly over the roar of *player, player, player* pulsing in my veins.

"Straight up call him out on it," Finley said with a squeeze. "What he's doing is so messed up, not to mention hella insensitive."

"You deserve to know the truth," Lucas said, kissing the top of my head. Tears of anger, of embarrassment, of disbelief fell as he leaned close to my ear and whispered. "And if he *is* playing you, we'll make him pay."

Three

Laughter replayed from my dreams as the sunrise tiptoed through the window. I blinked against the light, fighting the immediate itch to feel for my phone in the sheets. My mind was torn between wishing Presley had messaged me back and hoping he hadn't. I didn't want to deal with last night's revelation about him, but . . .

A quick glance at my screen showed no new notifications.

I forced myself to lie there, sadness spilling in with the rays through the curtains. They danced off the black-and-gold plaid comforter I'd kicked onto the floor. The mounted #9 Nyberg jersey crooked above my bed. Old rom-com DVDs of distressed damsels haphazardly stacked on my desk. Sweaty gym clothes piled on the floor from yesterday's run. The mirrored closet door and its reminder of puckered stretch marks. And beyond all that, the four boring gray walls surrounding the mess my life had suddenly become.

You're Ezra Hayes, I reminded myself. *Boring and messy and average.*

With a sigh, I rolled out of bed in frustration and ignored the nonexistent Snap messages. After getting dressed, I shoved my phone in the back pocket of my jeans and grabbed my favorite hoodie. The will-he-or-won't-he-reply question weighed heavily in my thoughts as I rushed to get out of my bedroom, away from this bad dream.

I could smell smoke the moment I shuffled into the hall, and I knew my dad was awake. The greasy haze curled up the stairs like it did most mornings. By the time I made it down to the living room, the smoke detector was beeping furiously. I followed it to the kitchen, where he stood at the stove, spatula in hand. The skillet sizzled with extra (extra) crispy bacon as he looked over his shoulder at me.

"Mornin'!" Dad called over the alarm, jumping as grease splattered his Hayes Railroad Construction shirt. "Didn't hear you get in last night."

"You were zonked out on the sofa," I pointed out, and looked up at the smoke detector. "Didn't know you were planning to burn the house down today."

"Look who has jokes!"

I grabbed a dish towel and cleared the air. "I'm here all week," I deadpanned in the ringing silence that followed. "Unless you *actually* burn the house down."

He shook his head, cutting his eyes back to his phone. He'd propped it up on the island with the weekend edition of *Good Morning America* streaming. Both the show and the potential risk of a fire were part of his daily ritual.

"Bacon sandwich?" he asked during the commercial break.

"I'll just grab a banana." I sat down at the island and reached into the fruit basket with a growling stomach. The corners of his mouth turned down. "What? I'm not that hungry."

He was unconvinced, thoughtfully scratching at his beard. We looked so much alike with the same brown hair, hazel eyes, and wonky Hayes nose. However, when he wore his "responsible father expression," it reminded me how different we actually were. There was the faintest hint of red in my hair, a slight curl that made it messy—as messy as his past, in which he'd become a single father in high school, choosing to raise me on his own instead of adoption like his then girlfriend had wanted. I worried he saw his sordid history when he looked at me like he was right now.

"Everything all right, bud?" he finally asked, wiping his hands on a napkin. I nodded, taking a bite. "You've been off the last few months. Not eating. Pushing yourself to go running."

He knew me all too well. Too perceptive to ignore when something was bothering me. He wouldn't be happy with all the secrets I'd been keeping.

"I swear on the Slammers winning the playoffs that I'm fine," I lied, swallowing the mushy, overripe banana.

"Don't joke about the Stanley Cup," he said, crossing his fingers.

"I know, too far." I swiftly crossed mine. "Immediately regretted it."

"He didn't mean it, Iceberg." Dad patted Nyberg's chiseled face, stretched across my chest, and I squirmed away while he chuckled. "We on for wings and rings with the Slammers season opener tonight?"

I nodded, stomach already growling in anticipation. Chicken wings and onion rings with hockey had started back in the depths of the pandemic. I'd watched old games with him during the 2020 lockdown, and it'd been a tradition ever since.

"And we both know you aren't fine," he said, taking a seat beside me. "I can't help if you don't tell me what's going on. Even if it's about a boy, don't be embarrassed to talk to me about anything."

That was the thing—I *was* embarrassed. Presley's laugh reverberated through me. I knew I had to eventually check my messages, call him out on it. But I didn't know how because I loved him and didn't want to blow up our relationship.

"What . . . what if there's someone you really care about, hypothetically speaking," I ventured, staring hard at the streaming show on his phone. "And you need to tell them how you feel, but it might make them mad?"

"If this person cares about you," he began, clapping me on the back, "it'll be okay. Tell them how you feel. If they do get mad, it's their loss. You're Ezra Hayes. Don't forget that."

I nodded, the haunting laughter roaring even louder in my ears. *What do I tell him . . . that I love him in hopes it'll fix everything or that I'm scared the rumor about him is true?*

Seemingly satisfied, Dad bit into his brittle sandwich and watched the weekend edition. I dug my phone from my jeans, swiping out of the camera app that always seemed to be on, and typed out another message to Presley in hopes he'd reply. Once I sent it, I forced myself to finish eating as the *GMA* correspondent interviewed Tennessee librarians on book bans. My stomach turned while I sat there, a nauseous mix of nerves and worry. I pretended talking to him would make it okay—that maybe I wasn't boring and messy and average.

The ornate clock above Magnolia Bookstore and Café's entrance ticked loudly. Each second carried the weight of a tied hockey game's third period. My head and my heart were racing to win. *Tell Presley you love him* would take a swing, slapping a shot, only to be denied by *He's a player* tending the goal.

Back and forth all weekend.

I didn't want to believe Finley and did my best to ignore what he'd said. But it was all I could think about while I cleaned my room. And each time Dad and I did our lucky dance when the Slammers scored in Saturday's season opener. And as I lay awake all last night wondering what Presley was doing, checking for his reply. No matter how many times my heart tried to make a point, my head stopped me from getting my hopes up.

And now Sunday was winding down like the last few seconds of the game. I was relieved Jackson wasn't working today. He'd only be a painful reminder of what happened in the hall on Friday.

I was too focused on the clock. Time was running out until Presley showed up like we'd planned after he (finally) replied. Soon I'd have to take my final shot and tell him how I felt, one way or another.

The new coat of nail polish was gone, splinters of gold and

black flaking the countertop, by the time the clock struck seven. It was now or never. A knock on the glass front sent my pulse hammering. The final buzzer had sounded, and I still didn't know what I was going to say as I slowly walked to the door.

"I missed you," Presley breathed as I let him inside.

He tells guys to keep it on the DL . . . so he can hook up with whoever he wants.

"Presley," I said over Finley's voice in my head.

"Need you now . . ."

His voice was hushed and thick as he flicked the lights off and backed me against the counter. His mouth found mine in the dark with lips so sweet, so gentle. His cologne filled my nose with sandalwood and citrus and *him.* He held my face as he kissed me, and a soft whimper in the back of his throat coaxed a decision to the tip of my tongue.

"I love you," I gasped, a perfect rom-com declaration.

"You love me," he teased with a devilish grin, breath hot against my face. "That's what you want to talk about?"

I nodded, my throat tight.

In the dim light, he smiled as I waited for him to say something, anything to show me we're good. Instead, he shucked off his varsity jacket and tossed it on the floor. My eyes swept up his arms. How they arched in a beautiful curve and disappeared into the yellow sleeves of his polo. The fabric raced along broad shoulders to his neck, throat swallowing as he drank me in.

"We should go to the back room," he finally said.

His eyes glowed, and he pulled me fast. Pushed me through

the staff door. Deft hands unbuttoning my jeans in a rush. Then I heard it over the thunder of heartbeats. *He's a player.*

"I love you," I repeated.

Fat ass resounded in his silence.

"I love you," I whispered as he laid back on the old table.

No one can find out that I'm with you.

"I love you," I mouthed against his skin.

It'd be embarrassing if you . . .

No reply as he shoved a condom in my hand. My fingers trembled with the foil wrapper, my voice shaking as I started to ask, "How do you feel—"

He silenced me with a kiss. I searched for an answer on his lips, but they were sloppy and rushed. "Hurry up," he groaned in annoyance. "I don't have time for this bullshit."

The dismissiveness of his reply slapped me in the face. "It's true, isn't it?" I heard myself ask, voice hollow. "That you're keeping us secret so you can hook up with whoever you want?"

His eyes slitted, and this secret version of him was gone—*my* Presley was gone. My vision blurred as he pushed me back roughly. "I don't know what you heard," he began, hopping off the table, "but I thought you trusted me like I trust you."

"I . . . uh . . . I'm . . . sorry?" I was ashamed of the wobbliness in my voice. All I could do was stand there helplessly in front of him, hating myself for ruining yet another moment.

He yanked his underwear and jeans up, tugging on his zipper. "I need you to trust me," he said as I wiped away a tear. "I thought you *loved* me."

"I—"

"Look, I didn't come here for you to pick another fight. I wanted to have a good time, but you ruined it. Again. I'm out of here, Ezra."

He turned from me, heading toward the front door. An unyielding desire to apologize, to get his attention, forced me to chase after him. I tried to call out but couldn't form words.

"I don't know what's gotten into you, but maybe you should chill," he threw over his shoulder before the door slammed shut behind him.

He left me in the dark. My heart was numb, my head racing to make sense of how fast it all fell apart. How he had bolted instead of actually talking to me.

I kept replaying his reaction while I went through the motions of closing the store. My eyes burned as I locked the door and clocked out. I wiped at the tears with my shirt, noticing a soft glow lighting up the dark. Presley's forgotten varsity jacket lay crumpled on the floor, and his phone had slid from the pocket. Without thinking—*too much damn thinking*—I picked it up.

New Snapchats from user HVHS157 flashed across the screen. I could find out if there was validity to the rumor. . . .

The passcode prompt appeared when I tapped the screen. There was only one number that mattered to him, the one he wore with pride on the football field. The same one he used in his Snapchat. I typed out 0-0-0-7, and a message thread loaded.

elvislion0007:
let's hang

HVHS157:
on a Sunday?

elvislion0007:
8:30? only time i can slip away from my parents
and i kno a great place to star gaze in my truck

HVHS157:
that sounds romantic 😍

elvislion0007:
i miss you
send a pic

HVHS157:
new snap image
just showered can't wait to see you

Bile hit the back of my throat as soon as I tapped the image. A chiseled torso appeared on the screen, the complete opposite of me. Embarrassment burned in my stomach. The dusting of hair across his muscled chest. Rivulets of water running down his happy trail. Three moles forming a constellation by his belly button. All of it added up to more than I would ever be.

Sudden banging on the door startled me. Presley stood under the awning, waving for me to let him inside. A few minutes ago, my heart would have leaped and bounded at the sight of him coming back to me. Now I knew the truth.

Presley was a player.

Holding his phone tightly, I crossed over to the door. He stood there expectantly, waiting for me to let him inside. Like I'd done for far too long.

"Forgot my—" he started, but I held his phone so he could see the Snapchat thread.

"Who's HVHS157?" I asked, raising my voice.

"You looked through my shit?" His voice vibrated through the glass door.

"Does he know about your secret? How he's supposed to keep quiet so you can play others?"

"You're acting crazy right now."

"Don't call me crazy."

He looked down at me, shaking his head. "Thought I could trust you—"

"I trusted *you*," I cut him off, stepping closer.

He laughed, the same laugh that followed me down the hallway on Friday. The gold of his hair caught in the streetlights as he shook his head, a misleading halo. "This is all your fault."

"My fault?" My voice was shallow, breaths rattling through me.

"You were begging for it when I first came in here. Following me around. Wanting me to notice you. You wanted to hook up with me so bad—"

"Stop!" I yelled. He glared at me, his wide stance looming over me. Willing me to do what he wanted. Manipulating me all this time into believing he was mine, when really . . . "You were never my boyfriend. You played me."

His breath fogged the glass as he laughed. "Maybe I did. What are you gonna do, tell everyone?"

"I—"

"It'd be my word against yours, and let's face it—your dick game's bomb, but you're just a fat-ass nobody. Who'd believe you? People like *me* don't date people like *you*."

People like me, a punchline. That's all I'd ever be. A fire burned in my heart, throat, eyes. Anger flickered through me as the last five months replayed yet again. All the times he'd made me believe in promises he'd never keep propelled me forward. I gripped his phone in my fist and shoved it through the door's mail slot.

"I don't want this," I said over its clatter on the concrete stoop. "I'm done."

Four

My dad's old Jeep whined as I pulled into a parking space at HVHS on Monday morning. It shuddered with a twist of the key, and silence rang between drops of rain. I didn't want to go inside or see Presley or deal with the fact that last night was real.

Dread weighed me down in the seat, and I glanced in the rearview. The familiar varsity jacket hung across the back headrest. It'd been left behind at Magnolia just like I'd been. Now I didn't know what to do with it. Was I supposed to give it back? Maybe throw it at him in the hallway and cause a scene?

The lion's eyes on the HVHS emblem stared back at me in the mirror, knowing full well my favorite memories were tied to it. Those nights burned the brightest, every detail rushing back. How I'd clutched at those black leather sleeves that first time, the red wool of the jacket front rough under my fingertips as I held him afterward. Night after night, he'd been mine until I'd lost count.

But those memories were a lie.

An exhale forced itself from my lungs when a familiar silver BMW pulled in beside me. I blinked the past away and opened the door to climb out. The October morning held the promise of cooler weather, making me hopeful. Anything to make me forget the summer.

I grabbed my backpack and crammed the jacket inside, hurrying as Lucas slammed his car door. He pushed rose-tinted, heart-shaped sunglasses up into his hair with a defeated expression. "We desperately need to take you shopping," he said with a flick of his wrist. "There is more out there than being a Bama Slammers fan."

"This is my comfort tee," I admitted weakly, looking down at the words *QUEER HOCKEY HERO!* spelled out over Nyberg on the ice. If he was brave enough to be himself, then I could be brave enough to face whatever today brought.

"How're you doing post-breakup?" He shouldered his bag and opened his umbrella.

"It sucks. Really fucking sucks." I crossed my arms and wished I could hide from today and tomorrow and however long it would take until the suckage didn't hurt so much. "I was so stupid to think he could . . ." *Want me? Had he ever wanted me like that?* "I wanna go back to May and stop him before he played with my head and made everything so blurry."

"I understand the feeling," Lucas grumbled. "It makes me want to punch Cass right in his stupid, chiseled face."

"You okay?" I asked. His shrug was lost in the bagginess of his oversized sweatshirt. "How are *you* doing now that you're done with him?"

"It feels like"—he waved a hand, his fingertips barely visible beneath the long sleeves—"I dunno, like I've transcended from that breakup/makeup drama and reached a higher level of pissed off and don't know what to do. . . ."

He fell into silence as Finley whipped his crew cab into a parking spot nearby in a flash of blue. The white font of LEWIS AUTO SALES that usually marked the side door was scratched through with jagged lines spelling out *FLOP*.

This is bad. Really bad.

Finley loved his truck almost as much as he was afraid of being humiliated again.

"What the hell happened?" I asked when he opened the door.

"*He* did," Finley said, jumping down. "Logan James Michael the Fucking Third keyed my ride last night. Pop shit a brickhouse when he saw it. Now everyone else will see it and it'll be like last spring all over again."

He slammed the door in frustration. This was worse than a typical shitty day. He was shaking, the muscles in his neck Hulking out. Finley didn't get mad like this.

Lucas let out a low whistle. "LJM3 holds grudges like none other."

"If anything"—Fin tore his gaze away from the etched letters—"*I'm* the one who should be angry. He broke up with me because he thought I'd cheat on him with a girl, proceeded to both out me as bi *and* call my performance in the spring musical a flop, and is now actively trying to ruin my life."

"I still have secondhand anxiety from *The Lightning Thief*," I said as we huddled under Lucas's umbrella. "Grover stopping a dance number to yell at Percy Jackson for not being gay enough—"

"Don't remind me." Finley let out an exaggerated huff. "His overreaction was as bad as his overacting." He gave LJM3's tiny car the middle finger as we walked by it. "I'm never, ever doing another musical again . . . unless it's a genderbent *Mamma Mia!* because, duh."

"You should get him back, Fin." Lucas hip-bumped him as we walked toward the building.

"Key the shit out of LJM3's turd wagon," I added, eyeing Presley's truck. So many memories were made in the back.

Finley turned toward me, considering my telltale signs of no sleep. He clocked the red-rimmed eyes and dark smudges underneath. "Sorry, Ezra." He took a deep, calming breath. "How're you holding up after last night, dude?"

An angry dread sloshed inside my stomach with each step up to the school. I forcefully yanked open the lobby door and looked over at him. "I was up all night replaying everything he's ever said to me," I admitted, pushing inside. "I'm so embarrassed and mad at myself for being so damn stupid."

"Welcome to the club," Finley said with a huff. "Don't take it out on yourself." He nodded at #7 on the Lions Pride football poster. "Be pissed at him instead."

"I know, but . . . I'm still processing what it means."

"Processing is good." Lucas pushed a strand of his hair back. It was greasy, unwashed, and unstyled. Very unlike him. "I processed all the way through the Maeve Kimball breakup challenge, but dropkicking Cass's shit onto his front porch didn't feel like *enough*."

"Maybe we should—" Finley started to say, but lurched against me as someone pushed past.

"Sorry, *dude*. Didn't see you hiding there."

Logan James Michael the Third shot a death glare over his shoulder, flipping his blond waves. Finley squared himself and gripped his truck keys. Then I saw it, the last straw in his glare.

"That's. It." Finley's tone crackled with decisive anger. "I don't know how, but I *have* to get even with him."

Lucas watched him, his face reflecting the intensity of his thoughts. "Glitter Bomb," he confessed as the first bell rang. "I haven't stopped thinking about getting revenge on Cass since we watched that movie." He turned toward me, his eyebrow arching elegantly. "Have you thought about making *him* pay for what he did?"

Wet sneakers squeaked on the tile floor as I picked at my fresh coat of nail polish. Getting back at Presley would make it feel real that he really had played me. I wanted to hide from this new reality. Go back to when it was only us three sticking together without boyfriends threatening our quiet, small-town existence.

"I dunno," I finally said with a shrug. "It, um, hurts. To even think about him."

Finley gave me a side hug like he could read my thoughts. "We'll help you get over him," he said, rubbing my back.

"Remember what I told you at the diner," Lucas reminded me as they started toward class. "I wasn't joking about making him suffer."

I tried to smile as they disappeared down the South Hall, and then I let out a shaky breath before turning around. Each wet-sneakered squeak toward physics sent tremors through my facade of playing it cool. Because there he was, right outside of anatomy with Jackson F'ing Darcy and the other dude-bros.

Presley's smile tilted upward when he saw me. My heart took a soaring leap. *Maybe he's sorry and—* The malice in his eyes sent whatever vestiges of hope I'd been holding on to plummeting.

"Keep moving, fat ass!" one of the footballers yelled, and Presley threw his head back, howling in laughter.

He never cared about me.

Shame clenched my insides, and I kept walking. Kept holding on to the truth—Presley Daniels had played me. My heart was trapped in his fist. Each echoing laugh squeezed it tighter and tighter.

"Wait up, Ez," a familiar, deep voice called behind me. "Don't listen to those idiots."

I was tempted to run toward physics. Ms. Abernathy's no-talking-sanctum would keep Jackson F'ing Darcy from pestering me. His long legs caught up to me before I had the chance, and he nudged me like we were friends. We were the furthest from it. He was one of *them,* a junior on the Mighty Lions, a fucking golden retriever of a person.

"You okay?" he asked.

"I'm fine," I said curtly, not in the mood for his pity. His creamy skin was flushed, floppy brown hair stuck to his forehead with sweat. I'd been working with him at the bookstore long enough to know he'd probably been in a rush (running late as usual).

"That's a sick shirt, brah," he continued, determined to make small talk (also as usual). "He's the best trade the Slammers have ever made."

"Thanks . . ." I turned toward him in surprise, slowing down. "Didn't know you liked hockey."

"Correction, I *love* hockey." He wiggled his bushy brows and grinned in excitement. "Did you see the way Nyberg denied the Wrens' forward on Saturday?"

"Uh, hello. It was such a se . . ." The comment died on my tongue. Because the play *was* sexy, but he didn't need to know that. "Season. Such a kickass season opener. They're gonna dominate."

"Especially with such an iconic defenseman, brah." He motioned at my shirt for emphasis. "He has been their lucky char—"

A snap of fingers cut him off. We both startled as Principal York hurried our way. He made a sweeping motion with his arm, waving us down the hall.

"Hurry up, gentlemen," he ordered. "The late bell is about to ring. Superintendent Bett is due any minute, and . . ." His wiry, gray eyebrows twitched as he followed Jackson's hand, still outstretched toward my shirt. "Ezra Hayes, do you know you're breaking the dress code?"

"How?" I asked in confusion. "All it says is 'Queer Hockey Hero.'"

"It's a perverse statement against the district's Watch What

You Say initiative," York explained with a toothy smile that didn't reach his eyes. He pointed to the bathroom sign. "You'll have to go and turn your shirt inside out."

Perverse? The word sounded vile in my head as I glanced down. "But Rolf Nyberg *is* a hero. He believed in himself enough to come out and take a stand for queer rights—"

"I get it, really I do. You kids and your issues, but not everything is an attack on your *rights.*" His voice was oil-slick as it oozed around us, and he held his hands up in surrender. "I'm on your side here. However, it's my job to uphold the rules, and you have to follow them."

"How's that fair—" Jackson started.

"You should go on to first block before you're tardy again, Darcy," York cut him off, exhaling roughly through his teeth. He stood straighter then, adjusting his name badge lanyard as he looked down at me. "Ezra, you're usually a quiet student, but you're promoting agendas not authorized by the Acheron County Board of Education." I opened my mouth to protest, but he held up a finger in warning. "Either fix your shirt or get detention. Those are the rules."

Despite my best efforts to control my expression, my jaw clenched in anger. "Fine," I bit out, turning on my heel.

I shoved the bathroom door open and dropped my backpack on the tile floor. With shaking hands, I gripped the edge of my shirt and ripped it off, yanking it back over my head inside out as the tardy bell rang. I stood there breathing heavily while embarrassment and anger rioted in my stomach.

The Mighty Lions had put a target on my back thanks to

Presley. Now Acheron County's Watch What You Say initiative wouldn't let me find comfort in one of my favorite shirts because it was *perverse*. I was running out of hiding spots at HVHS.

With a sigh, I grabbed my backpack and started to push open the door. Voices drifted in from the hallway, and I stilled when I heard his name. "Daniels won Homecoming King I see," a thick, Southern accent drawled.

"Yes, Superintendent Bett," York replied, his oily words slipping through the cracked open door. "He'll certainly win Winter Formal Lion King, too."

"Daniels is a good student. It'll be an honor to have the right kind of representation for HVHS. . . ." Bett's reply faded as they drifted down the hallway.

Amid the confusion roiling inside me, I knew one thing for certain: first impressions meant nothing. People were far too complex, too good at hiding themselves. It was those second, third, fourth impressions that mattered. They revealed who a person really was behind the facade of who they pretended to be. And Golden Boy Daniels, with his golden Homecoming King crown, wasn't a good student. Much less a good person. If only everyone could see how tarnished Mr. Popular really was underneath that shine . . .

He's just a fat-ass nobody.

Presley's words ricocheted through me. He had doused me in his kerosene lies, and now the superintendent had struck a match with his assumptions. The fire ignited an anger inside me, blazing away all my doubt. There was no way Luc, Fin, and I could go back to how it was before, like we hadn't been affected by our shitty exes.

There was only one way to make it stop hurting.

Those First Wives in that movie had it right. It was unacceptable how Presley had treated me like shit without consequence, and I wanted him to burn. Make him regret the day he made me feel like I wasn't enough. *What are you gonna do about it?* he'd asked, and York had just given me the answer. If they thought Golden Boy Daniels was the perfect student to wear the Winter Formal crown, then I had to just prove how much of a consequence a nobody like me could be.

The anger spread through my chest with every breath. Sizzled the blood in my ears as I grabbed for my phone, pulling up our group chat. I was tired of pretending. Tired of being boring and messy and average.

Best Besties

Today 8:11 AM

> **Ezra:** We need to pull a First Wives Club and get revenge on our exes

Lucas: hell yes booboo!!! 😲

Finley: For real?

> **Ezra:** They need to pay for how they've treated us

Lucas: They are so canceled 😈

Lucas: We'll be the last boyfriends of their nightmares

Finley: Meet tonight to discuss?

Ezra: Let's do it

Lucas Rivera has renamed this group chat to "Last Boyfriends Club"

Five

Rivera Furniture was part of the South Shopping Plaza on the edge of town. The double doors Lucas's dad had installed opened to a cozy sitting room with a fireplace, family pictures displayed on the mantel, and a reception desk along the back wall. The best part was the magnificent red carpet stretching past the television setup toward a hallway, zigzagging through more displays. Living rooms where we'd spent hours scrolling TikTok and kitchens where we'd pretend to be college roomies while eating takeout. As many times as I'd been here, though, never had we gone into the business cubicle in the back corner.

"Thought we could use this as a private home base for the Last Boyfriends Club," Lucas said, waving us inside. It was staged with a conference table in the center, bordered by a dry-erase board and a fake window view of a generic city skyline. "Plus, like, no one in this butthole town needs office furniture."

I dropped into a rolling chair, my bag thudding to the floor. A black sleeve of the varsity jacket spilled out as I searched for my notebook. I hadn't been able to bring myself to give it back yet,

47

unwilling to give him the satisfaction after his latest Snapchat message: *hey have u seen my jacket i can't find it.* That was it. No *I'm sorry* or *I miss you* or *Please forgive me for being such an asshat.* It had only stoked the fire inside me.

Finley sat down across from me, and I shoved the jacket back in my bag. "Dude, I'm starving," he said, opening a pizza box from Bubba's Shack. "Didn't get to eat dinner. Pop had me washing cars at the dealership to make up for Logan's handiwork on my truck."

"But it wasn't your fault, Fin," Lucas pointed out as he sat at the head of the conference table.

"Still doesn't change the fact he's making me ride the bus until it's fixed," he huffed around a bite of pepperoni-'n'-cheese.

Hunger made that familiar aching growl in my stomach, and he nodded toward the pizza in offering. I began to protest on instinct. But then the memories of Presley calling me a fat ass sent a bolt of rage through my body. "You know what," I said, reaching for a slice, "I *am* hungry."

Lucas nodded approvingly as I took a bite, grease dripping onto my chin. "Nice to see you actually eating. . . ." He tilted his head, studying me for a moment. "It was because of him." Not a question but a final piece clicking into place.

"Yes," I said, swallowing roughly. "He said I need to lose weight."

"And that's why you've been running," Finley surmised, and I nodded. "Don't let that asshead make you feel ashamed of your body. Thick is damn sexy."

Easy for him to say. He was naturally lean muscled like he

belonged on a sports team. His stare was heavy with seriousness as he locked eyes with me, though. I let out a small laugh to cut the tension.

"He did say my dick game was bomb, so it wasn't all bad."

"First off," Lucas said with an impressed nod. "That fanfic porn must've paid off."

"C'mon, I only read it three times," I argued as Finley nearly choked, saying, "Didn't think we were allowed to bring that Glitter Bomb up!"

"We can *always* talk about Nyberg's hockey ass," I pointed out.

"Secondly," Lucas continued, "I hope Golden Boy Daniels is ready for you to screw him one last time."

"I'm ready to do this damn thing." The sound of my voice got lost in the howls of hyena laughter in my head.

"Same, especially after what Cass did at lunch today." Lucas leaned back in his chair, clenching his jaw. "I designed his pretentious birthday-meets-Halloween party invitations, hand calligraphed the hell out of them too. Then he had the *audacity* to wad mine up in front of me and toss it in the trash?"

"Cass the Ass really out-assed himself again over his Hallo-Weird tradition," Finley offered.

"He is really out there doing the most." He spun back and forth, hands tented together. "Buuut it *did* give me an idea for revenge."

"Okay, dude." Finley dipped his head in encouragement. "Go off."

Lucas nodded once and stood, crossing over to the dry-erase board. I glanced down at the Winter Lion King nomination form sticking out from my notebook, remembering my dad's words of encouragement when I told him I was running. We were really doing this, getting back at our ex-boyfriends. A thrill ran up my spine as reality set in.

"What do you think of when I say Cass Jacobs?" Lucas uncapped a red marker and began writing as though he were the teacher, we the students. "Other than him being an insufferable asshole."

I shut my mouth, biting back an insult, and looked at Finley. He went wide-eyed in thought. "Uh . . . that he's a too tan, too bleached Greek god wannabe and apparently throws the best parties?" he ventured. "I heard they're all-nighters, and everyone gets shit-faced."

"Exactly," Lucas said, standing back to admire his loopy handwriting. "He used me to help him plan the best HalloWeird yet. I want to ruin the party along with his massive ego . . . and show everyone how big of an ass Cass *actually* is."

"How do we do that?" Finley asked.

"We've never been invited to his parties," I added.

"Easy," he explained, returning to his chair. His chest puffed with pride as he sat down. "I planned for all the cater waiters to wear masquerade masks to blend in. We can pretend to be them."

"And do . . . what?" I asked hesitantly, picking at my thumbnail.

"Still workshopping the plan of attack, but I have these old Snaps saved in my drafts. I secretly recorded him making fun of his friends. I thought they could prove useful." He passed the marker to Finley with a smirk. "Just clear your schedules for October twenty-third."

"Do you think we'll get caught?" I worried my nail polish at the thought. It'd be embarrassing if we did. Everyone would be there, including Presley and the other dude-bros.

"Don't fret, booboo. I'll make sure we don't."

I nodded and tried to push my worry away. "What about you, Finley?" I asked, not yet ready to speak my idea into reality. "What're you thinking for LJM3?"

He tossed the marker back and forth in his hands for a moment, looking up at the ceiling. "Know how my pop is trying to make up for what happened over the summer?" he finally asked.

"How could I forget?" Lucas held his hand up, clutching at his chest. Finley's dad had made him try out for varsity football, thinking it would help Fin be more manly after the whole LJM3 musical debacle. "The thought of having to attend all the football games to cheer you on *still* gives me heartburn."

"Yeah, yeah," he continued, standing up. "He's learning to be an ally, though, trying to make up for it. . . . That's why he's sponsoring the community college's drag competition."

"Wait." My mouth gaped. "There's drag *here*? How has *Harper Valley Tattler* not started a Facebook war over it?"

"Just found out today at work," he explained as he approached the board. "I'm sure that sorry excuse for a newspaper will have a lot to say about Lewis Auto Sales presenting the first annual So You Think You Can Lip Sync. First place is a one-year scholarship to Alabama Regional."

"Oh my god," Lucas said in awe. "We *have* to go."

"That's what I was getting at." Finley popped the cap off the marker and scrawled his plan in scratchy handwriting. "I also found out Logan is planning to enter, and since you can sign up as a group, maybe we should—"

"Are you telling me . . . ," I started, and Lucas finished with a high squeak, ". . . *that we get to give ourselves a drag makeover?*"

"I guess?" Fin shyly rubbed a hand over the back of his neck. "Deadass afraid to get back in front of an audience and have all eyes on me again . . . but I wanna make Logan see how wrong he is. Show him I can be bi and feminine. And *not* a flop."

"I'm sent." Lucas's voice was thick with excitement. "*You* in makeup? Padding? Tuck and all? I gotta see how this turns out."

"How hard can it be?" Lucas and I gave each other side-eye, and Fin looked dumbfounded. "What?"

"Oh, sweet and innocent, Fin. Despite our best efforts, you've never watched an episode of *RuPaul's Drag Race.* There's sooo much for you to learn."

"I don't understand the appeal of it."

"Oh, hon-neyyy," I said, shaking my head. "Obviously you're watching the season premiere with us for a strategy sesh."

"Shit, this won't be as easy as I thought, will it?" We both nodded, and he sighed as he sat down, dropping his head onto the tabletop with a thunk. "Not gonna lie," he muttered, "now I'm nervous. What if I embarrass myself? Oh my god. I *will* embarrass myself in front of my pop and Logan and an audien—"

"Relax," Lucas ordered, and he looked up.

"We'll teach you everything about drag extravaganza," I said, shoving away my own reluctance toward being onstage.

"And show LJM3 that you deserve the spotlight," Lucas added.

Relief eased the tense set of Finley's lips, and he smiled. "Thanks for always being there. Even at football tryouts."

"You say that now," I teased as Lucas cringed at the memory of watching sports. "Just wait until we have to tuck."

"Tuck?"

"Like with a shirt, but it's your . . ." Lucas pointed to his lap. "How do you not know this already?"

Fin blinked rapidly, processing what it meant. With a nod almost as though he were reassuring himself, he rolled the marker across the table toward me. It was my turn to add my revenge up on the board.

"So, uh." I cleared my throat and glanced down at the edge of the nomination form. "As we all know, Presley was playing me and hooking up with whoever he wanted."

The memory of the Snapchat image, that muscley torso and the constellation of moles, made me cringe. I tried to shrug it off, but it made my skin crawl to think I was just one of many. Another card he'd shuffled in his deck. How many had been tricked by his blue-eyed poker face?

"That's sleazy," Lucas said, his nose wrinkling. "Not slut-shaming at all, but he lied to you and made you think you were *together* when—"

"He had all the sidedick," Finley finished with a sneer.

"It's gross." Flashes of mouths and kisses and grasping hands flipped through my mind. "I feel gross."

"You were safe, right?" Lucas asked carefully.

"I always wore a condom." Dad had ingrained that in my

upbringing. "But, like, what about mouth stuff?" The horror was starting to sink in, and my voice rose an octave. *"How many guys have done that?"*

Finley nearly choked as he drank from his water bottle. "Oh god," he coughed.

"Don't freak out." Lucas held his hands up to calm me down. "I'll take you to get an STI check at the health department if you're worried."

"I'm fine," I said, and they both gave me a warning look. "I legit can't think about this right now, okay?"

"Promise me you will deal with it, though." Lucas cocked his head, Finley leveling his gaze. "It's not about him. It's about you."

"Sure . . ."

"I know you too well," Lucas began as he reached for my bag, "so I'll just put a little reminder in your phone."

"No, wait," I said, trying to grab it from him.

"Why are you freaking?" He pulled the varsity jacket out of my bag. "Uh . . . why the hell do you still have this?"

"It's not what it looks like."

"That you're still holding on to him?" Finley asked with raised eyebrows.

"The fuck? No. No, no, no." But there was a small voice in the back of my mind that pissed me off. *Aren't you, though?* "I just, uh, didn't wanna give him the satisfaction of returning it."

"You should do the Maeve Kimball breakup challenge," Lucas suggested, tossing the jacket onto the table.

"Yeah, dude. Toss his shit so he doesn't take up space in your backpack, *or* your mind."

"Eh . . ."

If I did that TikTok, then everyone would know I was with a football player. I stared down at the HVHS lion, Presley's threat weighing on me. Embarrassing me. *Who'd believe you? People like me don't date people like you.*

"I don't want anyone to know it's me."

"Just make an anonymous alt account like mine," Lucas said with a duh expression. "It might make you feel better."

"Maybe . . . but I'd def feel better about everything if I could play Presley like he played me." My eyes slid over to the notebook, and I pulled out the form I'd gotten from the front office earlier. "I overheard York and Superintendent Bett talking about how Presley was the 'right kind' of student to represent HVHS. How he was guaranteed to win Winter Formal King, just like Homecoming. So what if . . ."

Lucas let out a tiny, shocked gasp as realization set in. "You're gonna run against Presley for Lion King."

"I checked the rules, and there's nothing about juniors not being able to run."

Finley slapped the table with a loud *ha!* "With you campaigning against him, Presley will worry his ass off about you telling everyone what he did."

"I won't out him," I said quickly. "I'm not a snake like LJM3. But I want him to doubt everything he's ever done as much as I do. Show him, show this school and their stupid Watch What You Say initiative, that I can at least be one of the top two candidates on the final ballot. Be part of the Winter Formal Court. Represent HVHS as a queer student. As Presley's *equal.*"

"You're gonna be out there actin' up," Finley said with a gleam in his eye. "And I. Am. Living for it."

"Maybe if I get enough votes—"

"With us as your campaign managers," Lucas began, rubbing his hands together, "we'll get you on the Winter Formal Court, trust."

Nerves fluttered through my stomach as they both looked up at me. Could I really do this, put myself out there? It would mean no more hiding. But maybe I was tired of hiding. Tired of being a background character in my ex's story, tired of being forced to the sidelines by HVHS's stupid *rules*.

It was time to make our own rules.

A silent rage tore through the nervousness as I thought of Presley's dismissal, of York making me turn my shirt inside out. I stood and went to the board, the red marker squeaking as I added my part to our plan of attack. We were really doing the damn thing—*I* was doing the damn thing.

RULES FOR REVENGE

SABOTAGE HALLOWEIRD PARTY

ENTER DRAG COMPETITION

RUN FOR WINTER LION KING

An echo of familiar laughter made me cringe as I turned to the table, and my eyes locked on the varsity jacket. The HVHS lion stared back at me knowingly. All those nights wasted on

Presley came rushing back with a vengeance. I could still feel that rough wool underneath my fingertips, feel him in my arms.

And it felt so goddamn embarrassing.

I wanted it to burn. Burn all the times he'd lied. Burn every single moment when I'd been stupid. Burn those memories until there was nothing left.

"Do either of you have a lighter?" I asked. "I wanna do that TikTok challenge after all."

Six

"Look," he says, pointing up. "There's a shooting star. Make a wish."

I don't need a wish. Golden Boy Daniels is everything I could have wished for—the romance I'd only seen in movies. The summer night is just right with him straddling my lap. I'm lost in the smells of summer, my hands in his golden tangles. He grinds against me and he's real and we're real and it's the hard fact of being here together in this moment.

"I'm ready," he says breathily against my ear, his hands gripping my shirt. "I want you to be my first."

He reaches for his varsity jacket, a slow friction between our bodies as he pulls a condom from its pocket. Then his eyes are on me, his hands are on me. We're here together and it's real and I'm falling in love—

I startled awake with the roar of blood in my ears, my skin sweaty and crawling. I'm not in the back of his truck on County Road 233. Not out in the middle of nowhere. Everything I'd been dreaming had happened, but none of it had ever been real.

The plaid comforter was tented and wrapped around my legs. I felt for my phone in the tangle of sheets. The screen lit up brightly, cutting through the darkness: 6:13 a.m. on a Sunday. With a groan, I rolled over and tried to go back to sleep.

The longer I lay there, though, the dirtier I felt from the dream. All those nights came whispering back in the darkness. How he let me hold him in my arms. The magic of my first kiss, my first time. When I was the main character in my own love story with the perfect guy saying the perfect words at the perfect time.

My eyes snapped open.

Perfect had been a sleazy lie he'd tricked me into believing. *How many others have held him and touched him and slept with him and . . .* Anger and sadness thrashed inside me as I lay there in the dark, unable to sleep.

The restlessness forced me out of bed. I dug through the laundry and quickly changed into a pair of gym shorts. Grabbing my earbuds, I eased out into the hallway. Snores from Dad's room disguised my measured footsteps to the stairs. I didn't want to wake him. He'd give me hell for pushing myself, and I couldn't deal with that again. Not when a barrage of thoughts was weighing me down with worry.

So much had been worrying me lately.

I toed on my sneakers in the foyer and eased out the front door. The cool October morning wrapped around me as I stretched, eyeing the big hill in our Middlebury subdivision. My legs were sore from running it yesterday. Up and down and over again to silence the clink of the lighter, the whoosh of flames in the alley behind Rivera Furniture. But the burning crackle of his jacket was too loud.

I put my earbuds in and unlocked my phone. There were ten TikTok notifications, but I kept ignoring the red bubble and shuffled the playlist I'd made. Checking them would make it real, make the video Lucas convinced me to post *too* real. The wool was still rough under my fingertips, the metal lighter cold.

Balling my hands into fists, I took off. Houses passed by. My footfalls slapped the pavement to the beat of Olivia Rodrigo. I gulped in the dewy air while my legs burned up the hill. Each inhale brought the smoke, every exhale the scorching leather as my mind raced along with the pounding in my chest.

How many guys? Thump. *How many guys?* Thump. *How many guys?* Thump.

My panic was rising with the sun, its beams cutting through the lingering darkness. They burned bright on my face as I neared the top of the hill, burned with the smoldering heat of his varsity jacket. *How many, how many, how many?* I pushed harder, my calves screaming in protest by the time the sidewalk leveled out. A side stitch doubled me over, and I collapsed on the grass.

The dew soaked into my shorts as I tried to catch my breath. The angry-sad thrash was still there, nestled in between by ribs. *Why am I torturing myself?* He didn't want me anymore. But no matter how much I tried to purge him from my head, he was still there. His laughter mocking me, his jacket burning, his threat that no one would believe me, his other guys.

Too much noise in my head.

I reached to pause the music, and then I saw the little notification bubble. Fifty-three new TikTok notifications. My stomach sank as I sat there, breathing heavily. I was afraid to open them. Afraid everyone had somehow discovered the alt account Lucas helped me create was mine.

Who'd believe you? People like me don't date people like you.

I blinked sweat out of my eyes as the previous night came flooding back again. The *clink, clink, clink* of the lighter while I struggled to ignite the wadded-up jacket on the ground. A *whoosh* as the flame spread across the wool. Scorching leather and smoke that'd made me choke. The way the lion melted slightly, how I'd used my phone camera to zoom in on the HVHS logo as it disintegrated.

Unable to take the anticipation any longer, I clicked to check the now fifty-seven notifications. It was real. I couldn't deny I'd burned the last piece of him I had left.

The alt account we'd named Last Boyfriends loaded with new followers, comments, likes—all usernames I didn't recognize. Then I saw the play count. More than a thousand people had watched my #breakupchallenge.

The after-school shift at Magnolia was slow. Too slow. It gave me entirely too much time to overthink.

According to my most recent internet search, there wasn't much to running for Winter Formal King. The first step was the nomination, and that was the easy part. My form was filled out and ready to be turned in. The second step was hanging up posters to make everyone aware of my existence. That wasn't hard either. However, it was the third step that made me immediately pit out my shirt with a cold sweat. I'd have to campaign and explain why I wanted to run. Which meant actually talking to people instead of sticking to the sidelines. No matter which article I read, there wasn't a way around old-school campaigning. I cringed at the thought, swiveling on the stool.

A groan escaped from the back room for the millionth time, followed by squeaking. From the front counter, I could see directly through the doorway as Jackson agitatedly erased something in his notebook. He slapped his pencil down on the table, a hand tangled in his floofy hair as he flipped through the textbook.

"How the hell do you find the skidding distance?" he griped in exasperation.

He'd come in early after football practice to knock out some homework. Every few minutes he'd argue with himself over physics, and I couldn't witness the agony any longer. Even without small talk, he'd found a way to pester the hell out of me.

"Jackson," I called, and he looked up. His thick eyebrows made him appear in a permanent state of loss. "Do . . . do you need help?"

"Pleeeease," he begged immediately.

I hopped off the stool and crossed over to the back room, hesitating in the doorway. He was at the rickety table, the same table from that last night with Presley. I steeled myself not to think about him naked and me on the brink of shattering his perfect facade.

"Use the . . . uh," I started, but the memory was flooding back. My whispered *I-love-yous* and his screaming silence. I tried to shake them from my head. "Use the formula index. Back of the book."

"The *what*?" he asked, flipping more pages.

"Distance is"—my eyes slipped away from his textbook to the spot where Presley had lain back—"equal to initial speed plus final speed divided by two multiplied by time."

"How the hell do you know that?"

"How do you *not* know it?" I forced myself to step into the back room, pushing the memory to the recesses of my mind. "We literally spent two weeks on it."

"Don't even." He leaned back in the chair and crossed his arms. "We're not all as smart as you, Ez."

"Ha." I rolled my eyes. "What question is giving you trouble?"

"All of them," he stressed, and leaned forward to read from the worksheet. "Especially this one asking the skidding distance of a car traveling at 22.4 meters per second and stops in 2.55 seconds."

"Okay, it's given you the initial speed and the time," I explained, looking over his broad shoulder. "Obviously the final speed is zero, so you can use a formula."

"Which formula?"

"Damn, Jackson," I said, taking his pencil and writing it out. "You kinda suck at this."

"Tell me about it."

He tangled his hand in his hair again, and I caught a whiff of citrus that sent my stomach reeling. It smelled like Presley. Like when he pulled me to this table and pulled my clothes off and pulled me apart lie by lie.

"How about this second question?"

"Nice try," I said, holding my breath. "I'm not gonna do your homework for you."

"What if—just go with me here—what if you tutor me?"

He spun around, and our faces were suddenly close. The green of his eyes pleaded from under the flop of hair that'd fallen across his forehead. He smiled a lopsided smile, and all I could think about was what it'd feel like to close my eyes and get lost in that familiar citrus scent.

"Do I have to beg?" he asked, his breath hot against my face. As hot as Presley's had been in my ear. "Because I—"

"No," I said against the onslaught of memory, and his smile dipped as I stepped back. "I mean, no, you don't have to beg. I'll . . . uh . . . I can help."

"You're the best, brah." He grinned at me, and his chin dimpled. Why did I think it was cute? Had it always been cute? "I owe you big-time."

"N-no problem," I stammered as his phone vibrated on the table. Another step back to clear my head as he checked it. *Get your shit together.* Cute and Jackson F'ing Darcy didn't belong in the same thought.

He gawked at his phone, a familiar sizzle coming from the speakers. "No way," he said, tilting his screen toward me. "Have you seen this? Someone just sent it in the team chat. A HVHS varsity jacket was burned on TikTok."

"It was?" I asked evenly, shielding my reaction as he held the phone out. The Last Boyfriends upload now had 700 likes and way too many comments to count. *What the hell?*

"Brutal," he said, shaking his head. "The team's trying to figure out whose account it is."

"Damn." My voice was distant, my fingers itching to check the account's notifications as I backed away. "I should probably . . . uh . . . check . . . the front."

He said something in reply, but my heartbeat was thundering too loudly in my ears to hear. My fingers scrambled in a blur as soon as he was out of sight. I inhaled sharply, blinking several times to make sure I was seeing the screen clearly.

The video had 3,000 plays. Now the football team had seen it—*Presley* had seen it. A smile twisted onto my lips as I watched the fire burn, as I realized how much I'd wanted him to see what I had done.

Seven

"I. Am. Livid."

Lucas leaned against his car while I climbed out of my Jeep. Judging by the scowl and crossed arms, I knew he'd seen it too. The TikTok video had hit 100,000 plays overnight and spawned a new duet challenge, which Cass had taken part in. Now I understood what my dad meant when he said his blood pressure skyrockets during the news. My heart had quickened with every notification, frenzied beats pulsating behind my eyes, because the world was on fire.

"I can't believe he did #fireyourex with my Olivia Rodrigo tour shirt," Lucas muttered in complete disbelief. "Like *he's* the victim."

"Just when I thought he couldn't be any bigger of a dick," I said absently, pulling Lucas into a hug and scoping out the HVHS parking lot. Presley's truck was in its usual spot, but he was nowhere to be seen.

"Too soon." His words were muffled against my chest. "Below-average game it may be, I'm still mourning its loss."

Everyone around us had their phone out, flames dancing on the screens. I could feel the play count ticking higher and higher as news of the video spread. It was a wildfire out of control. I never thought anyone would see it, much less that it would start a trend. A nervous sweat beaded on my forehead as I tried to find him. What would he do when he realized he was the spark that had started all this?

"Damn him! That was my *favorite* shirt from my *favorite* concert too." Lucas pulled back, smoothing down a silvered tuft of hair. "Whatever. It's okay, I'm okay. I'll show him at HalloWeird."

"What's the plan there?" I asked as we walked toward the entrance, keeping an eye out.

"I'm thinking . . . maybe I could edit those mean Snap vids I have saved into a montage of his assholeness. He wouldn't know who recorded them. . . ."

"Sure," I said offhandedly as we passed by Presley's truck. The cargo bed was piled high with memories from last summer. But none of them were real. We weren't real. People like him didn't date people like me. He'd laugh at me for thinking I could fire him as my ex.

"And I wanna dump blood on him like in that old horror movie."

"Sur— Huh?" I turned toward Lucas as I processed what he'd said. "Like real blood?" He batted his lashes in reply. "That's kinda cringe. And basic."

"Ruuude." He rolled his eyes, tapping the Notes app on his phone. "I can do some readjusting. Fake blood will work just as well . . . I guess."

"What *exactly* are we doing?" I risked another glance around before trying to read Lucas's screen. "Is it illegal? Because I don't think juvey would look good on a brag sheet for college applications."

"Full details forthcoming—"

His eyes went wide for a split second as he looked over my shoulder, and then they squinted with anger. The pressure inside my head throbbed as I spun around, fully expecting to see Presley looming over me and hear those barking hyena laughs. False alarm. It was just Cass pulling his big-ass double cab into a space.

I exhaled raggedly as he hopped down from the lifted truck. As though on instinct, he immediately looked our way with the smarmiest grin on his smug face. He waved, a little wiggle of his fingers that said he knew Lucas had seen his duet.

"Can't wait. To see his face. When I destroy his party," Lucas said through clenched teeth, flipping Cass the bird.

He marched up the steps, and I raced to join him so I wouldn't be left alone. We pushed into the lobby, and I glanced up the hallway and down. No sign of Presley. Part of me was afraid I'd see him, and another part was hoping for a reaction if I did.

"Anyway," Lucas huffed, stopping by the Lions Pride poster. "Still good for *Drag Race* at your place tonight?"

"Yep."

"Thank god for drag." He rooted around in his bag and pulled out the stash of emergency Sour Patch Kids he always kept on him. The tartness settled his nerves. "It has already been. A. Day."

"What you said." I told myself to stop freaking out, to shake the nerves and focus on the good things about today. "I desperately need drag queens and sweatpants. Dad's gonna grab pizza on his way home from work too."

"Zaddy Kevin is a blessing."

"Also cringe that you call him that."

Lucas rolled his eyes, chewing a red candy as he unlocked his phone. "I wonder how Fin is doing on the bus with the middle schoolers. . . ." His face fell as he read the screen.

"What fresh hell is it now?" I asked.

"The HVHS update," he muttered while he read.

"You actually read the school emails?"

"How can you not with everything happening around here?" He took a deep breath, closing his eyes. "Principal York has issued a new list of banned books that go against Superintendent Bett's Watch What You Say homophobic bullshit."

"Let me see." I pried the phone from his vise grip and read through it. "Uh . . . these are almost all queer books." But they were more than that—a book about a girl falling in love for the first time, a memoir of growing up in the Bible Belt, a search to find meaning in life, and the list went on.

"Most are intersectional." Lucas's voice was hollow, his words terse as he stared at the Lions Pride poster. "It's all part of Superintendent Bett's sneaky plan to keep any kind of diverse representation out of schools. They're banning books to silence us. They want to erase our existence. Keep us from realizing we are actual fucking human beings with thoughts and feelings and identities."

My bag weighed heavily against my back. The Winter Formal nomination was still in there, still waiting for me to go through with it. Waiting for me to stop caring that Presley had called me a nobody.

I was tired of waiting, of being a goddamn bystander in my own existence.

"We have to force them to notice we're here," I said with determination, swinging my backpack off my shoulder. "I'll show them the 'right kind' of representation for HVHS."

The form was still firmly pressed between my physics and world history textbooks when I unzipped the bag. All I had to do was go into the front office and turn it in. *Easy,* I calmed myself. *I can do that. No one has to know I'm running yet.*

Cold seeped through my jeans as I knelt in the bathroom stall. Nerves ravaged my stomach, the dates swirling through my head. Winter Formal announcements were on the fifth of November, first round of voting the twenty-second. Then the final court announcement and voting after Thanksgiving.

I didn't know if I could do it. If I could stand up to Presley and the school with a queer AF campaign. If me running for the Lion King crown would even matter like Lucas said it would.

Principal York's oily voice cut through what little confidence I had mustered. *You kids and your issues* and *Not everything is an attack on your rights. . . .* The bacon sandwich I'd eaten earlier rioted with the nervous energy in my stomach, splashing up my throat even as I tried to keep it down.

It felt like I was moving in slow motion as I stood and flushed the toilet. Went to the sink. Let the water run until it was hot. Splashed my face and tried to exhale the pressure in my lungs.

My reflection stared back at me between breaths. I didn't know if I could do this. If I could run for Winter Lion King or sneak into that party or do drag. I was a boring, average, messy nobody.

The bathroom door creaked open while I splashed my face again. I looked up in time to see the blue dazzle gone from Presley's eyes, his mouth a hard line. Then he jerked me backward by my bag. Books went skittering across the tiled floor as it fell off my shoulders.

"You burned my jacket," he said matter-of-factly as he spun me around. "And you put it on TikTok."

I opened my mouth to say something, say everything I'd wanted to tell him since I'd discovered who he was. No words came out, though. There was only silence as he glared at me, his stoic demeanor slowly morphing into unbridled anger.

"What the fuck were you thinking?" he seethed, his voice breaking with rage.

He shoved me against the wall, and I tried to push him away. A flash of pain shocked through me when he grabbed my hands. As he pinned them against my chest and leaned in with a whisper. "Everyone has seen it now. The team's already asking questions."

My head swam with his strong sandalwood and citrus

cologne. He was too close. The same mouth I'd kissed countless times was right there. All he'd have to do was lean in slightly. Like we'd done so often, like he'd done with so many others. My skin crawled, and I struggled to break away from his grasp.

"S-stop," I managed to say, finally finding my voice.

His fingers dug into my hands harder. All those perfect lines of his body I'd once traced were now pricking me. Stabbing me. I slumped against the wall, unable to breathe. The bathroom spun, and my rib cage threatened to explode with each agonizing heartbeat.

"You better not say a word about us being together." His voice was quiet. So soft, so intimate. "No one will belie—"

He was cut off by a flying blur pushing him sideways. "Leave him alone!" Lucas yelled, standing tall. Taller than I'd ever seen him. With a thwack, he hit Presley once more across the face with his bag. "You sorry piece of shit."

Presley blinked in confusion, shielding himself. Blood dribbled down his chin. He lifted a hand to his busted lip and eyed Lucas. "I'm gonna kick—"

"Save your toxicity for someone who gives a damn," Lucas cut him off, sparing me a quick glance. Then he got a better grip on his bag. "Touch him again, and everyone will find out what a pathetic player you are." He nodded toward the exit. "Go be you somewhere else."

The threat hung in the air as the bell rang. Presley held Lucas's gaze until its shrill echo faded; then he made for the door. With a parting glare at me, blue eyes so cold they stung, he slipped into the hallway.

Lucas breathed heavy for a moment, and then he spun around to me. "I saw him follow you into the bathroom," he explained, rushing over. "You okay?"

"I'm fine," I tried to say, but I wasn't. His hands were still on me, his fingerprints dirty on my skin. I forced myself back to the sink, to pump soap in my palms and lather as the faucet ran hot.

"Ezra?"

I couldn't say anything as I scrubbed and scrubbed and scrubbed. My stomach turned, the too-familiar smell of his cologne stuck in my nose. But he'd become a stranger. The last five months really did mean nothing. I felt the tears on my cheek while I rinsed my hands in the scalding water, his grip still lingering.

"Hey." Lucas stopped me from pumping more soap and tore off a paper towel. "That's enough. Dry your hands, and then we're skipping first block because you're not fine."

"Can you . . ." I sniffled, wiping snot on my sleeve. "Can you take me to the health department . . . for an STI check?"

"We'll listen to Taylor and sing as loud as humanly possible on the way."

He smiled at me reassuringly, and I dried my hands even though I could still feel Presley's grip. Even though I could feel him using me and wadding me up and throwing me away.

Eight

There is a framed photo of me hanging in our living room. In it, I'm seven years old, sitting in the old farm truck with my grandma. The straps of a purple tank top cut across my sunburnt shoulders, and a wide smile is plastered on my reddened face. It was one of those days I could remember vividly. Every detail and every sense.

It'd been a hot day in August, the smell of dried grass and earth still strong in my memory. Dad was helping Grandpa load up hay bales for the horses. My job had been to steer the truck while Grandma worked the pedals. We went through the fields while they tossed bale after bale from the hitched trailer, and I'd been so proud in that picture because I'd helped drive.

That was how I felt now.

The health department had been scary at first, but I'd done it. I had done something important. I answered personal questions with Lucas holding my hand. I went back to the exam room and held my breath while the doctor examined my junk.

The entire time I kept chanting *I'm a big boy* to myself just like I'd said that day way back then.

Seven-year-old me held my gaze as I chewed a blue Sour Patch Kid. My mouth burned from the sugary tartness, from the grin I was wearing, just like the one I'd worn in the picture. I was proud of myself for going through with the screening. Relieved that nothing was out of the ordinary. Grateful for Lucas and car karaoke and Finley's introduction to *Drag Race*.

I shifted on the sofa and looked over at Lucas on the other end. His head was bent over his phone, swiping back and forth between his messages and the Notes app. Whatever he had planned for his ex-boyfriend, I'd stick with him no matter what. I owed him that much and more.

"Luckily, the caterer at Longleaf Farm doesn't know about the breakup yet," he said, looking at us with a glint in his eye.

"What did she say?" Finley asked from the side chair. His body was tightly wound on the edge of the seat in anticipation. He'd even brought a notebook for a crash course in drag.

"She confirmed the timeline for the party." Lucas chuckled lowly, scribbling as rain pelted against the windows behind him. "Waiters will be there at five p.m. in all black. We can sneak in and pretend to be one of them. That'll give us an hour to rig the cake's confetti cannons and break into the audio-visual room before the party starts." He cut his eyes toward me as my mouth opened. "Before you ask, nothing's *technically* illegal."

"Good to know," I said, my voice scratchy from belting out

how we were never (ever, ever) getting back together over and over again.

"The time was the last puzzle piece," he added, typing in his note. "Let's get there before five to be safe. Finley and I will swipe the cake from the kitchen's walk-in fridge and fill the confetti cannon cake toppers with fake blood. Ezra, you will take the flash drive of the Snap videos I edited and hook it into the AV computer. Then we wait until seven-thirty-three p.m. Eastern time for his parents' 'tribute' video to play while the candles are lit."

"That's an oddly specific time," Finley commented, scratching the dark stubble on his chin. "Why does it matter?"

"It's the time he was born," Lucas explained, and I couldn't contain my eye roll. "Timing is everything. We'll need to blend in until then and be ready. His parents will think it's the video they programed to auto-play, but instead it'll be my edit of Cass being an ass to his friends before anyone can stop it. By then, the candles will have ignited the confetti cannons and sprayed him in fake blood. I'll get a picture—"

"Hold up, a blood cake sounds kinda cool," I pointed out.

"I know, right? That's what I told him, but he didn't want to mess up his costume." His lips curled into a smirk. "It'll be a message, so he'll know it was me."

"But, like . . . what if he comes at you?" Finley asked. "Or rats us out to someone?"

"*I* don't care what he does," Lucas stressed, waving a hand with indifference. "Besides, no one will listen to him after the video plays. I'll make sure they don't forget about it either. When we design the Senior Life yearbook spread, the picture of him and his ruined costume—and reputation—will be the main feature."

"Ms. D won't let us get away with that." I turned toward Finley for a second opinion. "Would she?"

"Maybe?" He thought for a moment and then nodded in assurance. "I think she'd understand. She's one of us."

Lucas typed in the Notes app with a quick succession of finger taps. "Check. Ex-boyfriend mission number one is officially ready to go, and soon Cass will *finally* be out-assed."

"It's about damn time," Finley said with a snort as his phone lit up. The laughter died in his throat while he watched the screen intently. Then he closed his eyes and took a deep breath. "Speaking of asses, Logan just dueted that challenge on TikTok. With my Roll Tide hat. And *tagged* me in it."

He passed his phone to us, and Lucas's eyebrows dipped in disapproval as we watched. "I've never punched anyone before," he said, "but there's something about LJM3's arrogant face that makes me wanna hit him."

"Same," I added with a grimace, watching the video replay.

The casualties from my video were racking up with the view count, and all I could hear was Presley asking what I was thinking. I didn't think anyone would notice, that's what. But now the video had a life of its own.

"Sorry about the #fireyourex thing. . . . I didn't think any of this would happen," I said.

"Not your fault he's dick scum." I watched as Fin clicked through to my Last Boyfriends profile and did a double take. "Damn, dude! The video has five hundred thousand plays!"

"I know." I breathed heavily through the mounting tension in my chest, side-eyeing my phone on the sofa cushion. "I can't even keep up. The notifications are out of control."

"Let me see." Lucas grabbed my phone and keyed in the passcode. His eyes went wide as he scrolled through the never-ending list of comments and follows. "I'm shook people from school are posting conspiracy theories about what happened." Then he gasped, a light bulb practically going on above his head. "You *have* to post a second video and spill the tea—"

"I don't want anyone to know it's me!" The thought of bringing more attention to it, of Presley's threat in the bathroom, set off alarm bells. "That'd be bad. Really bad. You saw how fast that rumor about Presley spread since this morning."

"Yeah, yeah." Lucas rolled his eyes dramatically. "He told people he busted his lip in a 'fight' when he was mugged for his varsity jacket."

"This video must have him spooked if he's out there covering his ass," Finley said. "Still can't believe he came for you."

I could still feel his grip on my hands, his fingers burning like scorch marks. *You better not say a word about us being together.* If he'd been that upset, maybe Finley was right.

"Dude, you have an absolute choke hold on him," he added. "Trust me, after what Logan did to me, I know Golden Boy Daniels is afraid you'll out him and everyone will know he's a player."

I shook my head. "I'd *never* do that. Outing someone is such a low blow. No matter how scummy they are."

"He doesn't know that, though." Lucas tilted his head in thought as thunder rolled in the distance. "This most def helps with your campaign for Lion King. He's afraid of what you could do. Your voice actually has a shot of being heard now."

"But what if . . ." I squirmed under both of their stares, under the pressure of what it meant to stop hiding. "What if nobody cares that I'm running?"

"There are people who care." Finley rubbed a hand over the back of his head. "People like me last year, too afraid of what coming out means. Seeing you *be* out might help them."

"We can do posters, flyers, campaign buttons!" Lucas added enthusiastically, clutching my phone. "Do you have any good selfies we can use or—" The lock screen lit up with notifications, and his eyes went wide. "Jackson Darcy is sliding into your DMs?"

"Jackson Darcy?" Finley asked, his brow dancing. "The same Jackson Darcy who bugs the shit out of you every day?"

"His name has been said way too many times for my comfort level." I reached for my phone, but Lucas held it away with an insinuating smirk. "Don't even go there. It's *not* like that."

"Then what could it be?" He posed, clicking to read the message. "Ahem . . . 'Hey, Ez, when you wanna get together?'"

"Shut up," I said before Finley could say anything. "He asked me to tutor him. That's all."

Lucas squealed, clapping his hands. He and Finley shared a silent look. "Fin, are you thinking what I'm thinking?"

"Y'all—"

"That Jackson could be Ezra's date to the Winter Formal?"

"Our little boy is growing up!" Lucas pretended to wipe a tear from his eye. "Wait . . . do we know if he's into guys? More importantly, would he go full bully mode if Ezra asked him out—"

"I most certainly won't be doing *that*." I snatched my phone back, the thunderous rolls of every hurtful dig Presley had thrown at me syncing with the storm outside. "Because it's *not* like that."

"That's too bad," Finley said with a slow grin. "I saw him changing in the locker room during football tryouts . . . and he looks good naked. Like *really* good."

I blinked slowly, caught off guard over the thought of Jackson F'ing Darcy without clothes. Then Lucas burst out wheezing with, "You were totally creeping on him!"

Finley slapped Lucas with a throw pillow, and then it was on. We were waging war, tossing laughs and pillows. Much too loud to hear a key rattle or the front door open. Right as I hauled back to smack Finley, Dad cleared his throat from the foyer.

"What's so funny?" he asked, shaking the water from his curling hair.

Lucas let out another wheeze of laughter, muttering something unintelligible about zaddies. "You don't wanna know," I said, and hit Lucas with the pillow instead.

He hummed in agreement and looked at Finley in surprise. "Didn't see your truck out there. These boys finally talk you into *Drag Race* night?"

"Something like that." Finley cocked his head with a huff.

"My truck got keyed, and Lucas is giving me a ride until it's out of the shop."

"Sounds like that Logan twerp struck again," Dad said, and Finley nodded. "That kid needs his ass whupped."

"Kevin, let me tell you something." Lucas held a hand to his chest, clutching at nonexistent pearls. "It has been an *ordeal*, but Fin's here to gag on eleganza and come for him."

Dad grinned with uncertainty. "Well. That's nice. I'll just go put these pizzas in the kitchen." His smile faltered into a stern line as he met my gaze. "Think you could help me for a sec, bud?"

"Sure . . ." I trailed off, unsure of his change in mood.

With a shoulder shrug, I padded through the foyer. The wind chime on the porch clanked wildly as more thunder rolled. I paused as leaves swirled outside the windows, summer slowly being swept away. *If only I could let go as easily* . . . I pushed the thought from my head, shoving it deep down with my hands in my hoodie's pocket, and continued into the kitchen. Dad was seated at the island, locked in a staring contest with the Bubba's Shack logo in front of him.

"How was work?" I asked cautiously.

"Ezra, listen, bud," he said after a beat, hands fidgeting. "You know I don't like being the bad dad, but why did you skip class today?"

"What?" My stomach dropped as he waited for an explanation.

"I got a voice mail from the office administrator. You were absent for first block."

Shit. Shit. Shit. I'd completely blanked on that.

"Look, I know something's up. You haven't been acting like yourself. I've tried to respect your boundaries, but now you're cutting class and—"

"IwenttogettestedforSTIs," I blurted, cutting off his panic mode. Unable to lie to him, too tired of pretending to be okay.

"You what?" He blinked several times as the confession sank in. "Oh *god*. I haven't made it that far on the PFLAG's resource materials. Okay, uh—"

"I was safe." The admission felt like cotton in my mouth. I just told my dad that I'd done it. Capital I.T. The sex. *Kill me now.*

"Okay," he said again, mostly to himself. "What made you want to get tested?"

"I was . . ." I didn't want to tell him that I'd been secretly dating someone, but the vulnerability in his eyes made me stall. We were supposed to talk about these things. He'd *begged* me to talk to him. "There was this guy and one thing led to another and we were safe, but I just wanted to make sure that I'm good and yeah." I said it all with my eyes trained on the floor.

"Hey," he said gently, and then he wrapped me in a hug. "I'm proud of you. You're smart to get checked. Thank you for telling me."

"Thanks, Dad," I said warily, waiting to see how this would go. "Am I in trouble?"

"Not for taking care of yourself." He patted my back. "Just don't skip class again, okay? I'm required by parental law to say that."

"Promise."

"So, uh. Pizza." He turned to the island, not sure what to do with himself. "I got your old favorite. Spicy sausage with hot honey. Didn't know what the boys would like, so I got pepperoni and supreme. Do you think they'll like it? I could go back out."

"It's fine," I said, thankful he didn't press with too many questions. "Hey . . . you wanna watch *Drag Race* with us?"

"And be the 'old dad' hovering while you're with your friends?" He laughed at his self-pitying humor. There it was, the awkward reality that he was old enough to have a sexually active son.

"You aren't old." I picked up the pizza boxes and nodded toward the living room with a grin. "C'mon, we'll fill you in on the drag competition we're entering."

Before I could turn the corner, he was out of his seat. "Wait, you can't drop a bomb like that and walk out," he called, raising his voice in delight. "Boys, when are y'all doing drag? Better yet, where do I buy tickets? This I've gotta see."

Nine

@lastboyfriends is just gonna post and ghost so who got theories?

♡ 1.2K

It was the top comment, the most replied to by everyone at HVHS. I'd woken up to an incessant influx of notifications that lasted all through physics. Before the bell could stop ringing, three new ones popped up as I grabbed my bag to leave:

she got knocked up and he bailed

who said it was a she?

omg who's gay on the football team?

A wave of whispering voices rose around me, a hush of expectant theories. I could feel the weight of all those notifications in my back pocket. All demanding an explanation. Lucas was in favor of a second video, but how could I do that without outing Presley—or myself as the alt account?

No one would believe me anyway.

I slipped through the hallway with my head down, too nervous to make eye contact. Too worried someone would somehow know it was me. Too focused on my feet to see it coming.

A hard shove slammed me against the old lockers. Their hollow clang echoed through my body as I slid to the floor, kneecaps cracking against tiles. My mind raced to catch up with why I'd fallen. Then I heard it, that stabbing laughter as I picked myself up. Presley smirked over his shoulder. His self-satisfied expression went stony as his focus shifted to somewhere behind me.

"Brah," Jackson said, approaching me, none the wiser. "I totally dozed off in first block. Did I miss anything?"

I shook my head while trying to shake off the ache in my side. The blue-eyed glare kept looking back as Jackson fell into step beside me.

"What?" I asked while he side-eyed me. *Did he see Presley knock me down?*

"You gonna leave me on read like that?" he countered instead, stifling a yawn.

"My bad, I got . . . distracted."

"I see how it is."

His laugh sounded tired. I hadn't noticed how distressed he looked when he'd rushed into class late. Up close, though, I could see the dark smudges under his eyes and the deflated floof of his hair. Like he'd stayed up all night running his hands through it.

"You okay?" I asked.

He draped an arm around my shoulders, pulling me close

as we passed the Lions Pride poster. "Real talk, I bombed my extra credit. Ya boy is gonna fail physics if you don't help me understand this."

He smiled pleadingly, and that dimple was back. It was doing things to me that it had no right to do. "O-okay," I stammered, looking away before I could consider it *cute* again. "Let's hang—"

That blue-eyed glare cut me off like a dagger to the throat. Presley was standing outside the economics classroom watching our every move. His busted lip was jutted, jaw set as Jackson ruffled my hair. The way he stood, shoulders high and arms crossed in a tangle of coiled muscles.

Finley was right. I *did* have a choke hold on him.

"Next week?" Jackson asked, backing toward his second class. "After practice?"

"Sure thing, man!" I called to him like we were friends, and my skin prickled from the analyzing glare. "You owe me big-time."

He winked, giving two thumbs-up, and headed down the hallway. I watched him go for a count of three before turning to see Presley's reaction. But he wasn't there. He'd disappeared into the classroom.

My lips twitched in a satisfied smirk, and I continued to world history. Golden Boy Daniels was afraid of what I could do to him. When he found out I was running for Winter Lion King, he'd freak even more. Everything was out of his control now.

I'm *out of his control.*

He couldn't stand over me or grip my hands or threaten me

or keep me quiet. He couldn't make me feel bad for being myself. The realization coursed through me as I sat down at my desk, as the bell rang, as everyone took their seats.

"What has you grinning?" Finley asked, slipping into the seat beside me.

"You were definitely right," I said with a nod. "About the whole choke hold thing."

"I *knew* it!" He beamed, pleased with himself for calling it; then he lowered his voice. "I bet the comments are freaking him out too."

Maybe the flood of notifications wasn't as bad as I'd thought. Because I'd done that, caused him to freak out. I reached for my phone in my back pocket to check them again, but the camera app was already launched in an accidental video. The last five minutes had been recorded from where my phone had been sticking out my jeans. Enough time for me to leave physics, get slammed into the lockers, and make Presley nervous. Five minutes that could have captured the effect I had on him.

Making sure Coach Rogers wasn't looking, I clicked to play the video. It began as I stood with a focus on the desk seat and then on the students packing up their books, Jackson waking from an impromptu nap. The camera had recorded as I left the classroom and joined the crowded hallway. Students carried on like normal, Principal York lurking in the background as he monitored the class change. A shadowy blur crossed the frame. The person was unrecognizable, but I knew it was Presley as he collided with me and sent the phone tumbling.

Watching the video play back, the satisfaction I'd felt over

Presley's reaction boiled into rage. He'd lashed out at me. Again. And this time there was proof. All I had to do was show Principal York and then . . . *Daniels is a good student. It'll be an honor to have the right kind of representation for HVHS.* If Superintendent Bett thought Presley could do no wrong, everyone else would too.

No one would take my side.

I'd have to do it myself.

The accidental pocket recording would be the perfect second video. Fear had stopped me as he'd gripped my hands in the bathroom, but not anymore. There were so many things I wished I had said. So many things he needed to hear. If burning his jacket had caused such an uproar, then putting his actions on blast would too. He'd be forced to listen then. Forced to feel the way I'd felt at Magnolia the night I confronted him. How I'd felt when I found out he'd played me—stupid and embarrassed and scared. A blurred nobody.

"I'm the last boyfriend of a cheater."

I watched as my new upload replayed; my voice disguised by a narration effect. The video began in the crowded hallway. Hushed whispers and sneakers on the tiles echoed in the background while I exited physics.

"He told me we had to be a secret, but that's his game. He hooks up with whoever he wants, gaslighting them into silence.

Now he's trying to keep me quiet because I found out he's a player. He's attacking me, but I won't back down."

Then the blur hit me, Presley's features hidden save for his new Mighty Lions jacket. The camera shaking, the frame zoomed down the hall where Principal York stood watch and Jackson made his way through the crowd. Slowly, it faded out to the Lions Pride poster with the football team listed.

"There is no pride here. HVHS wouldn't do anything if I reported what's happening to me. I have to take matters into my own hands."

The video stopped and started over again. It posted five minutes ago for the 2,000 followers of the Last Boyfriends account to see. I nervously kept checking for a response, but there were only three plays so far (two of which were from me). My legs jangled as I sat on the edge of my bed, as I tossed my phone to the side, as I tried to concentrate on English homework.

My eyes read and reread the opening page of *The Great Gatsby*. Every few words, though, they'd shift slightly to the darkened screen in anticipation. I shook my head and trained them back on the 1920s. Another sentence, paragraph, page, two pages before the itch to check overpowered me.

I sighed, leaning back against the pillows to read. Three more pages until I got distracted by the crooked jersey. Memories replayed of being forced to turn my Queer Hockey Hero shirt inside out. If Rolf Nyberg believed in himself enough to come out and take a stand for queer rights, then I could too. He wouldn't just sit around and wait for the world to notice him.

"He'd get shit done," I said aloud, sitting upright.

The book fell to the side, bouncing shut against my Spider-Man sheets. The same sheets that'd once been under Presley. Bile splashed up my throat at the thought of us naked. Sweaty. Wrapped in them.

I stood up and hurriedly stripped the bed. Stripped that memory away.

After cramming the bedding into the hamper, I looked around my room for more reminders of him. Everything was the same as it had been, though. Same four boring, gray walls. Same haphazard stack of rom-coms piled on the desk. Same pile of laundry that really needed to be put away.

But *I* didn't feel the same.

I started with the DVDs, white-knuckling their cases as I tossed them on the floor. Reese Witherspoon stared up at me from the cover of *Sweet Home Alabama*. Her grand declaration on a stormy beach made me hesitate. *So I can kiss you anytime I—*

"No," I said forcefully, shaking my head. There was no more need for damsels distressed by forbidden loves or secret loves or slow-burning loves. I kicked the movies as far under the bed as they'd go, pushing their fake promises out of my mind.

Next was the laundry. I opened the closet to put it away, and the mirrored door caught my reflection. I stood there frantic and sweaty. Same wonky nose. Same thick body. Same hair that didn't know if it was brown or red, straight or curly. I stepped closer, right up to the cool surface of the glass. The same hazel eyes looked back at me, but now they knew—they *knew* what he'd done, and what *I* was capable of doing.

Ten

"The *nerve* of that man—no, boy," Lucas was saying as he pushed into the HVHS lobby, "to think I'd still want his below-average dick game." Cass had apparently Snapped a picture asking Lucas to come over last night. "Can't wait to wreck his ego. We'll run through the plan tonight at the furniture store. . . ."

He trailed off, stopping both midsentence and in the doorway. I bumped into him as a rush of voices met us. "That was on TikTok," someone said in the crammed lobby. "Who posted it?" another asked. "Last Boyfriends did this," claimed a third.

Did what? When I had woken up, the video still hadn't received many responses. Confusion pushed me forward through the crowd, Lucas on my heels. Then I caught sight of spray-painted arcs of rainbow through the bodies swaying with furtive whispers.

THERE IS NO PRIDE HERE

Lucas tugged at my sleeve with a silent question flashing across his face. I shook my head, thoughts fighting their way to the front of my mind. *I didn't do this* and *Who did this?* and *Why would they do this?*

I read the graffiti again. What I'd said in last night's upload was sloppily spelled out in a hurry across the Lions Pride poster that hung in the hallway. Each letter dripped and dribbled down over the football players' names. It sent my head and heart into a battle over the puck that had just dropped in my stomach. My fingers worried over my polish as I picked at my thumbnails. Someone at HVHS was *actually* paying attention to what I had to say.

Wildfire accusations spread around us. I searched for a hint, an idea of who might've done this. All I found was uncomfortable confusion etched on the faces of the students of HVHS. They weren't in any rush to name it, to acknowledge the lack of pride at our school.

My gaze locked on a pair of green eyes looming over everyone else. Jackson stood just inside the lobby. He paused and read the sign, the door opening behind him. Presley stepped up beside him as he stared hard at it. Their lips moved inaudibly, and then annoyance knitted Jackson's bushy brows. He shot Presley a sharp look while the bell sounded, and he edged around the crowd.

Golden Boy Daniels stood there, hands fidgeting in the pockets of his new varsity jacket. It looked the same as the burned one, but it wasn't. He wasn't the same. The smile I'd once found so alluring was strained, the hair I'd loved to run my hand through was greasy and tarnished. He briefly glanced at Jackson before he saw me watching. Slightly, almost imperceptibly, he shook his head. An accusation.

He blames me for the graffiti, I realized as a sharp thud quieted the dull roar of voices. My attention snapped to the front office. Principal York pushed his way through the horde of gathered students, the blinds on the door still swinging where he'd slammed it.

"Break it up!" he shouted, his eyes darting. "You know the rules on fighting. . . ." He stilled as he saw the poster. I watched him mouth my words, his lips pursing. "Who vandalized *my* school?"

He marched toward the Lions Pride poster while too many voices began talking at once. Then someone shouted, "He knows who did it!"

Lucas went rigid, gripping my hand as heads rippled toward Jackson.

"He was in the TikTok!" a girl yelled as York tore down the poster.

Jackson froze, helpless and lost while accusations hurled at him. All because he'd been in the background of my new TikTok. Another casualty I didn't think through. I didn't think the video would lead to him being the center of attention or someone using my words to graffiti the school.

"Silence!" York bellowed, and the roar died. He wadded up the poster as he walked toward Jackson. "Darcy, do you happen to have any insight as to who might've posted that TikTok about one of your teammates?"

"N-no, sir," he stammered. "I don't know who posted it."

"Are you sure?" York pressed. Jackson nodded, and York studied him for a moment before scanning the crowd. "Superintendent

Bett is calling for me to punish whoever posted that video last night. It's in direct violation of the Watch What You Say social media policy." York plastered on a fake smile despite his angry grip on the balled paper. "I'm sorry the student feels that way, and my office door is always open. I'm here for you. That's why I'm willing to let this destruction of school property slide and not inform the superintendent *if* the video is removed." He gulped, his throat working to swallow. "The student has by the end of fourth block, or there will be consequences out of my control. Now get to class."

Anger rooted me in place as York's dress shoes clacked on the tile floor, as the office door slammed, as students began scattering through the hall. The school district was up in arms over people actually listening to what I had to say. My body was on fire, burning with fury. York wasn't here for students like me. Not if he was enforcing their rules.

"Can't believe Fin's bus-ridin' ass missed this shitshow—don't move," Lucas ordered, and then the flash of his phone's camera startled me.

"The hell?" I asked, blinking away the brightness.

"The perfect campaign picture." He pinched the screen to zoom in on it. "You're so pissed off, and TBH it's hot."

"Not funny."

"For real." He turned his phone to show me the photo. "Look."

It was a picture of me, but it didn't look like me. It was a photo of someone new. Strong and standing tall with shoulders squared, mess of hair pushed back off my face, a scowl-furrowed brow, eyes burning in the fluorescent light, mouth a taut line of seriousness—and I knew I wasn't the same, not anymore.

"Duuuude," Finley said, swiping through the TikTok comments. He leaned back in the office display chair with his feet kicked up on the conference table. "Some detective wannabe started a thread identifying everyone in the video."

After this morning, the theories had only snowballed. Everyone was trying to suss out who was behind the account. I braced myself for an impending freak-out with each notification, waiting to be found out. But every new comment fed the flames of my anger. Fourth block had come to an end, and I'd refused to delete the video. Neither Presley nor York could stop me from taking matters into my own hands. I was a *nobody,* after all. Last Boyfriends had become the perfect hiding spot.

"You def missed out this morning," I said smugly, helping myself to a slice of spicy pesto pizza. "My words got *everyone* riled up."

"At least Pop said I could have the truck back tomorrow." He breathed out in relief, puffing his cheeks. "Thank god. Don't get me wrong, I've binged an entire season of *Drag Race* while being stuck on the bus, but with the middle schoolers?" He shivered, snarling with a grimace. "Those kids are brutal. At least they don't know what happened at the spring musical."

"That's nice," Lucas said absently, too absorbed with his Notes app. He'd been typing, deleting, and retyping with an anxious energy ever since the lobby incident. It was putting me on edge.

"Nice?" Finley kicked his feet off the table and leaned forward. "Middle schoolers are lethal. And full of farts."

"That's nice."

"Are you okay?" Finley waved a hand in front of his face.

"Huh?" Lucas startled, eyes glazed over as he looked up. "I'm fine."

I watched him carefully. His mascaraed lashes blinked slowly as he looked from Finley to me. Something was wrong, and I couldn't let him call off our revenge plan. I couldn't go back to being a bystander, not after this morning.

"Glitter Bomb," I said, and grabbed his phone. "I think you're full of it."

He opened his mouth to deny it, but I widened my eyes and dared him to lie. "Fine," he admitted. His hands fluttered like moths toward his bag, and then he pulled out the emergency stash of Sour Patch Kids. "I'm anxious as hell."

"Why?" Finley asked.

"You don't wanna stop, do you?" I added.

"Do you for real think I'd back out now?" he replied, much to my relief, and popped a handful of the candy in his mouth. "It's just . . . I didn't think this through."

Think this through reverberated through me. Everyone paying attention, the graffiti, the uproar with Principal York—how could I have thought any of this through, let alone expect it to feel so damn good?

"What makes you say that?" I asked warily. "Did Cass find out about the sabotage?"

"That boy doesn't have enough brains to figure me out," Lucas huffed, biting down aggressively on the sour chewiness. "It's . . . Okay, so what's gonna happen after the video plays and his cake is ruined? What's gonna happen at school? What will everyone say?" His voice rose an octave as he went wide-eyed. "Ohgodcouldwegetintrouble?"

"Why are you pulling an Ezra?" Finley asked, cutting him off mid-ramble.

"Hey!" I said. He arched an eyebrow, and I backed down. "Okay, fair."

Lucas shoved another handful of gummies into his mouth and asked, "What if something happens?"

"What could go wrong?" I countered.

"Nothing that I've planned for." He turned to read the dry-erase board where he'd detailed his plan. "Step one, we arrive at Longleaf Farm at five. Ezra stands guard while Finley and I rig the confetti cannons with blood—"

"*Fake* blood," I interjected.

"Any. Way," he continued, side-eyeing me. "It'll take five minutes, max, to rig the cake toppers."

"Get in, get out. Sounds easy." Finley gave him a reassuring grin. "No reason to be nervous, dude."

"If anything, it's step two that makes *me* nervous," I offered while reading the board. "How am I supposed to blend in as a waiter until it's time to change out the video? Presley will undoubtedly be there and then he'll notice me. What if he says something and ruins our cover and—"

"You need this." Lucas cut my ramble off, tossing me the emergency Sour Patch Kids. "There's nothing to worry about, booboo. All *you* have to do is hold a serving tray until seven and then slip into the AV room to load the video on the computer. You'll be fine. With face masks and all black outfits, no one will care who you are, not even Golden Boy Daniels."

"If you say so." I nodded and picked out a blue candy. He might've had a point, but the bluntness of it still stung a little.

Lucas pointed back to the board for emphasis. "Now, that brings us to step three. The cake will be brought out at seven-twenty-five for Cass to welcome guests." He rolled his eyes so far back I could see the whites of them. "It'll be something like 'My name is Cass and I'm a massive asshole, yadda yadda.' His parents have scheduled the video to play at precisely seven-thirty-three as the candles are lit, saving the confetti cannons for last. When they go off, he'll be standing onstage humiliated over the Snaps and covered in blood. I'll get a picture before we make a mad dash back to your truck, Fin. Voilà. Revenge complete."

It was as straightforward as all our plans. However, he bit his shiny-balmed lips and studied the board, hands anxiously tapping his thighs. He was seeing something I couldn't. Maybe what happened this morning wasn't a good thing like I'd thought. Maybe starting that TikTok account knocked our plans askew. Maybe I really don't need people listening to me.

"Something wrong?" I asked him, the secondhand tension raising my shoulders. "You're starting to make me worry now. . . ."

"It's step four that's giving me grief."

"Step four?" Finley arched an eyebrow and turned to reread the board. "There isn't a fourth step."

"That's the problem." Lucas took a deep breath, exhaling evenly through his nose, and lowered his voice. "I *know* I said that I didn't care what Cass does afterward, but . . . now I'm worried what his reaction will be."

"Dude. I get that. Ever since I submitted our registration for the drag competition, I've been bracing myself for Logan to find out."

"You turned it in already, Fin?" I asked.

He nodded with a wide grin, clearly pleased with himself. "We are officially part of the first annual So You Think You Can Lip Sync."

"Obviously we need a group name. Let's talk details. We can practice makeup and—"

"Stop, I can only handle one tailspin at a time," I interrupted Lucas, holding my hands up. My mind couldn't handle the fact that I was about to crash a party (possibly illegally), get onstage in full drag in front of an audience, and start campaigning for Lion King. I shook off the pressure and tried to focus. "Let's back up . . . you're worried about Cass's reaction?"

"Wouldn't say *worried*." Lucas stuffed a red Sour Patch Kid in his mouth, swiveling back and forth in the chair. "I want him to know it was me, but maybe I also don't want him to know it was me." His hands gripped the armrests tightly, as though he was bracing himself. "Glitter Bomb . . . I've been holding on to hope that something would change. That he would want more than just to get into my pants again." He swallowed, gulping down the emotion rising in his voice. "But after tomorrow night, it will be final. There's no coming back from this. We're officially over at seven-thirty-three."

I reached out and covered his hand with mine. "That's why I kept Presley's jacket after I ended it. Hanging on to him was like trying to keep a hold on empty promises. Nothing to grasp." I could still feel the rough wool as I let go of him and flicked the lighter. It had felt better than those five months added together. "It's okay to hold on to what you lost, but when it's time to let go . . . you have to *let go*."

"Damn, dude," Finley said, reaching for another slice of pizza. "Ezra coming in hot with the harsh truths."

Lucas turned toward me, tension showing on his face. The depth of his dark eyes filled with uncertainty. "What happens next, though? I was falling in love with him and now?" He shrugged. "I'm just a last boyfriend. That's all I'll ever be to him."

"Not true!" Finley's words were muffled through his mouthful of pizza.

"You are more than who you've dated," I pointed out. "We are all more than who we've dated. Yeah, we might be their last boyfriends, but I guess that's the aftermath of those disaster relationships. We might as well grow from it instead of letting it drag us down. . . ."

My rant died as I inhaled, exhaled through what it meant. I didn't want to go back to Presley. Not now. Not when it felt better to be the one in control.

Both of them gawked at me, and Lucas leveled his gaze. "Whoever *this* Ezra is," he began, waving a hand at me, "it's the type of confident persona you need for campaigning. It'll match that bangin' picture of you. When the hell did you get so damn insightful?"

"Maybe the emergency sugar high is kicking in."

I shrugged it off and reached for my phone for a distraction. I didn't want to think about what would come next for me or Winter Formal, not right now. It was almost time to start campaigning. And then I couldn't keep hiding. Campaigning wouldn't be like starting an alt TikTok—I'd have to show my face.

The screen lit up with the familiar horde of notifications, stoking my hate fire. Another popped up on the screen. Then another. And another. Too fast for me to keep up.

"Uh, guys, I think something's up on TikTok." I panic scrolled down and down and down through the list of notifications, worry sending my thumb swiping faster. Did someone figure me out? Was all this over before it had a chance to really start?

My stomach dropped in a roller coaster of misfiring neurons as I read the first notification. As I read it again. A third time with my mouth agape. The verified queen of TikTok herself had tagged *my* account in a post.

"Maeve Kimball," I said breathlessly, the air gushing out of my lungs. "She dueted my hallway video."

Lucas screamed, springing out of his seat as Finley bellowed,

"Are you fucking for real?" They hovered over my shoulder as I clicked the notification.

"Hey, Kimball Crew," she began in her winsome voice. She smiled from one side of the frame, the HVHS school hallway on the other. "I saw this post from Last Boyfriends and immediately deep-dived to find out more. Whoever they are, a spineless ex is attacking them at school. As you'll see right now." One side of the video spiraled as I fell; then it faded into the Lion's Pride poster. "It's Harper Valley High School in Harper Valley, Alabama. I'm tagging the school's TikTok in the comments. Let them know how pathetic they are for letting this harassment happen."

Maeve smiled wide and looked directly into the camera. She did her signature move, sipping from a cup of tea while flipping her brown curls over a shoulder, and looked right at the camera. It felt as though she were looking at me. As though she were telling me I had been right, that everything I had done was worth it.

"P.S. brav-fuckin'-o to Last Boyfriends for burning that abusive asshole's jacket in the breakup challenge. Give this badass account a follow."

Eleven

The lush green hills of Longleaf Farm rolled and rollicked up to the main estate. From the service hallway window, I could see Thoroughbred horses grazing on either side of the winding drive. Headlights intermittently sliced through the settling dusk as the party guests pulled up. With each new arrival, my anxiety sent me checking on Lucas and Finley again and again.

"How much longer?" I called, pushing on the kitchen's swinging door.

They both looked up from the cake. It was covered in black icing, sugary skeletons decorating the base of each of the three tiers. Lucas made brief eye contact with me as his hands worked to bury a confetti cannon cake topper.

"Nearly finished," he said with a smirk. "When these go off, it will be horrific in the best way."

"Well, *hurry.*" I checked over my shoulder. "It's getting busy out there."

The stream of costumes to the pavilion was steady with rock stars, superheroes, and the line kept going. No sign of Presley yet, though. Unless he was the zombie clown that had entirely too much swagger.

"We're working as fast as we can," Finley said. He aggressively stabbed a red-filled syringe into a cake topper. Then he went wide-eyed as a splatter sounded through the kitchen. "Dudes . . . dudes! It's leaking. Oh my god, the confetti cannon is leaking—"

"That was *not* part of my plan!" Lucas yelled in a panicked frenzy. "Get some napkins to soak it up!"

I let the door swing shut, breathing evenly through my nose. Maybe this revenge mission wasn't as straightforward as I'd thought. I checked the hallway as guests continued to arrive, readjusting my mask. Any minute the real waitstaff would be here and . . .

Breathe, I told myself, patting the back pocket of my slacks again. The old flash drive with the edited Snap videos was still there. *We got this.*

I picked my nail polish into nonexistence as I paced back and forth. Jangled nerves had me keeping an eye on the hallway and the kitchen through the door's circular viewing window. Inside, Lucas and Finley rushed to clean up the murder scene.

Another exhale as I reached for my phone. It was 5:52. They had less than ten minutes to go. Below the clock, the screen was full of TikTok notifications from thousands of new followers in the last twenty-four hours. The satisfaction of those upward-ticking numbers made me forget about the stress of tonight. More and more comments were stacking up, one after another repeating what Maeve had said in her duet. Each new outcry only doused me with vindication. HVHS hadn't replied to her tag, and the continued silence made my face flame.

A soft tap on my shoulder sent me scrambling. There stood a girl in all black, her mask slid back over her short, blond hair. "We aren't supposed to have our phones out," she said, nodding to my hand.

"S-sorry," I stammered as she stepped toward the kitchen. The swinging door creaked as she went to push it open, and I could see Lucas look up in terror through the view window.

"Uh, hey," I said.

"Hey?" she replied, hesitating.

"Sorry. About the phone, I mean."

Over her shoulder, I could see Finley run across the kitchen, hands full of blood-soaked napkins as Lucas shoved in the last cake topper.

"It's my first day. Any, uh, any tips?"

"Yeah." Her pale blue eyes sized me up. "Don't let Ms. Mary see you on your phone."

"Cool," I said, nervously glancing back at the window. Black icing was streaked across Lucas's face, but he was nearly finished. "Cool, cool, cool . . . she's the . . . ?"

"The caterer." *Duh* was written on her face as she studied me. "Hang on a sec. You go to HVHS, right?"

"Uh . . ." We weren't supposed to have our identities known tonight, but desperate times and all that. "Yeah, I do. Go there."

"You're Ezra from yearbook, right? You took all the pictures during Spirit Week." If she heard the metal clank in the kitchen, she didn't acknowledge it. She stood there expectantly, waiting for my answer.

I shifted my gaze from Lucas's mad dash to pick up spilled utensils and looked back at her. She had recognized me despite the mask, but she hadn't called me "Lucas's friend Ezra" or "Finley's friend Ezra." *I'm Ezra from Yearbook.*

"That was me. . . . Sorry if I bothered y'all—"

"You took a lot of pictures of me and my girlfriend when you were documenting the freshman class," she cut me off with a grin. "Hopefully Principal Numb Nuts won't ax them from the yearbook since he's a doormat for the superintendent's BS."

"I'll try my best to stop him from doing that." As soon as I said it, I knew I would.

She smiled at me then, nodding appreciatively. "I'm Samantha, by the way, but you can call me Sam."

I never would have known she went to HVHS, much less that she was queer too. It wasn't like we ran around with flashing signs that identified our orientation. Especially not now, with that damn initiative making it so hard to be out and proud at school.

"Nice to meet you, Sam."

She nodded and started into the kitchen. The door jammed, causing her to look down at what might be blocking it. Lucas appeared in the view window. He frantically waved with bloody palms and mouthed, "GET RID OF HER!"

"What's wrong with this door?" she asked, pressing on it harder.

"Sam," I said, sidestepping in front of the window. "Did you . . . get the, uh . . . thing from . . . Ms. Mary?"

"The thing?"

"The . . . uh . . . checklist?"

"We never have a checklist."

"Oh. Uh. She gave me one. And I thought maybe we all needed them?" She tilted her head skeptically. "Maybe go check and see. Since it's a big night. I'll figure out what's wrong with this door."

"Valid point." She shook her head, turning around. "That asshole probably invented another new rule for his birthday party."

If it had been a less tense situation, I would have laughed because he *was* The Ass after all. Instead, my insides clenched as she headed down the hallway. When she disappeared around the corner, I rushed into the kitchen.

"You better be ready," I said, and then, "What in the actual hell?" Lucas and Finley were on the ground, wiping up fake blood. Both of them had sticky red smears on their faces.

"I knocked over the container," Finley explained with a gag. "Ugh, it's everywhere, and it smells, ugh, bad."

Voices sounded in the hallway. Sam and someone I didn't recognize. "Shit, that's the caterer!" Lucas yelped. He stood, slipped, and landed on his ass as Finley dry-heaved.

"Hurry," I said, grabbing the gloopy napkins. "You two get that three-tiered monstrosity back into the fridge."

Lucas stood, rushing to the cake. He and Finley hoisted it up and began to walk it toward the fridge in a jumble of legs. "Sorry,

Ms. Mary," Sam was saying as the voices drew near. "I could have sworn we needed a checklist for tonight."

"I wouldn't put it past them," Ms. Mary replied. "It has been one thing after another since the client apparently fired his event planner without notifying me."

Lucas stuck his head out of the fridge with the stankiest expression on his face. "*Event planner?*" he repeated snidely. "That *mother*—"

I motioned for him to hurry and tossed the bloody mess of napkins in a bin. Finley rushed out of the fridge, shutting it softly. We all froze as Sam and Ms. Mary's faces appeared in the view window. "Let me just do a final check on the cake," Ms. Mary was saying as the kitchen door swung open.

"Hide!" Lucas hissed in a panic, and we all took off in different directions through the back exit.

The Longleaf Farm estate was made up of too many overly decorated corridors. I took a left, then a right, then another left into the main ballroom. I got turned around as voices drifted around the corner, and I opened the nearest door, darting inside a storage room full of linens and stacked chairs. Muffled footsteps stomped by in a hurry.

"Don't walk away from me."

That was Presley. *Who was he with?* My heart hammered with residual feelings of jealousy, breath catching as I squatted down to look through the keyhole.

The first thing I noticed was the familiar black and gold of the #9 Nyberg jersey. Next, the guy's bubble butt in a pair of athletic pants. He gripped the hockey stick slowly and turned around. I didn't think it was possible for my heart to beat any louder. Jackson F'ing Darcy.

His costume accentuated assets I've never noticed before. *What the hell is wrong with me?* I shouldn't be this attracted to him. But he carried himself proudly with his head held high and a determined gleam in his eye just like Iceberg in a game. The whole package was doing something to me. *When the hell did Jackson F'ing Darcy get so damn sex—*

"What do you want now?" Jackson's curt reply cut through my thoughts.

"Why won't you talk to me?" Presley pressed, coming into view. He was dressed as Superman, the tight bodysuit hugging his ass in a way that made me both nostalgic and disgusted.

"Because you keep blowing up my phone every night," Jackson said in exasperation, taking a step back. "Stop pressuring me."

"C'mon," Presley urged, and I could see the side of his face pinch in a smile. I knew that smile. It had been the one he wore for me, *my Presley.*

"I'm not ready." Jackson leveled his gaze at him. They were the same height, but Jackson was twice as thick.

Presley hesitated for a moment, his smooth composure tensing. *Am I witnessing a drug deal?*

Presley stepped forward. He grabbed Jackson by the front of his jersey. Shoved him backward against the wall. A thud sounded, and I forgot how to breathe as Presley reared back to hit him.

His hand swung forward, but the punch never came. Instead, he grabbed Jackson's face and crushed their mouths together.

My brain short-circuited, nausea coursing through me. They were *kissing,* and that meant they were together now and Jackson was closeted— *Wait.* Jackson pushed Presley away, wiping his mouth with the back of his hand.

"Stop." He shook his head. "I told you I'm done being your secret, too."

"And I told you it wasn't me," Presley shot back, shaking his head. "Why are you acting so stupid about it?"

"I'm. Not. Dumb." His eyes glowered underneath the hockey helmet. "I know those TikToks are about you. Everybody else might've bought the rumor that you were mugged, but you're a player just like Last Boyfriends said."

"It was nothing, okay?" Presley rolled his eyes, squaring his shoulders. "Just a lame nobody who's jealous because I wouldn't give him the time of day."

"Who was it?" Jackson pushed Presley to back up.

"Some loser who doesn't matter."

I cringed as he looked at Jackson lovingly. Tears splashed down my face. He'd pulled the knife from my back just to stab me in the chest.

"You're the one I wanna be with."

"Being with me and pressuring me into having sex aren't the same thing." Jackson shook his head with a morbid laugh, shouldering past him. "Those TikToks were right about you."

"Wait, don't go, babe. *Please.*"

Presley was left alone in the hallway as Jackson disappeared from my line of sight. He punched the wall with a bark of anger. All because Jackson wouldn't let him catch the dick.

I reached for my phone to send a message to the group chat, but my hands stilled. Jackson obviously wasn't out yet, and I couldn't say anything knowing that. But he'd been with Presley the moment when my relationship had gone to shit— *Oh my god.* The realization hit me, and I didn't know what hurt worse: the fact that Presley had called me a nobody or the fact that Jackson had been the shirtless guy on Snapchat.

From the darkened AV room, I crouched down to watch the HalloWeird party through the window. Music thumped and bodies gyrated underneath the pavilion's roof. Everyone was completely unaware of Lucas and Finley hiding in plain sight, guests picking at the fancy hors d'oeuvres on their trays. Everything was on schedule, and all I had to do was hit play on the computer at precisely 7:33 p.m.

I tried to stay focused, but my eyes kept zeroing in on the hockey player alone at a table in the corner. The twinkling orange lights caught the exhaustion in Jackson's eyes, the ruffled hair from where he'd taken off his helmet. The expression on his face was clear misery. I had to make myself look away, not feel sorry for him. He didn't deserve my sympathy when he was the reason Presley had played me.

Across the room, Superman and his Justice League of dude-bros were dancing with the cheerleaders. I clenched my hands into fists, knuckles white, and forced myself not to march out there and punch Golden Boy Daniels in the dick. My veins boiled with rage as he threw his head back in laughter. I slid down to the floor, resting my back against the wall.

Some loser who doesn't matter replayed over and over as I sat there. Traitorous tears made their escape again as the DJ's voice interrupted the music. "Everyone put your hands together for tonight's guest of honor!" she announced.

I wiped at my eyes and reached into the pocket of my slacks for my phone. The glow of the screen cut through the dark as I pulled it free. Dad had sent a flurry of texts with updates on the Bama Slammers game and Iceberg's plays. I forced myself not to think certain thoughts of Jackson's costume as I scrolled through TikTok notifications. At least all the Last Boyfriends followers didn't think I was a *nobody,* even if they didn't know who I was.

@HVHSOfficial is gonna catch some hands

I'd burn more than his jacket ngl

fuck **@HVHSOfficial** for being so backwards!!!!!

make that pathetic loser pay for treating you this way

Each new comment only fanned the flames of my anger. The more I read, the more clarity it gave me: both Presley and

HVHS had to pay for what they'd done. Just running for Winter Formal Lion King wasn't enough—

A thud hit the window above me, and I nearly dropped my phone. I stood up quickly as a bacon-wrapped shrimp slid down the glass. Out under the pavilion, Lucas waved erratically to get my attention. The black mask couldn't disguise the *WTF* arch of his eyebrows as he gestured toward the projection screen. Cass was onstage in his pristine angel costume, and Ms. Mary had already lit the 1 and 8 candles on the cake.

"Shit, shit, shit!" I berated myself, rushing to the laptop to press play.

"It's an honor for y'all to be here celebrating me . . ." Cass trailed off as someone in the crowd gasped. The video projected onstage, and giant words spelled out HAPPY BIRTHDAY ASSHOLE! in all caps. He looked behind him, dropping the microphone to his side as he read it. Then his recorded voice echoed through the pavilion.

"I swear to god this school is full of dumbass losers," he said in the first Snapchat. *"Our football team might win another state championship, but they're just a bunch of rednecks peaking in high school."*

There was stunned silence for a beat, and then someone booed him. More boos ensued as a clip of a very drunk Cass played. *"Look ath me. I could sweep with anyone I want, ya hear meh. I'ma fuckin' god in this shmall assh town."*

"Who did this?" Cass yelled, spinning around as the first confetti cannon went off. Fake blood sprayed across his white costume. "What the—"

"You deserve that!" someone yelled.

"All of my friends are so pathetic," his recorded voice announced. *"It's sooo obvious they're jealous of me."*

Another cannon sprayed, a mix of confetti and fake blood drenching Cass's blond hair as he stood there in shock. The video continued with him trashing each of his friends. A guy dressed as a ladybug threw a drink at him, and cheers erupted as it splattered, congealing the fake blood.

More guests tossed their drinks at the stage, the spiked punch no doubt intensifying their rowdiness. His father shielded him and attempted to calm the crowd with raised hands. However, it was too late. The tides had already shifted. HalloWeird was successfully ruined with everyone turning on Cass.

"Someone stoo000p that video!" Cass whined as he was pulled off the pavilion's stage.

It was time to make an escape and meet at Fin's truck before someone caught us. I started toward the door but paused when I saw Lucas still in the crowd. He was grinning like a kid opening presents as he took pictures of Cass the Ass's fall from grace.

If it felt this good helping destroy someone, it'd be even sweeter when it was my turn for revenge.

Twelve

The Last Boyfriends account was targeting shitty exes.

That was the rumor even though I hadn't posted anything new. By Monday morning, everyone at HVHS was blaming my alt account for what had been dubbed "Bloody HalloWeird." They uploaded their TikToks of the confetti cannons in action. Even Cass added his own reaction video tagging Last Boyfriends in his hot take. Commenters went on to speculate how many actual last boyfriends were behind the account and who would be next.

They aren't wrong, I thought, pushing my way down the hall. We had been the reason for Cass's party catastrophe, for his ego imploding, for the rumors running rampant. But the theories weren't anywhere close to the truth.

"I heard he was trying to date a bi-curious freshman," someone whispered as I pushed through the lobby.

"He really thought he could upload that TikTok and play the victim?" came a reply. "I wonder what he did to get put on blast."

"Well, my cousin at the University of Alabama said she heard from her roommate, who graduated from here last year, that he was dating a college student."

"I bet Cass cheated on him with that really pretty junior guy."

"Shut up! You think a college student is behind this?"

For some reason, the gossip made me bristle. I was the one who set fire to the jacket, and I'd been the one attacked in the hallway upload. They were *my* videos going viral. Now Lucas's revenge had been lumped in with mine. There was a chance that Cass would call Lucas out for it—he didn't exactly have the same concerns over discretion that Presley did. And then what? Everything that I'd done to get back at Presley would be forgotten.

I searched the hallway for a bleached head of hair, stained pink from fake blood. Cass had his face turned down as he maneuvered to fourth block, dodging the speculation. *Has he figured it out?* His reaction video hadn't hinted that he knew it was Lucas. I was hesitant, though. At any moment things could change and—

"Ezra!"

The sound of my name made me stumble. *Have the rumors gotten back to me?* I glanced around and cringed when I saw Jackson across the lobby. He hitched his gym bag over his shoulder with a wave, and I nearly stumbled again as I rushed toward the Media Center. I'd been avoiding him all day, unable to deal with the mental image of him in the hallway with Presley. Unable to process the torrent of emotions I felt because of him.

"Hey, Ez!" he called out again, but I didn't stop.

I wanted to be mad at him—*needed* to be mad at him. Then

I'd know exactly how to feel. Anger was tangible, something real. Not spinning like the third wheel I'd been in my own damn relationship, if I could even call it that. One second I was right side up, the next upside down. Tumbling over and over as I rolled downhill.

My thoughts continued to spin as I made my way into Yearbook Club. I knew it technically wasn't Jackson's fault Presley had played me. He was just another victim, but he'd been smarter than me. He'd been able to shut it down before he got in too deep. Though he had every right to be pissed about what happened, Presley had still hurt me because of him.

And now I couldn't stop comparing myself to Jackson F'ing Darcy.

Jackson Darcy was athletic. Jackson Darcy was tall. Jackson Darcy had been able to make Presley beg for him. Jackson Darcy was everything I wasn't.

I hung my bag on the back of the desk chair, and Finley turned from the window. "You're just in time for my favorite preshow," he said as a group of cheerleaders crossed over to the gym.

He looks good naked, Finley had said, and I immediately thought of the Snap Jackson had sent Presley. I backed away from the impending *One-Thirsty PM* and the Mighty Lions and the reminders that I'd never be good enough.

"I think I'll just get started on work and—"

A flash of silver cut me off as Lucas bounded up beside us, pulling me toward the window. "I neeeeed jock butt today," he murmured, letting his bag fall on the floor with a thud.

I opened my mouth to protest, but Lucas shook his head.

Tightened his grip on my arm. "Shhh," he said, tapping a manicured nail on the window. "My stories are on."

The Mighty Lions marched out like normal, but it wasn't the same. This was a new reality in which Jackson had stargazed out on County Road 233 too. He had undoubtedly stayed up late Snapping Presley and had fallen for the romance in those blue eyes. Looking back from the sidelines, they'd probably been more real than me and Presley ever were.

"You know," Lucas began as he turned to me, "the cake on Daniels hasn't had the same effect on me since I found out he played you."

Since he played us, I mentally corrected, clocking Jackson in his athletic pants. Unable to forget how he'd looked dressed as Nyberg. Unable to look away as he angrily shoved Presley out of his way to type in the field gate code.

Lucas sighed and picked up his bag. "So . . . did y'all hear the newest rumor?" He raised his eyebrows as he took a seat.

"That Last Boyfriends have been planning to ruin Cass since he didn't invite one of them to last year's HalloWeird?" Finley asked as he pulled a chair over.

Lucas huffed, blowing a strand of hair out of his face. "It keeps getting wilder and wilder."

"But does Cass suspect anything about *who* actually did it?" My words were strained with bitterness, edged in selfishness as I sat down. I cleared my throat and forced myself to look away from Jackson F'ing Darcy. "I mean, you wanted him to know the fake blood was because of you."

"His head is too far up his own ass to realize it was me."

Lucas blinked rapidly, eyes glassy. "The truth is . . . I don't register as a threat to him. He never cared about me enough to pay attention. Guess I know what step four is now."

"If he's too stupid to consider you, Lucas," Finley began, pointing at him, "then he's a bigger ass than I thought. You're beautiful, brilliant, bold. Who else would think of such a sickening stunt?"

"You're sweet, Fin, but everyone already thinks Last Boyfriends did it—wait a sec!" Lucas turned toward me in excitement, and I could see the spark of an idea in his eyes. "I am a last boyfriend, though. So, what if the Last Boyfriends account takes credit for it?"

No, absolutely not! was my immediate thought. If I took credit for Lucas's revenge plot, that would only increase the likelihood of Cass finding out we're behind the account. Then where would that leave me?

"I . . . don't think that's a good idea," I ventured. The theories and rumors and comments pressed down on me from all sides, giving credit where it wasn't due. The TikTok account was *mine*. Hundreds of thousands of followers, including Maeve Kimball, cared about what *I* had to say. It was the only thing I could control.

"Why not?" Finley asked, eyebrows creasing as he looked from Lucas to me.

"C'mon," Lucas added teasingly, "it's the least you could do for nearly messing up the video."

Both of them laughed as though it was an inside joke they shared at my expense. It rubbed me the wrong way. They didn't know what I had been dealing with. But I wouldn't out Jackson. Even if I were to stoop that low, the entire situation was too embarrassing, too enraging to make them understand.

There was too much pressure inside my head, and I snapped. "It worked out in the end, didn't it?"

"Geez, he was joking, dude."

"Sorry. It's just . . ." I blanched, struggling to find the right words. "Like what if Cass figures out who's behind it? Then he'd ruin everything I've done to get even with Presley. Everyone would find out. . . ." I wasn't ready for this newfound TikTok fame to go away. Every time another user called out HVHS and my shitty ex-boyfriend, it made me feel vindicated.

Lucas didn't try to put up a fight as he sat back in his chair. "I guess that's fair," he said a bit dejectedly.

I noted how he hadn't bothered styling his hair or wearing eyeliner today. He was taking step four harder than he was letting on. As though he could feel me watching, he cut his eyes toward me. I knew that frantic expression. It was the same one I'd had after posting the hallway video. After I'd torn apart my room and realized I wasn't the same Ezra anymore. Lucas wasn't the same either, and I knew how important it was to get in the last word.

"But," I started begrudgingly, "what if you stitched one of the videos Last Boyfriends is tagged in and put Cass on blast like Maeve Kimball did for me?"

He shrugged as I reached for my backpack. At least this way I was in control of my TikTok. Uploading the stitch would show the world there was *one* person behind Last Boyfriends. Then it'd disprove the swirling rumors of multiple people, and Cass would be discredited if he ever did remove his head from his ass. I'd be safe from being discovered.

"There are so many posted videos of him onstage," I pressed, pulling my phone out. Lucas smiled weakly as I slid it across the desk to him. "Pick whichever one you want, and then use one of the pictures you got of him on the stage to stitch with it. I have them saved."

"Am I gonna find any spicy ones on here?" he asked, typing in my passcode. "I might've seen you naked that one time we burst in on you changing, but warn me if I'm gonna see—"

"No!" I cut him off, crossing my arms over my chest. I would never, ever be anything like Jackson Darcy standing in front of his bathroom mirror.

"Not shaming at all." Lucas chuckled, but it died quickly as he looked at the screen. "Oh my god."

"What?" I asked, snatching the phone from him.

There was the usual list of TikTok notifications on the screen. At first, I thought Lucas was amazed by my popularity. Then I saw that the latest was from the official HVHS account. I swallowed roughly and clicked it. That familiar fire burned through me as the hallway video loaded, and it intensified when I read the comment.

HVHSOfficial: Remove this account or face the consequences. This is your only warning.

Thirteen

Magnolia's door opened with a chime, briefly letting in the patter of rain before it thudded shut. I mumbled a welcome to the lady hurrying toward the café. Like everyone else, she sought an escape from the approaching November chill in pumpkin spice warmth. And tracked puddled footsteps across the hardwood floors.

With a resigned sigh, I stood from the front counter and grabbed the mop. My entire shift had been spent making sure no one slipped. I'd barely had any time to scour the shelves to set up a new center display. It was an exhausting monotony, and I was beyond ready for *Drag Race* night.

The bell chimed again before I could clear the puddles, and I fought the urge to scream. It was only Jackson, though. He shook rain from his hair and smiled at me. My eyes zeroed in on the soaked hoodie plastered to his broad chest. My heart spun into another confused blur, and I was angry all over again. Too aware of his existence taking up entirely too much space.

Jackson F'ing Darcy.

"You're late," I griped.

"I'm so sorry, Ez," he said with a grimace. He swiped at the wet flop of hair stuck to his head. I noted how his creamy skin was more flushed than normal, and those red-rimmed eyes gave me pause. *Has he been crying?*

"It's . . . it's fine." My anger deflated. "Are you okay?"

"Coach Carter made us practice in the storm."

I waited for him to say more, to explain what drove him to tears. Instead, he did the most outrageous thing possible and peeled off his wet hoodie. It made his shirt ride up. Right there, hidden beneath his happy trail, was a three-mole constellation beside his belly button. Just like in the picture he'd Snapped to Presley.

I spun upside down again. Or right side up. I didn't know anymore. It pained me in too many ways to look at him.

Oblivious to my torment, he tugged his shirt back down and noted the center display. " 'Don't Watch What You Read,' " he read from the sign I'd made. " 'Books HVHS doesn't approve of.' That's ballsy in the best way."

"I know." I shoved the mop at him, not in the mood to talk. "Here. Clean up your mess."

"Shit." He looked down at the puddle beneath him and tangled a hand in his hair. "Sorry, I always do that. Make a mess."

I tried to ignore the apology, but it was difficult to block out the wave of sadness coming from him. Saturday night flashed through my mind. How he'd ended things with Presley. *Is that the reason he's—*

"How was your weekend?" I blurted, unable to stop myself.

"Fine." He spared me a tight-lipped smile and propped the mop by the door. "Went to the HalloWeird party."

"I saw what happened on TikTok. . . ." I watched his face for a glimmer of insight.

"Kinda avoiding TikTok right now." His bloodshot eyes glowered. "Someone tagged me in that video about HVHS. Now I'm getting all these cringe mentions."

Heat flamed my cheeks as I turned away. I immediately knew which ones he meant. The comment section was simping over him, and I'd hate-read each of them, pathetically comparing myself. Every *@jacksondarcy010507 could get it* made me think of Presley begging him to stay, every *@jacksondarcy010507 could spit in my mouth and choke me* reminded me of his hockey costume.

"Sorry," I said with a scowl, grabbing my things.

"Not your fault."

If only he knew.

He leaned back against the counter and crossed his arms. The white fabric of his undershirt stretched tight across his pecs. "I, uh, should go," I rambled, lost in their trance as I self-consciously hid behind my rain jacket. "Lucas and Finley are coming over. *Drag Race* night."

"Nice that your boyfriend and Lucas are friends," he said, not looking at me.

"Shut up!" For a second, I forgot to be mad and laughed at the absurdity. "Finley *and me*? I love him and all, but no. He's like a brother."

"My bad." Jackson ran his fingers through his wet hair again, blinking several times. He took a deep breath and locked eyes with me, the emerald green reflecting the light. "It feels like you've been avoiding me or something, and . . . I dunno." His exhale was ragged as though it pained him to continue. "Are . . . are we friends?"

I hitched my backpack onto my shoulder, wanting to tell him we weren't. That I despised him, envied him, thought too much about him in the last forty-eight hours to admit. But then he swallowed roughly as tears welled up.

"Hey," I said, awkwardly patting his arm. Hating myself for what I was about to say. "Of course we're friends, Jackson. What's wrong?"

He sniffled and stared down at his soaked Converse. "What you said to Principal York that day in the hall. About your shirt. How Nyberg believed in himself enough to come out and take a stand." He took a quick glance around the store. "I'm still figuring out what it means, but . . . I'm pansexual. Just wanted to tell someone, a friend, because it's lonely, I guess."

"Oh." That was all I could say. Jackson Darcy was coming out to me, but he had no right to make me sympathize with him.

"Sorry, I shouldn't have—"

"Don't apologize!" I rushed, trying to convey surprise. "I wasn't expecting you of all people to come out to me." *Especially since you're a dude-bro Mighty Lion and my ex-boyfriend cheated on me with you.* "Thank you for letting me in."

"I've been wanting to come out because I *am* confident in who I am. It's just, like, okay. I constantly see how hard it is to be out at school and that Watch What You Say shit. I can't deal with that stress. Not with football and scouts next year for college and now . . ."

"Now?"

"Only one person knew. A friend until we kinda sorta dated. Or I thought we were dating. I ended whatever *that* was."

"You miss him?" I asked, emotions spinning again. "That's why you're so upset?"

He screwed his face up in offense. "Hell no. He told me I was stupid for wanting to come out. He even begged me to stay closeted like him. . . . I guess he wanted me to do a lot of shit I didn't wanna do."

Their fight at HalloWeird made more sense now. How Jackson wasn't ready for sex. How Presley played him like he'd played me. "I'm sorry," I said, and meant it. Without thinking, with all the anger I had for him draining, I stepped forward and gave him a hug.

"Thanks, Ez."

His arms wrapped around me, and I could feel the heat of his body. Smell the sweaty boyness from football practice. Hear the frantic rhythm of his heart. It was a reminder that Jackson was a person, and I couldn't be mad at him for what'd happened. I couldn't leave him alone in the mess Presley had left for him to clean up.

Jackson F'ing Darcy was a last boyfriend, too.

"Duuuudes, these heels hurt," Finley complained, collapsing in my desk chair. He'd been walking in them ever since the *Drag*

Race episode had ended. By the looks of it, he'd need way (way) more practice.

"How do you *not* know how to walk in heels?" I scoffed, sitting on my bed. Heels were the easy part. It was the whole being in front of a crowd, people watching us business that would be the hardest. "You played the mom in *Hairspray* freshman year."

"For your info, I had to wear flats because I was too tall." He groaned, looking down at his feet. "Now my toes are gonna plot revenge against me."

"Just wait until you have to tuck," Lucas said from the floor, and Finley went wide-eyed. "Relax. We aren't gonna tape your dick tonight. Baby steps."

"Literally," I added, leaning back against the headboard. "You sound like a herd of cattle, and my dad's asleep."

"Relaaaax. He's been conked out since the maxi challenge. Didn't even flinch during that epic lip sync." Lucas grinned as he looked up at me. "Besides, finding our inner divas will help you with the campaign. The world is a runway, after all."

"I'll try to 'sissy my walk' like Mama Ru says," I joked, ignoring the spike in my nerves and checking my messages with sweaty palms. *Let me deal with one havoc-wreaking thing at a time, damn.*

Jackson had been texting me ever since he'd asked for my number. His coming out had left the tumble of my emotions at a standstill.

Jackson: soooo what're you up to now?

I looked over at Finley as he toed off the heels. He'd bought them online and misjudged their height. "Damn it," he whined, rubbing at his foot. "I already have a blister."

> **Ezra:** Finley wanted to try walking in heels and yeah 😬

> **Jackson:** bet he ate that 😄

> **Ezra:** He left crumbs everywhere tbh

"Earth to Ezra!" Lucas yelled, smacking me with a pillow. "Who are you talking to?"

"Uh . . . I . . . um," I floundered, locking my phone. They still didn't know about Jackson, and I couldn't tell them I was texting him. Couldn't even begin to describe *exactly* how I felt angry yet happy, simultaneously sad and confused over the entire situation. "No one. I was just . . . checking on the hockey game. What's up?"

It was a small lie, but Lucas didn't know enough about the Bama Slammers schedule to call me out on it. He obliviously squealed as he flashed his phone screen at me. "Look at my For You page! The Queen of TikTok dueted my stitch!"

"Technically, it's *my* video," I pointed out.

"And technically," he replied with side-eye, excitement nose-diving, "it's *only* a dumb TikTok that did nothing for me. Cass didn't even react to it."

I ignored him and watched Maeve Kimball's signature

brunette curls sway as she sipped from a steaming cup of tea. It was a reaction to the HalloWeird video. When the cake toppers sprayed blood, she snorted with a laugh and snapped her fingers in praise.

"I didn't know she did this," I said, quickly opening TikTok. "Everything is getting lost in all the notifications, and . . . Oh. My. God!"

"Good 'oh my god' or—"

"My account hit one million followers!" I cut Finley off, laughing in disbelief. "Is this real life?"

I clicked the Last Boyfriends inbox with the maxed out "99+" notification bubble. Comment after comment about how badass I was, how sexy Jackson was, how someone had set their ex's leftover junk on fire. Then there were the replies to the HVHS account's comment. Just reading the threat again yanked the levity from my lungs, and I fell back into burning rage.

"Still cannot believe HVHS thought it was a good idea to comment," I said while scrolling through the replies. My eyes caught one, and reading it fed the flames. "Listen to this: 'I hope they get revenge on you next.'"

"Really, though," Finley pointed out, absently scratching at his stubbly chin. "HVHS deserves it. Coach Carter was such an asshat to me at tryouts. Not that I actually wanted to be on the team, but still. Principal York didn't even try to help me."

"York's a dickhole," Lucas added. I could feel his eyes watching me as I clicked to play the hallway video again. "Our school is full of them lately."

The dickhole in question was there in the background,

always watching but never doing anything to help us. Not caring what happened to students like me. Then Jackson entered the frame with his sleepy eyes and tight shirt. My mind drifted to our conversation earlier. How he'd admitted to being lonely, and the thought of that golden retriever of a person being lonely was . . . sad.

Shoving those confusing feels down deep, I swiped to my texts. No reply from Jackson. I huffed and tossed my phone on the bed. Then I noticed how silent it had become. When I looked up, Lucas and Finley were staring at me.

"What?" I asked sheepishly, crossing my arms.

"Fin was just saying how he had an idea for the drag routine," Lucas began, shaking his head, "but you were zoned out. Again. What's up?"

"Nothing is—"

"I'm callin' BS, dude," Finley cut me off. "You've spaced out a lot lately."

"No, I haven't."

"Yes, you have," Lucas added, his tone salty. The serious set of his glossy lips was a reminder of how I'd nearly messed up his revenge on Cass. "You're giving off big dickhole energy with the attitude, and you're not telling us something. . . ."

An unasked question lingered between us, and it was triggering. Because I couldn't lie my way out of it without them knowing. Couldn't tell them Presley cheated on me with Jackson. That Jackson came out to me because I'd tried to stand up to York at school. That I was on edge because all of HVHS will know I've thrown my name in for Winter Formal this week. It was growing increasingly difficult to disappear in plain sight now, and it was a lot to deal with by myself.

"I'm fine," I said, refusing to look Lucas in the eye.

"Booboo, don't—"

"I *said* I'm fine," I snapped, immediately regretting the flare of anger in my voice. We were supposed to stick together. However, it felt like the pressure of *everything* was driving us apart. "Sorry, can we please just . . ." I took a deep breath, unsure of what to say. "What, uh, was your idea for the drag routine, Fin?"

He and Lucas shared a furtive glance, an exchange in which they decided to let it go. Then he slowly spun around in my desk chair. "Uh . . . just that I think I might have the most epic idea . . . but I need your laptop. My phone is dead."

"The password is 'nybergsthickthighs.'" I tried to smile as he looked over his shoulder with a slow blink, ignoring how much I related to Jackson's loneliness. "All one word. No apostrophe."

"Yesssss, it's on YouTube," he said after a moment, motioning for us to join him. "Come watch."

We scrambled to the desk, and he clicked play on the video. A clip from the ending of *The First Wives Club* began. Bette Midler, Goldie Hawn, and Diane Keaton had just celebrated the successful opening for their women's center. They began to sing along to some old song while dancing around in all-white power suits.

"What if we re-create this?" Finley asked with brows raised.

Lucas was silent for a moment, tilting his head in consideration. A lightbulb went on behind his eyes as he clapped in excitement. "Then we'd literally be like the First Wives in the movie—that can be our drag name!"

"It says here the song is 'You Don't Own Me' by Lesley Gore," Finley read from the caption. "The dance doesn't look too hard." He glanced down at the pumps. "I could totally break it down in these heels."

"Oooh, Fin," Lucas cooed. "You're gonna break something all right."

"With practice," he amended.

"What do you think?" Lucas asked me. He rested his head on my shoulder and wrapped his arms around my waist. It was a truce hug, his version of keeping the peace.

"Maybe we could wear white like them," I suggested, dissolving our almost-fight. I could do this, focus on getting drag ready instead of on the upcoming Winter Formal nominee announcement (and *everything* else). "We'd just need to learn each of their moves."

"I'm definitely Goldie." Lucas shook his ass. "I wanna dance like that."

"You're the main star," I told Finley. "Learn Diane's dance moves, and I'll take Bette."

"What about wigs? There's Party Cit—"

"Costume wigs are a hard no," I said, and Lucas added, "We don't want to look cheap. Let me handle the hair. I'll find us each the perfect shake-and-go to match the actresses."

Finley nodded, almost as though he was reassuring himself. "I'm doing this," he said, swiveling back and forth in the chair. "I'm performing drag revenge on my ex-boyfriend while my pop watches."

"Did you prepare him for how gag-worthy it'll be?" Lucas asked.

"He says he's excited, but we'll see how he reacts when I'm in front of an audience again."

"What about Logan?" Lucas pressed. "Does he have any clue that we've entered?"

"He'll find out when we all show up in the theater's dressing room to get ready."

"Trying to decide if I *want* him to cause a scene for the sheer entertainment value or not," Lucas said, thoughtful for a moment. "LJM3's theatrics go zero to a hundred real quick. . . ."

Finley laughed, and I snuck a glance down at my phone again. Then Lucas mentioned a makeup plan they'd already decided on. Without me. I tried to focus on their conversation instead of the growing tension between us. Tried to force my stage fright down along with the confusion about Jackson. But I couldn't stop myself from spinning as they planned to boots the house down like I wasn't there, as I kept checking for Jackson's reply, as that familiar ache of loneliness panged inside me.

Fourteen

The bell sounded to end second block, and I grabbed my bag. In the wake of its ringing trill, I could hear the comment someone left under HVHS's reply. *I hope they get revenge on you next.*

I couldn't shake it for some reason. It lurked in between my thoughts, growing louder during silent moments all week. Between the doorbell ringing and handing out Halloween candy. Each breath I'd held in wait of the Slammer's goal horn to sound. Those few seconds before the next song played on my morning drive to school. Now here it was again, creeping through the hush of Principal York's watchful gaze in the lobby.

He stood guard at the new Lions poster, daring someone to tag it. I kept my head down in case he could see the comment written on my face. *I hope they get revenge—*

Presley's laugh cut through the thought as he left economics. We made eye contact as the many versions of him I'd discovered jumbled into a montage of disappointments. I fought the urge to run like I'd done before and held his gaze. Tomorrow he'd know I was competing against him for Lion King, but it didn't feel good enough, big enough, loud enough. Not after everything that had happened.

He swaggered toward me without a care as he laughed with the dude-bros. As though no one could beat him at his own game. The memories of what I'd witnessed at the party resurged—how he'd acted made me see red. He shouldn't get to strut around after everything he'd done.

Golden Boy Daniels deserved to feel that same pressure that was crushing me.

I gripped my phone and held it up, reminding him that I wasn't powerless. "You're going down," I mouthed slowly, tightening the choke hold. His smooth stride hesitated, his smirk slipping into chagrin before he hurried past. *Let him lose sleep wondering if I will or won't destroy him,* I thought, twisting to see where he went. But he was already gone.

When I turned back, I found Lucas's silver hair bobbing rhythmically with his steps. "Ezra!" he called, waving excitedly as he hurried toward me. "I was about to text you, and—boom— here you are!"

He was breathless and wild-eyed. "Okay, what's—" I started, but he continued hurriedly.

"Get this, we were working on an essay during second block, and I was *obviously* procrastinating while checking the view count for our TikTok."

My TikTok, I corrected internally as Lucas fumbled for his phone. He was stealing the shine I'd created for myself, as if he didn't have enough of his own. If it wasn't for me, the Hallo-Weird video wouldn't have received those millions of views and the entire school wouldn't be in suspense about what would happen next.

"Then I had the best idea for your campaign while reading the comments." He held his phone out, brandishing a brightly colored image. "Look at what I designed for your poster!"

It took a moment to register what I was looking at. The angry picture he'd taken of me had been edited in black-and-white, and behind it was a rainbow fire background.

"'Show HVHS *real* Pride,'" I read. "'Vote Ezra Hayes for Lion King.'"

"What do you think?"

"It's . . ." I had felt weak and helpless when I first read the threats from HVHSOfficial, but the poster made me feel the opposite. Strong and unapologetically queer. "It's . . . Lucas, it's perfect." Guilt shot through my irritation as I looked up at him. "You're like my fairy godmother."

"I mean, *someone* needs to help you. Even if you can be an ass sometimes." He winked in jest, but the dig still stung. "Fin and I are hanging out at the store tonight if you wanna come over. We can make copies with my dad's mega printer. Get a head start and hang them up tomorrow after the announcement."

They're hanging out without me? I thought. *Since when do they do that?*

"Can't," I said defensively, irritation returning. They'd obviously planned to hang and only invited me as an afterthought. What else are they doing without me knowing?

"Why not?"

"I have plans to hang with Jackson."

"Excuse me?" His eyebrows did a dance, glossy lips grinning. "Why didn't you tell me? Is *hang* code for *bang*?" he asked, heavily stressing the insinuation. "Because Fin said he looked good—"

"I *know* what he said." I willed myself not to think about it again. Because if I thought about it, I'd only start comparing myself to Jackson. And I'd been drowning in too many comparisons since HalloWeird. "I'm *only* helping him study for our physics test."

Lucas gave me a skeptical smirk. "Someone's awfully snippy again . . . Wait! Do you *like* Jackson?"

"Don't even go there," I said in frustration. He had no idea that his teasing only twisted the knife Presley had stabbed in my chest. "Besides, you and Finley are the ones making plans."

"Like you said, don't even go there." His ears turned pink as the bell rang again, and he started toward precalculus. "See you in Yearbook."

I tried to shake off the ache as he disappeared in the rush of bodies and shuffling feet. The hallway was clearing, and York was still standing guard in the lobby—a reminder there wasn't any pride at HVHS. A reminder that my campaign announcement for Lion King tomorrow meant more than just getting back at Presley.

The pressure was growing heavier.

Jackson's floofy hair fell over his face as he scribbled in his notebook. "Physics is stupid," he said with an irritated huff.

"Just state the known and unknown variables first," I said, leaning over the dining room table. "Then see which equation they fit into. It'll help on the test."

"I knooooow," he began, pushing his hair back, "but can we take a break?"

He stared at me for a moment, a pleading arch to his thick eyebrows. I hadn't considered them *sexy* until recently. "S-sure." I cleared my throat, my voice wobbly as Lucas's smirk appeared in my mind.

He groaned and leaned back in the chair. "My brain has been soupy ever since York pulled me from athletic training."

I could still feel York's eyes tracking me in the lobby, looking down on everyone. "What did . . . uh . . . what did he want?" I asked cautiously.

"Superintendent Bett is upset about that TikTok account." He laughed sardonically as I sank in my chair, weighed down with dread. "And York assumed I was straight. Like I was on *his* side and would tell him if I knew who was running the account."

I forced a neutral expression on my face despite the chaotic freakout brewing underneath. "Do you, though? Have *any* idea who it is?"

"Even if I did, I sure as hell wouldn't tell him." He rolled his broad shoulders, irritated by the idea. "Especially not after he threatened me."

"He *what*?"

"Said it'd be a shame if I got kicked off the team for interfering with Watch What You Say."

"What a doormat," I said, chipping away harder at my nails. Blood pounded in my ears, but all I could hear was that TikTok comment. *I hope they get revenge on you next.* "I'm sorry."

"It'll be okay, Ez."

But it wouldn't. I'd thought these casualties were piling up because of me, of what I'd started. I was wrong, though. They'd been here all along, hiding in plain sight right along with us. All because of Acheron County's stupid "family values."

The furrow in my brow unraveled as Jackson reached out. I glanced down at the sudden warmth of his hand covering mine. His giant hand. Thoughts spun from *His big hand!* to *Do big hands mean a big . . . ?* to *He's touched Presley with this same big hand!* I stood up quickly, pulling mine away.

"D-do you want something to drink?" I asked, my face hot as I escaped into the kitchen.

"Water's fine," he called.

He followed me, and I busied myself to avoid looking at him. To avoid *those* thoughts that had no right being in my head. I fiddled with my phone as he drank, ignoring the bob of his Adam's apple. The screen lit up with a new message notification from the group chat. I pretended to be engrossed in checking it and opened the thread to the two photos Lucas had sent. The first was of him and Finley at the front desk of Rivera Furniture. They were holding up a stack of printed posters, and I zeroed in on how close they were sitting. How Lucas was practically in Finley's lap. How Finley was watching Lucas with a grin on his face. How they were having fun without me—their third wheel.

I angrily swiped to the second photo. It was a close-up of the poster, my face determined as I stood tall with shoulders squared. The new version of me who knew exactly what he was doing and didn't give a fuck—

"Did you get a good text or something?" Jackson asked, wincing as I looked up. "Not that I'm all up in your business! Or that I care. But you were staring really, really hard at your phone. And okay I'll shut up now."

"It's . . . uh," I started, confused by his embarrassment, "just a campaign poster Lucas made for me."

"What are you campaigning for?"

I took a deep breath. *Might as well tell him. Rip the bandage off and get ready for tomorrow.*

"Winter Lion King," I admitted, holding my phone out with a trembling hand. He leaned closer to inspect the enlarged picture. "It's a long story but I thought I could do something for queer people at HVHS and yeah . . . I know you probably think I'm being stupid."

"No, I don't. I think you're brave." He cleared his throat. "So this means you're running against Pres—people who always win. . . . Can I help you campaign? It'd be nice to see someone else get some shine for once."

I was suddenly overwhelmed by the fact that I knew more than I should. I couldn't comment on him and Presley. I couldn't say I knew exactly what he meant. "Yeah. If you want," I said instead, thinking back to that first photo of Lucas and Finley. I was more than ready to get some shine of my own.

"I want you to win." He smiled, and I refused to acknowledge the fluttering in my stomach. "And that picture of you . . . it's hot. Like for real."

Jackson Darcy was complimenting me, and for some ungodly reason I was blushing. My hands had a mind of their own, pushing my hair back like it was in the photo. I wasn't a fan of the confusion he caused. *Get your shit together!*

I flinched as keys jangled in the front door followed by an opening and closing thud. Dad was home. I'd forgotten to tell him that Jackson was coming over to study. He'd make a scene about this because that's what he did.

Suspense grew as he rounded the corner, as he took stock of the both of us and the panicked expression on my face. A slow smirk pulled his lips to the side. He set the takeout bags on the counter and opened his mouth to make a comment.

"Dad," I said before he could embarrass me. "This is Jackson, and I am *only* tutoring him for our physics test."

He narrowed his eyes like he wasn't buying my story, holding his hand out to Jackson. "I was wondering whose sporty hatchback that was in the drive," he said. "Nice to meet you, Jackson."

"You too, Mr. Hayes," he said as they shook.

"Ezra never has boys over."

He winked at me, and I shot him death glares, warning him to knock it off. "That's a lie," I pointed out, grabbing the bags. Anything to keep my hands busy. "You know Lucas and Finley identify as male."

"That's different," he said under his breath, and then to Jackson, "Guess it's a good thing I got extra for wings and rings tonight."

"Am I supposed to know what that is?" Jackson asked.

"Bama Slammers game night tradition," I explained, and his face lit up in excitement.

"I've got my fingers crossed"—he held up a hand for proof—"that Juicebox shuts out the Macaws tonight, brah."

"You're a hockey man." Dad beamed, pointing at me. "You brought home a hockey man, Ezra?"

"Proud member of Slammer Nation."

Dad's grin was too big for my comfort level. "Jackson," he began with a nod of appreciation, "you down to watch the game with us tonight?"

Jackson didn't answer as he turned toward me questioningly. I knew he wanted to stay, and I also knew if he did, Dad would do the most. He'd assume things that shouldn't be assumed. But I was beginning to like Jackson. We were kind of . . . friends.

"Yeah," I said, smiling at him. "He's staying."

Fifteen

The fifth of November had finally arrived, and with it a chilled fog. I watched the clouded eeriness while painting my nails. Last night's game had chipped away at what little polish I'd had left, and today was *the* day. A fresh coat was necessary for the Winter Formal announcement.

Footsteps thudded on the stairs, and then Dad swung around the corner. He startled for a second, sleepy eyes registering me at the kitchen island. "Mornin'," he said through a yawn, checking the clock on the microwave. "Did I wake up in one of those weird *Doctor Strange* dimensions, or are you really up this early?"

"Couldn't sleep," I muttered, gliding the gold polish onto my thumbnail. *I hope they get revenge on you next* had seeped through my dreams much like the fog, and I'd woken up to check TikTok. To read the thousands of comments calling for accountability from HVHS.

"Ahem. So. How *late* did Jackson stay?" Dad's cheeks flushed, and he busied himself with putting grounds in the coffee maker. "Do we need to have a talk about boys in your room, bud?"

"Absolutely not." My face was hot, and I focused too hard on painting my other thumb. "He left after the final buzzer anyway." Which technically wasn't a lie. He did leave the house, but we stayed on the porch talking for an hour more.

"Seems like a good guy." I could feel his eyes on me. "Is he the boy trouble you were having?"

"*What?*" I startled, missing my nail with the polish. "Noooo." Dad's expression was doubtful as I grabbed the bottle of remover. "He came out to me and needed a friend and so we're friends now and *only* friends."

Silence followed my rambling, and I risked a glance at him. He was grinning, head tilted as he set the skillet on the burner with a clank. "In case I haven't said it lately, you're a good guy too."

I cleaned up my nail, focusing too hard on making it perfect. "Do you really think so, Dad?"

"Yeah," he said, propping his phone up for his morning ritual. "Good guy *and* he's a looker too."

"Don't attempt humor before coffee," I deadpanned. "It's never funny."

He considered this for a moment while the *Good Morning America* stream loaded. "And all across the state of Georgia, student protesters are gathering to boycott the ban on transgender girls participating in female sports," one of the anchors said while Dad studied me.

"You *are* a good guy," he said, jokes aside. "Why do you ask?"

A deep breath expelled itself as he leaned against the island. I wanted to tell him about our rules for revenge, the surrealness

144

of the TikTok account, that one comment racking up thousands of likes. But I didn't know how to make him understand, not yet.

"They're announcing the Winter Formal nominees today," I diverted, hand shaking as I tried to paint my nail again. "And I'm nervous."

"Don't be nervous." He took the brush from me and held my hand still, looking up in between swipes. "Like I told you before, you're more than good enough to run."

"I know, but . . ." I trailed off, nodding toward his phone. The anchor was still discussing the sports ban. "It's *that* . . . and Lucas made those really, *really* queer posters for me, and I dunno. What if something happens at school because I'm running?"

Anger contorted his face as he finished my nail off with one last stroke and capped the polish. "Don't be afraid of a fight if someone harasses you. You remember those self-defense moves I taught you, right?"

"Yes, I remember," I said, forming a fist with my dried hand. "But . . ."

What-ifs began piling up. What if York found out I was behind Last Boyfriends? What if I got expelled? What if I never got into college *because* I got expelled? What if I gave up now and became a bystander in my own life? What if I didn't?

"But?" he asked, opening the pack of bacon.

"It'll be a fight with Watch What You Say." I shrugged and fought the urge to pick at the slowly drying coat of polish. "I just don't wanna get in trouble."

"Campaigning for Winter Formal won't get you in trouble, and if it does, that's for me to worry about." The slap of thick slices on the skillet punctuated his sentence, and he turned toward me. He cocked an ear toward the *GMA* stream. "Do you hear that?" he asked, and I nodded. "There are students fighting the only way they know how. That's showing up and being proud of who they are. People are gonna tell you what you can't do in this life. But there is one thing they can't ever stop you from doing, and that's trying. The best revenge is believing in yourself. Don't let them take that away from you."

I nodded as the sound of frying bacon filled the kitchen, as his words settled into my mind. Campaigning and hanging up my posters wouldn't get me in trouble. It was everything else—the TikToks, the ruined Lions Pride poster, Maeve Kimball blasting HVHS. It was all adding up to something bigger than Winter Formal. I just didn't know what yet.

"If you were *only* tutoring Jackson Darcy, then why was he at your house until midnight last night?"

Lucas stood beside his car, one hand on a jutted hip and the other clutching a stack of posters. The toe of his Chelsea boot tapped impatiently as I shut the Jeep's door. "Good morning to you too," I said, pulling my bag over my shoulder.

"Yeah, yeah." He waved his hand, dispelling the pleasantries. "I need all the juicy details."

"There aren't any—" I began, but his eyes widened in a silent threat. "He stayed to watch the hockey game." His eyes widened even more. "And we talked on the front porch before he left." His staredown was unwavering. "He wants to help me campaign for Winter Formal."

"What *else* aren't you telling me?" His boot tapped faster.

That Jackson came out to me. That he was the guy Presley was cheating on me with. That Jackson and I are strangely becoming friends now.

"What's with the third degree?" I asked in a huff.

"Mmm-hmm." The skepticism was evident in the valley between his arched brows. "If you wanna hit that, I don't blame you. He's tall, has that adorable grin and nice man tits—"

"Can you not?" I cut him off, crossing my arms. The last thing I needed today was a reminder that I paled in comparison to Jackson F'ing Darcy.

He held my gaze for a moment and shook his head, a promise we weren't done discussing my attitude about the entire situation. Then he held the posters out to me. "Good thing he wants to assist in campaigning. We'll need all the help we can get to hang these up and paint HVHS gay today."

I took them from him carefully, studying the picture of me. Strong. Unapologetically queer. Ready to show HVHS real pride. *The best revenge is believing in yourself.* Dad's words resonated as I stared at the rainbow flames. They twisted and turned as I shoved the stack into my backpack.

"Don't forget the tape," Lucas added, tossing me the roll. "Finley and I can take the South Hall. You and your *friend* Jackson can do the North."

"I heard that." I rolled my eyes, sparing him a sarcastic glance as we started toward the school.

"All I hear is how you're keeping something from me again."

I knew he was just being his usual brassy self, but the way he said it cut through what little resolve I had. "And all I saw from the photos last night," I began in the same tone, "is that y'all are having fun together without me."

"What does that mean?" he asked as we came to the steps.

"Just that you and Finley are suddenly hanging out and forgetting to invite me until the last minute." I hitched my bag onto a shoulder, too aware of how vulnerable I felt saying it aloud. "You're leaving me behind, just like you did when you both had boyfriends."

"What?" he asked in disbelief, hands on his hips. "What are you even talking about right now?"

"Just an observation."

"You wanna know what I'm observing?" he asked, continuing before I could reply. "That you're not acting like yourself lately and you're shutting us out. The last time you did this, it was because of Presley. I get that you don't like talking about feelings, but you've been such a dickhole and weirdly possessive ever since *your* alt TikTok that *I* helped you create started getting attention."

I gripped the straps of my bag tight and faced him. "No, I'm not fine, Luc. Is that what you want to hear? Between the pressure of running for Winter Formal and trying to keep up with everything on TikTok—"

"Then stop it," he said gently, putting a hand on each of my shoulders. "If it's affecting your mental health this much, delete the Last Boyfriends account and focus on why you wanted to get even with Presley in the first place."

Delete it? My head began to spin as his eyes searched mine. Last Boyfriends was all I had. Lucas and Finley were leaving me on the sidelines again.

"I won't do that," I said, pulling away from him. "It's too important."

He nodded once, pity filling his eyes. "Then I hope you're ready for today. The moment your name is announced, everything will change here in *real life*. As gag-worthy as that TikTok has been, those view counts and likes and followers won't protect you from reality. Trust me, it's not as easy as you think it'll be."

"Whatever," I said, leaving him to wait for Finley.

He didn't call after me as I took the stairs. I almost turned around to tell him he was wrong. How the last thing I needed was more pressure from someone who was supposed to have my back. Just because his revenge didn't unfold as he'd hoped did *not* mean he knew better than me.

I am focused, I reaffirmed without a glance back. *I'll show him.*

My heartbeat was heavy and growing heavier with each step closer to the lobby. Today was supposed to be about showing up proud of who I was, proud that I was trying. Only everything else—TikTok and my so-called best friends and *I hope they get revenge on you*—kept weighing me down as I stepped inside.

York was standing guard at the Lions Pride poster again, scowling at anyone who passed by. A sleazy smile spread across his face when he saw me, sending red flags waving. "Ezra," he called. "Just the young man I was waiting for. Care to join me in my office for a moment?"

He didn't wait for my reply, clapping his hands to motion me forward. Was York about to threaten me like he had Jackson? Did he know I was behind the TikTok account?

I gulped and followed him into the front office. He led me around the counter, through his looming doorway. *Oh god.* I panicked as he directed me to sit. *This is it. He knows.*

"How are we doing this morning?" he asked, pulling out his chair.

I hesitated, unsure if it was a trick question. "Fine . . ."

"That's great!" His tone was too friendly. "Listen, Ezra. We're preparing to announce the Winter Formal nominees." His gaze locked on mine while he adjusted his name badge lanyard. "Much to my surprise, I came across your name."

"Yes, sir?" I said, voice rising.

"Ezra." My name was too saccharine as he said it, leaning forward. "I admire you thinking you can win. That's certainly the Mighty Lions pride!" A chuckle. "I do worry that you will only embarrass yourself, though."

"Embarrass myself?"

"You're just a junior, and—"

"There aren't any rules that juniors can't run," I pointed out.

"That aside, you do realize those who make the final ballot will represent the school in the Winter Formal Court?" His toothy smile nauseated me. "Our superintendent has an image to uphold for the Acheron County school district. Don't get me wrong here because I am on your side . . . but are you certain you're the *right* type of student to represent HVHS?"

There were those words again, only this time they weren't being used to compliment but to demean. My hands stilled, and I gripped the chair arms as the first bell rang. Silent rage coursed through me while I considered what he said, what he didn't say, what I've been wanting to say since he'd made me turn my shirt inside out. They didn't want people like me to be seen. To represent the school or interfere with Superintendent Bett's Watch What You Say initiative.

"Sir," I began, fighting to keep the anger out of my voice, "I'm not here to represent HVHS because *there is no pride here.* I'm representing myself and those like me, and I'm extremely certain I'm the right kind of student to run for Lion King."

His placating smile dropped, the friendly facade instantly dissolving. "Know that it isn't an attack on your *rights*," he began with exasperation in his voice, "if you're not chosen for the final ballot." He eyed me slowly, clocking my body and now-chipped polish. "We both know you're not the best choice for Lion King, and you're not making my job any easier. I'm trying to help you before the superintendent gets involved."

Dad's words churned inside me. *The best revenge is believing in yourself.* I breathed out evenly, standing up. Tall. Strong. Unapologetic.

"If that's all, I have some campaigning to do."

He clenched his jaw and nodded to the door. "You're dismissed."

151

My feet propelled me out of his office, past the front counter, out into the empty hallway before I let myself cry. Angry tears spilled over as I stared at the Lions Pride poster. As I remembered York ripping the graffitied one down in anger. As *I hope they get revenge on you* collided head-on with *The best revenge is believing in yourself.* As the two thoughts warped and melded together.

I hope they get the best revenge on you.

Once I thought it, I couldn't take it back. These posters and running for Lion King—they were reminders we were here, no matter the lengths they would go to erase us. The school was threatened by me, by what I was doing. *You used to be a quiet student,* York had told me that day, and now I'd have to show him how loud I could get.

If they wanted to be sneaky with the Watch What You Say initiative, then I could too. My hand shook as it undid my backpack's zipper, the *tck-tck-tck* echoing loudly in the hallway. I reached inside and grabbed a poster. My heartbeat sped up as I checked over my shoulder before slapping the poster over the football players' names. I hurriedly taped the corners, knowing it wouldn't be there long.

I was betting on it.

With a parting glance at the front office, I crossed over to the bathroom and kept the door cracked. Waiting for York to make his rounds. Watching as the intercom crackled with the morning announcements.

"Good morning, HVHS!" the administrator said cheerfully. "It's my pleasure to announce the nominations for your Winter

Formal Court. For your consideration as Queen . . . Yasmin Spencer, Terri Lakely, Ashley Gonzales, Jessica Chung."

She continued on to congratulate the nominees for Lion Queen, and my heart thundered in my ears. Everyone would know in a few seconds. There wouldn't be any going back. But I wasn't nervous anymore. I had my sights focused on something else.

"For King . . . Presley Daniels, Jesse Saros, Filip Peterson, and Ezra Hayes."

The announcement went on to include voting dates while the front office door opened. It banged off the wall, and York stomped out. I gripped my phone as he held his in mid-conversation.

"Yes, sir," he was saying. His eyes darted down to the Media Center first, sweeping to the cafeteria on the other end of the long hallway. "He didn't back down—I'm sorry, sir. I understand, sir. I'll try to convince him again. . . ." Then he did a double take.

I watched as his face reddened and he quickly ended the call. He spun around, neck straining to see if anyone was in the hall, and then he forcefully ripped my poster down. He kept ripping it into smaller pieces while I recorded every tear.

Sixteen

"Ouch. Ouch. Ouch!"

A thump sounded in the adjacent stall of Rivera Furniture's bathroom display. Finley had been in there for the last thirty minutes attempting to tuck. Lucas's hand stilled with the glue stick, half of a brow coated. The other one rose in a slicked purple arch as his reflection eyed mine. I brushed back my wig's wavy curls and avoided his gaze. Ever since our parking lot spat, the vibe between us has been too tense, too all-knowing.

"You good in there?" Lucas called. Fin's answer was another thump followed by a muffled, "Ouch! Shit! Damn!" Then the ripping shriek of the medical tape.

"Finley?" I asked, knocking on the door.

"Dudes," he yelped. "Are y'all *sure* this is how to tape your dangle?"

"Push 'em up, pull it back, and wrap the sack," Lucas called, blocking the rest of his eyebrow. "That's how we did ours."

"I don't understand how . . ." The commotion stilled for a beat, and then the knob rattled. I watched in the mirror as the

154

door opened slowly. Finley stuck his head out with a tight smile. "Funny story, I need a favor."

"Are you about to ask what I *think* you're about to ask?" I shook my head in disbelief, turning toward him.

Finley nodded solemnly, and Lucas flipped his shaggy blond wig over his shoulder. "Let me see what we're working with," he said, huffing into his hands to warm them up.

"Deadass?"

"You're lucky we're besties . . . Oh my god."

"Oh my god," I echoed as Finley stepped out from behind the door. He was wearing his Lewis Auto Sales polo, a bobbed wig, and nothing else.

Lucas immediately rummaged around in his makeup bag. Even from under an ungodly amount of foundation, I could see him blushing. He found the emergency Sour Patch Kids and crammed a handful into his mouth. Chewing roughly, he squared his shoulders and glanced down at Finley.

"Hand me the tape."

The awkward vulnerability in Finley's expression as Lucas got to work made me look away. My hands fidgeted in the emergency candy on the counter, sour-then-sweet on my lips as I unlocked my phone.

"Ooooh." Finley's voice climbed higher. "This feels hella weird."

The TikTok draft was still there, still ready to be posted. The camera zoomed in slowly, focusing on my campaign poster. Pausing long enough to read the words. Then a hand reached from out of frame and ripped it down. York's angry face grew more and more red as he aggressively tore it up, rainbow pieces falling in front of his name badge lanyard.

It was York's voice in the back of my mind keeping me from tapping the post button. *I do worry that you will only embarrass yourself.* The rage had worn off, and now all I felt was doubt. Would anybody even care what he'd done?

"Low-key impressed you baited York like that," Finley commented as the video replayed. I lifted my gaze and saw him in the display vanity. He was watching over my shoulder, fake lashes flinching at the sound of ripping tape. "Also high-key shocked Jackson was so offended on your behalf."

"That's what *friends* are for, apparently," Lucas commented from below.

"He was only mad because . . ." I hadn't been able to tell Jackson it'd been a setup, and he'd been infuriated that York had lashed out. He'd taken most of the remaining posters and plastered them all around the Lions Pride poster as a fuck-you. "Because he thought someone was trying to harass me for being queer."

"Which *is* what happened," Lucas pointed out, tearing off another piece of tape. He looked at me with another tense glare. "You aren't really gonna post that, are you?"

It was a loaded question I wasn't ready to answer, especially after our argument. Instead, I shrugged and lay my phone back on the counter. Nerves rattled through me as I finished blocking my brows, hand unsteady. There was a chance York would find out the TikTok account belonged to me if I posted it, and Lucas had said as much when I'd showed them. But I couldn't get *I hope they get the best revenge on you* out of my head.

In the vanity, Finley studied my expression as I slicked on the glue. "Are you worried what Presley will say about you running against him?" he asked, mistaking my apprehension.

"He's too much of a chickenshit to say anything," I said while he cringed, Lucas threatening him to be still. "He's gone out of his way to avoid me since the announcement."

"Probably still scared you might out him," he suggested.

"Stop moving," Lucas mumbled with a yank of the tape.

"Dude!" Finley gasped, peeking down to see what'd happened. "Wait . . . it doesn't feel that bad."

"Not what I usually hear when I'm in this position," Lucas said with a wry grin as he stood.

Finley swallowed roughly as we all three stared down at his tuck. "Just gonna put my pants back on and, like, not be naked anymore." He shuffled toward the adjacent bathroom, the tips of his ears reddening.

Lucas's eyes widened at me in the mirror when Finley disappeared. "So that happened," he whispered after a few deep breaths, checking his phone. His blocked brows shot high as he read his notifications. I was already on edge from our argument, and the sharp slam of him throwing it on the counter made me jump.

"What was that for?" I asked carefully, already afraid I knew *who* it was for.

"Cass is being so extra right now," he grumbled, and reached for the setting powder.

"He's blowing you up?"

Lucas patted his face in a heavy cloud, still managing to roll his eyes. "Trying to dick me down again. Swearing Last Boy-friends made him realize how much of an asshole he is. Even said, and this is priceless, that he's *sorry*."

I turned my head so quickly the wig flipped back. "Cass the Ass *apologized* to you?" I asked, momentarily forgetting the tension between us.

"Still shook." He dramatically pointed a makeup brush at me. "Don't get me wrong. Totally glad he did it *after* we ruined his party. That felt soooo good, but now? It's weird because the apology feels good too."

"Weird?" I asked, afraid of where this was heading.

"I thought I'd get this big moment of pleasure watching him learn the error of his ways. But it was just an apology. A short message that he was changing for the better—don't give me that look, Ezra." I kept my purpled and slick brows narrowed as he held his hands up in surrender. "I swear on Taylor's Version that we're neeever getting back together."

"Good," Finley said, clacking through the doorway in his heels, fully dressed. "You deserve top-notch dick game."

Lucas met my stare in the mirror, and I furiously began beating my brows with the powder. He bit his lip to keep giggles from escaping, and I knew we were both thinking the same thing.

When the silence couldn't get any more deafening, Finley leaned against the counter and cleared his throat. "Okay, I get it," he said, eyes darting between us. "Y'all saw it."

"And he touched it," I blurted with a tiny laugh.

"*All of it,*" Lucas emphasized, waving the concealer brush. "The dangle. The dangly bits."

Finley opened his mouth, closed it. Turned his face downward and laughed once, twice, three times until he couldn't stop. "That happened," he gasped. "I can't believe *that* actually happened."

"It was. The least sexy. Encounter. I've ever had," Lucas managed between his giggles. "With a penis."

I snorted through the powder cloud and couldn't stop. It felt good to laugh. The longer we stood there teary-eyed and wheezing in half drag, the more it felt normal. Like it used to be before we all got caught up in ex-boyfriend dramatics.

Finley leaned his head back with a dazed smile on his face. He cut his eyes over to us, wiping his tears with the sleeve of his shirt, and picked up the glue stick. "For the record," he began, "I don't let just anyone touch my dangle."

"I feel honored to be in the same ranks with LJM3." Lucas pursed his lips with sarcasm and took the stick from him. "Let me show you how to do that, and then we'll contour that strong jaw of yours."

"You rank above Logan," Finley muttered as Lucas slicked back his thick brows. "He's a turd person."

"What has he done now?" I asked, dabbing more concealer on my brows.

"Ya know, still holding a grudge and being an overall turdy person." He rolled his eyes. "It's because he's a Scorpio—"

"Astrology isn't an excuse for a shitty personality," Lucas pointed out.

"I know." He breathed out roughly. "He def isn't gonna apologize after this competition."

"Do you want him to?" I turned toward him, one brow blended in perfectly. "Like Cass did?"

He was silent, the display bathroom quiet except for the sticky slide of the glue. Then he glanced up at Lucas, over at me. "No," he decided. "I wouldn't forgive him anyway." Another pause as he thought. "I'm gonna do this for me. To prove I can get back onstage, that I'm not afraid of being out after what happened."

"You *are* already doing it," I told him. "All that's left is to get our outfits, and then LJM3 really will be gobsmacked over how much of a star you are."

"Just hope my pop doesn't get all weirdly embarrassed like he did during *The Lightning Thief.*"

"If he does, those antiquated views on masculinity are on him." Lucas caught his attention with a smile. "I'm proud of you, Fin."

The tips of his ears went red again, and he cleared his throat. "Proud of you too. For, um, not getting back with Cass."

"Same," I added, recalling what Lucas had said about it being weird. How I was feeling weird about all of it. "So . . . what did you mean, Luc? About the apology feeling good?"

He shrugged, sucking air between his teeth as he searched for the right shade of brown. "I guess because his next boyfriend will have it better than I did. Because I did something about it."

What he said, how he had done something, reverberated through me as I fiddled with my phone. As I watched the TikTok draft replay again. "Should I post this video?" I asked suddenly, looking up from the screen. My mouth went dry as I gripped the brick of a phone weighing in my palm.

Lucas's nonexistent eyebrows narrowed, his posture stiffening. The vibe between us reverted to tense, as though we hadn't just been laughing. "You already know what I'm gonna say," he said tersely. "If you're gonna take your campaign seriously, then you need to—"

"I *am* taking it seriously," I cut him off, matching his tone. "That's why I want to upload this to Last Boyfriends. Can you imagine how much campaign help I'd get if it trends like the other TikToks?"

If it did, I'd have an advantage over Presley and get my name out there for millions of people to see. The more views, the more people would talk. Maybe Maeve would even do me a another solid too. I could see the comments now from the entire school, theorizing why York would rip down my poster—

"Dude." Finley's voice cut through the reverie, and I looked up. He chewed on his bottom lip and nodded once at Lucas. "You were right, Luc."

"Right about what?" I asked.

Lucas tossed the makeup on the counter without looking at me. He inhaled deeply as though he was preparing himself. "Fin and I have been discussing it," he began on an exhale, "and we're worried you don't care about what we're doing anymore."

"What the actual hell?" I asked, taken aback by the audacity. By the fact that they'd *discussed* me like I was a problem. "Why would you even say that?"

"Because it's true, dude. You got distracted at HalloWeird and you've been spacing out at almost every brainstorming session for the drag routine. It's like you're too busy focusing on yourself to care about us. . . ."

"And now you're too wrapped up in the attention you might get from posting that TikTok to worry about the implications it could have," Lucas added.

"Like what? Proving that I'm the right kind of student to represent HVHS? That the school district's Watch What You Say shit isn't fair?"

"More like how it could shine a giant spotlight on *who* is running the account." Lucas gestured between us. "If you get caught, we all go down. Not to mention it'd be the end of everything we'd planned."

"We won't—"

"You don't know that." He shook his head, a morose laugh escaping. "It's one thing to be loud and proud with your campaign. I'm obviously all for the fabulosity. But it's another thing to give them a reason to target you. They've been looking for someone to blame ever since that Lions Pride poster got graffitied. Have you *even* paid attention to what's really happening with that initiative?" He held up a finger, jabbing it toward me before I could tell him I had. That I couldn't stop paying attention. "You're only thinking about yourself, and now you're leaving Finley and me hanging."

I nodded once, twice as I looked from him to Finley. Neither of them thought I cared. It made my eyes burn with angry tears, and the pressure on me hit a breaking point. "Well, I guess now you know how I've felt," I snapped, each word ragged with indignation. "You both left *me* hanging when you got boyfriends, and now you're doing it again. Only this time, you're jealous I'm actually getting attention with my TikTok—"

"That's right, it's *your* TikTok." Lucas threw his hands up in exasperation, turning away from me. "I can't believe you're acting like this."

"Like *what*?" I pressed.

"Obsessed over likes and followers," Finley began, holding up fingers to count, "not telling us what's bothering you, pushing us away—"

"Y'all aren't listening to me!" My voice came out in a shout, much too loud for the confined space of the display room. It startled all three of us, and I almost cowered back in apology. But I was pissed they didn't understand me. "Look, I can use my fame to show Presley and York and everyone watching that someone like me *deserves* to be Winter Formal King."

"Do you, though?" Lucas let out a long sigh, pulling his wig off. His red lips parted, and then he stopped himself. He looked to Finley and nodded decisively. "Glitter Bomb, your 'inner saboteur' is showing, Ezra. It's obvious you're not gonna listen to us, so why even bother. Post that video. Do whatever you want." He started toward the door. "We're out."

"What do you mean y'all are out?" I called as he stomped out of the bathroom display.

I turned to Finley in search of something, anything to make sense of what was happening. He stared at me in resignation before turning away. "Fin," I begged. "Don't be like this too."

His measured steps hesitated, and he paused in the doorway. "Ezra," he said sadly, casting me one last glance. "The rules for revenge were your idea, but you're not doing it for us anymore. You've made it all about yourself. You're so focused on how hard things are for you that you've forgotten that things aren't exactly easy for us, either." Finley exhaled like he was making a decision. "Listen, don't even bother getting ready for the drag competition. We'll do it without you."

"What the hell, Fin?" I asked as he turned to leave, but he didn't reply. I could hear his steps rushing to catch up with Lucas, their soft whispers trailing through the store. I'd thought we were getting back to our old selves, but now they were teaming up against me.

"Whatever," I muttered to the sudden emptiness of the room.

With a yank, I ripped off the wig and tossed it at the vanity. The mirror showed me standing there red-faced, nostrils flaring, with my phone tightly clenched in my hand. I glanced down as the video continued to replay. As York ripped up my face again and again. That was how I felt right now. *You're bringing this embarrassment on yourself,* he had said.

Did anyone care what I had to say? York didn't. Lucas and Finley certainly didn't. I met my reflection's gaze, those same hazel eyes bloodshot and angry staring back at me.

"'Proof there isn't Pride @HVHSOfficial,'" I read the caption aloud. Before doubt could slip through my determination, my thumb tapped the post button.

Seventeen

Heat blew from the Jeep's vents, chasing away the morning chill. Each breath fogged up the driver's window as I scrolled through TikTok. A measured inhale and exhale to keep my lungs from combusting with the unyielding desire to scream and lose my mind.

The video had been viewed 2 million times in less than twelve hours, accumulating nearly half as many likes. Comments were pouring in too fast for me to keep up. Each refresh was a rush of excitement as the notifications loaded.

ezra has my vote

does **@jacksondarcy010507** know ezra?

have u seen this **@maevekimball?**

@HVHSOfficial is a hate crime waiting to happen

joseph york needs to be fired

Ezra is right, we need to show **@HVHSOfficial** what real Pride means

The speculation went on as I read. It was all a mad jumble of shouts into the void that didn't add up to anything real yet. Not until HVHS responded. Not until I walked through those doors and saw what was happening in real life. Saw if my actions had any real consequence.

I wiped at the window and looked toward the school. A few people lingered on the steps, their breath clouded in the morning chill. Would they know me? Would anyone recognize me as that strong, pissed-off guy on the poster?

I took a deep breath, inhaling the warmth, and shut off the ignition. A gust of cold air greeted me as I climbed out. This was it. I was no longer Ezra Hayes, the guy nobody knew who hid on the sidelines. I was a Lion King nominee—one who was being targeted by Watch What You Say.

"You're late, Ez," called a familiar, deep voice that had once grated on my nerves.

Jackson rushed along the sidewalk to catch up with me. That floof of hair was more of a nest, and there were still pillow creases on his cheek. "You're one to talk," I said as he drew near.

"But I'm always late," he pointed out with a smirk.

"Yeah, well . . ."

I squinted at the glinting silver of Lucas's BMW in the morning sun. It had been here when I pulled in later than usual. I'd made myself dawdle this morning so I wouldn't have to talk to him and Finley. They'd only throw shade over the TikTok post.

"I can't believe Last Boyfriends caught Principal York destroying your poster," Jackson said. "You're gonna be TikTok famous."

"Please," I deadpanned as we walked. But a part of me secretly hoped it was true, that everyone would notice me today. Preferably in front of Lucas and Finley.

"Seriously, braaah," he said through a yawn, rubbing at the sleep still in his eyes. "Now you'll be the one getting those cringe comments about how hot you are."

There he went complimenting me again, and I hated the way it made me blush. And the fact that I'd deliberately done my hair like it was in my poster. "So," I said, ignoring the comment. Ignoring the confusion that was Jackson F'ing Darcy. "Do you make a habit of being perpetually late for class?"

He grinned sheepishly, a dimple appearing in his cheeks that I'd never noticed. "It's usually my brand," he said as his smile slipped. "I was up late last night, though. Argument with that friend I told you about."

Presley must still be harassing him. My stomach turned at the thought. "Everything okay?" I asked through the wave of nausea.

His stride slowed, and I looked up at him as we halted at the stairs. "Ez, can I ask for some advice?"

"Not sure I'm the best person to ask," I muttered, thinking back to last night. "But sure."

He took a deep breath, swallowing roughly. It made his throat constrict and relax in ways much too sexy for this early in the morning. "How do you do it?" he asked without looking up from his feet.

"Do what exactly?"

"Be out."

I studied him for a moment. How he ran his hands through

his hair, tangling it into even more of a nest. How the purple smudges under his eyes from not enough sleep made him look weary. "Does that have to do with the argument you had with . . . your friend?"

"Definitely my *ex*-friend after he told me I was stupid for . . ." He squinted against the sunrise, checking to see if anyone was around. "Seeing you be out and how you're showing HVHS real pride reinforced how comfortable I am identifying as pan. So I told my parents, and they are legit happy for me."

"Jax, that's great!" I said with a smile, clapping him on the shoulder. "I'm proud of you!"

"I'm not," he muttered, and my eyebrows rose in question. "Because I'm afraid to be out at school with the pressure of Watch What You Say. How do you do it?"

I thought back to what my dad said the morning of the Winter Formal announcement, how I'd been nervous. "Hey, it's okay," I said, resting my hand on his upper arm. Then I realized I was awkwardly gripping the toned muscle of his bicep and let go. "I'm afraid, too, but they can't stop me from being myself. All we can do is be proud of who we are. Don't let anyone take that away from you. Especially your ex-friend."

Relief washed over his face, his mouth softening into that smile of his. "Thanks. Seriously. I needed to hear that today," he said, hugging me. "You're like my own queer hockey hero, brah."

"Anytime," I muttered into his shoulder.

The warmth of his citrus cologne was overwhelming. *Too much like Presley.* It clicked as he pulled away, the reason why Presley had smelled like him. *Because they were together.* I braced myself for the pain of that realization. For it to send me spinning. But nothing happened as he stood there, searching his pockets.

"Shit," he said, craning his neck toward his car. "I left my phone."

Still, I waited for a flare of hate or jealousy. Nothing. Just an understanding that what'd happened was in the past. Jackson couldn't control how Presley had acted, just like I couldn't either.

"Tell Ms. Abernathy that I'm on my way?"

"What are friends for?"

I smiled at him as he backtracked, and I made my way into the lobby. The posters he had hung up inside the door were still there, still scowling and reminding everyone how pissed off I was. However, the Lions Pride poster was missing. On the tiled floor of the lobby were scraps of paper. Torn shreds covered in the names of football players.

Someone had given York a taste of his own medicine.

People were actually listening to Last Boyfriends, and I was responsible. My dad would've taken this opportunity to remind me of that crap about power and responsibility, but whatever. It felt incredible to know I'd caused someone to act out. Lucas and Finley didn't know what they were talking about. I *was* like Rolf Nyberg.

The last shreds of doubt I had about today dissipated as someone waved at me. *It's campaign time,* I pep talked myself, raising my hand in reply. *I'll show them it was a good—no, a great—idea to post that video.*

"Was that the guy from TikTok?" someone asked as I passed by, and another replied, "His name is Ezra, I think."

An uncontrollable grin spread across my face as more people noticed me. They gave me nods of acknowledgment as I walked toward physics. My head was high, my smile proud. I'd caused this. Me.

"Ezra?"

My name was a rushed whisper, and I turned around with a wave. Then I saw Presley standing in the bathroom doorway. His gaze darted as people passed by before motioning for me to follow him inside.

"I need to talk to you," he urged.

I could feel the way he'd jerked me backward, hear my bag slapping to the ground as he rammed me up against the wall. My instinct was to cower back, to make myself take up as little space as possible so he wouldn't hurt me. Then I remembered my poster, how empowered I felt, who I *really* was. Presley Daniels didn't dictate how I felt about myself. Not anymore.

"What do you want?" I demanded, following him.

"Why are you doing this?" he asked as the door closed. "Running for Lion King and making a whole scene about it on TikTok?"

"Because I can."

My voice was steady while I looked him in the eyes, daring him to say something. He swallowed roughly as his shoulders rose. The biceps that I knew too well coiled tightly, and he crossed his arms.

"Look," he began, glassy-eyed, "if you are going to out me on TikTok, then please—"

"I'm not," I cut him off.

"But you threatened me the other day . . . said I was going down."

I started to tell him that I'd been screwing with his head, but he was acting cagey. His eyes darted from me to the door as he chewed at his thumbnail. It was clear he was scared. Scared of how I could ruin his game, his reputation, his golden boy status.

"I didn't mean to hurt you," he continued while pacing in front of the sinks. "I just . . ." He wiped at his nose, wiped at his tears. "I get it, okay. I'm a shit person. I was jealous."

"Jealous?" I asked, scrunching my face in confusion.

"Jackson told me he was pan back in May, and he'd been crushing on you for two years."

"What?" I leaned against the wall, nothing making any sense, a dull roar pounding in my ears. *Jackson likes me?*

"I was jealous, so I distracted you so he couldn't get a shot," he rambled quickly, wringing his hands. "And now he's gonna do the stupidest thing imaginable, even after I begged him not to, all because of that video you posted. He doesn't realize what it would mean, that it could ruin everything, Ezra. Think about what you're doing. If you post about me . . . I know I deserve it, but I'm asking you to please don't. It could ruin my football scholarship."

I gawked at him, still spinning from the revelation about Jackson. He sniffled again and wiped away tears. This version of Presley Daniels was new. He was terrified of me, another impression unfolding from the deck of cards he called a personality.

He'd begged me, apologized to me—and it *was* weird. Lucas was right about that. But he was wrong about it feeling good.

It made me feel like *I* was the shit person.

"Ezra, can you come in here for a moment, please?"

Ms. Dion's voice floated out of her office as I entered Yearbook. From the doorway, I could see her seated at her desk. Hesitation stilled my feet, but the warmth of her brown eyes was welcoming.

"I saw what happened to your poster," she said. "How are you holding up?"

"I'm fine," I said, stepping into her office. The firm set of her mouth told me she wasn't impressed with that answer, so I tried again. "I'm angry but not surprised about what happened. With York and my poster."

She exhaled, bringing her hands together in a clasped fist, and studied me as I stood there. "I'm a representative for the teachers' union, and what Principal York did is considered harassment."

"It was just a poster, Ms. D," I said, but she shook her head.

"We both know it's about more than a poster." She sat back, a bemused tilt to her brow. "Especially with what you're doing with that TikTok account."

Panic knocked me down into one of the guest chairs, and I gaped at her. "I don't . . . uh . . . I'm not sure what you mean . . . uh . . . It isn't—"

"Ezra, don't insult my intelligence." She smiled with a wink. "Besides, I saw your setup yesterday with the poster and York."

"I'm sorry," I said, my stomach churning. I felt like throwing up, like I'd admit to everything if I wasn't careful.

"Don't be!" She let out a high-pitched laugh, its trill slicing through my confusion. "The Watch What You Say initiative is one of the worst things to happen to this district. You caught York red-handed doing Superintendent Bett's bidding, and it has lit a fire within the teachers' union *and* the school board."

"Should I stop?" I grimaced as warnings sounded in my memory from Lucas, Finley, and even Presley. "Am I doing something wrong?"

She leaned forward in seriousness. "You're doing something *right*, Ezra. Don't back down now. Someone needs to stand up for students like you."

"Thanks, Ms. Dion," I said with a tentative smile. "Really. Sometimes it feels like . . . like nobody cares. Like there's not any support for queer students."

"Things haven't changed much since I went to school here, and it saddens me to see you kids having to fight the same damn—*dang*—battle. These so-called politicians have continued to screw up everything thinking they know best. I have your back, and I will say *gay* for as long as I'm a teacher. Let me know if there's anything I can do to help you."

"Thank you," I said again as the bell rang.

"And, Ezra, your secret is safe with me," she added seriously.

With mutual nods of appreciation, I left her office feeling at odds with myself. What Presley had said this morning pulled at me in ways I couldn't make sense of. Now Ms. Dion's encouragement was pushing me to keep going.

I dragged my feet to the back of the room, dreading the awkwardness that would ensue when I sat down. However, the workstation was empty like the lunch table had been earlier. A quick sweep of the room showed Lucas and Finley at a separate desk. Their heads were bent down over a notebook, both of them smiling at one another in a way that felt different than usual.

Lucas's high-pitched laugh carried across the room, and I caught a whisper of the conversation. "Your dad's football pads won't work," he was saying, playfully shoving Finley. "We'll find hip padding today when we go shopping."

I slammed my backpack on the floor with more force than necessary, and they both jumped. Their glares stabbed at me as I sat down and turned my back to them. It was absurd they were going through with the drag competition without me. Absurd they were so quick to abandon me. It felt like last spring all over again. Only this time, I knew what I was doing.

Think about what you're doing.

Presley's words pulled harder at me as I waited for *One-Thirsty PM*. He'd been *afraid* of me. The memory of him begging felt like yet another sucker punch. It had been all I'd wanted before, for him to finally see me as someone on his level. But now I *was* on his level and no better than him. He'd thought I'd ruin him out of spite. That I could be a player in my own game of revenge.

Each time I saw him in the hallway today, he'd skirted by me. Like I was the one who would knock him into the lockers or

174

bully him with names. It made me want to throw up. The cringe feeling outweighed the admission that Jackson once had a crush on me. In fact, it made me feel worse knowing it, and I didn't know why.

My stomach twisted as I watched outside the window. The door to the athletic building opened, and the Mighty Lions marched out with Presley and Jackson in the rear. If it was a normal day, Lucas would have quipped a vulgar observation and I would have laughed. But it wasn't normal. I had no friends, my chest felt tight with too much pressure, and . . . *Did Jackson really just knock Presley down?*

Presley stood back up and lunged for Jackson—no, he tried to pry Jackson's phone out of his hand. They heatedly exchanged words as the rest of the team turned around and took notice. I stood up and leaned closer to the glass pane. Presley tossed his hands in the air, backing away from Jackson and the scene they'd caused.

What the hell? I thought as Jackson hurriedly tapped on his phone.

A few beats passed, and then my pocket buzzed. I scrounged for my phone in my backpack. The screen was bright with the new text notification from Jackson. I opened it, hoping he might shed some light on what'd happened. Instead of an explanation, he'd sent a smiley face emoji with a link to a TikTok.

Someone gasped, and I looked around Yearbook. Another gasp as everyone watched their phones. Lucas and Finley were shaking their heads in disbelief, and I quickly tapped the link. Jackson had just posted a duet of the Last Boyfriends video of

York. I had a feeling I already knew why he and Presley argued again—why Presley was freaking out in the bathroom this morning.

"I'm Jackson Darcy," he introduced in the video. His face filled the second half of the screen, pillow creases still on his cheek. He must have filmed it in his car when he went back to get his phone. "As you can see, Principal York is ripping down Ezra's poster because he's queer, and it isn't right." He smiled that damn lopsided smile of his. "He's pretty amazing, and he's standing up for our rights. It's more important than ever for us to show our pride. I'm pansexual, and I'm not nervous about it anymore. All because of Ezra. He has my vote for Lion King."

A grin stretched across my face as I glanced over at Lucas and Finley. Their look of utter shock was the proof I needed. They didn't know a damn thing. Neither did Presley. All of them were playing games with my head. I wasn't a shit person. Ms. Dion had said it herself—I *was* doing something right.

Eighteen

Jackson Darcy wasn't hiding any longer.

His coming out video had racked up as many plays as any Last Boyfriends video overnight. Queen Maeve Kimball had even commented on it and applauded his bravery in standing up for me and himself. It felt surreal to know all this had happened because I'd burned Presley's jacket. That I'd caused this viral effect on TikTok.

I hadn't expected his upload to garner me even more attention, though. More and more students stopped to say hello, waved, thanked me for showing real pride. They associated my Winter Formal campaign with his coming out. Jackson Darcy and Ezra Hayes were now tied together, and it was all anyone wanted to talk about. However, the only person I wanted to discuss it with wasn't talking to me.

Jackson was avoiding me, and I didn't know why.

I anxiously watched the clock above Magnolia's entrance as it counted down to 7:00 p.m. Just two hours until my shift ended and he showed up. Until I could figure out what had changed overnight, if he now regretted siding with me on Tik-Tok. I looked back down at our text thread, scrolling through our last messages.

Yesterday 9:58 PM

Jackson: Just got back from a celebratory coming out dinner with my parents! wish you could have been there

Ezra: You deserve to celebrate after that TikTok!

Ezra: (and endorsing me for king) 😊

Jackson: I feel so freeeee . . . and exhausted from replies

Jackson: (so worth it)

Ezra: I bet!

Jackson: All right gonna crash. Good night, Ez 🌙

> **Ezra:** Good night, Jax 🌙

Today 8:07 AM

> **Ezra:** You skipping physics? 👀

Today 1:37 PM

> **Ezra:** You weren't at lunch . . . you okay?

Today 3:53 PM

> **Ezra:** Talk later at Magnolia?

Presley's voice weaseled into my thoughts as I read my unanswered messages. *It could ruin everything.* I still didn't know what he'd meant by that. Everything had been fine, but now Jackson's lack of a reply was bothering me more than it should. More than I was willing to admit.

The door chime sounded, shaking me from my thought spiral. I forced myself to look away from our thread and said the welcoming spiel. Then I saw the waiter from HalloWeird by the banned books display holding hands with her girlfriend.

"Sam, right?" I called.

"Hey, Ezra," she said with a nod. "This is my girlfriend, Kasey."

Kasey's beaded braids swung as she waved enthusiastically. "Ezra," she chirped, "I'm *so* sorry about York ripping down your poster."

"Thank you." Their smiles were warm, welcoming. "Just another day of Watch What You Say." *And every-fucking-thing else going on,* I mentally tacked on with a glance at the clock.

"Numb Nuts can take that bullshit and cram it up Superintendent Bett's ass with the stick he keeps there," Sam said, tucking a blond strand behind an ear. "We refuse to let anyone tell us who we can be."

Her voice was unwavering, inspiring. It cut through the pressure, and I heard myself say, "Me too," with the same defiance.

She smiled at me knowingly, pointing to her jacket collar. "That's why we're telling everyone to show their pride," she added.

On her collar was a lion-shaped enamel pin, the inside filled with the colors of the pride flag. It made me feel as strong and unapologetically queer as the version of me in the campaign poster. I smiled, their warmth filling me. I had caused them to do that. This was real life now.

"I made these so they can't pretend we don't exist," Kasey answered before I could ask.

"That's the only way to show 'lion pride,'" I offered, smirking at the thought of York flipping out over them. "If Numb Nuts does anything to you because of them . . . you know, because of Watch What You Say . . . tell me." *And then I'll take him down in another TikTok.*

"Oh, we have it under control." Sam laughed, sharing a secretive look with Kasey. They both nodded in agreement as the door chimed, announcing a new customer.

The welcome spiel died on my lips when I turned. Jackson had shoved through the door. His face was hidden, his hair a mess of tangles as he stormed across the store to the back room. I checked the time. It was barely five o'clock, and he was supposed to be at practice.

Something wasn't right.

"I should probably get back to work," I said with an uneasy smile.

They said their goodbyes and went to the café while I edged my way closer to the staff door. Taking a deep breath, I pushed through to the back room. Jackson was seated at the squeaky table with his head down, his hand bunched up in his hair.

I opened my mouth to ask what was up with him today, but he looked at me with bloodshot eyes. My steps stilled. I was afraid of doing something wrong, saying the wrong thing.

"Ez, it has been the shittiest day ever," he finally said in a small voice. "Like school is always shitty but it got a hell of a lot shittier." He wiped snot on his HVHS hoodie sleeve. "Sorry I haven't texted you back. . . . Please don't be mad at me too."

"I'm not mad at you," I said, ignoring the ping of relief. He hadn't ghosted me. "What happened?"

"I got pulled into York's office before I could even make it to first block. He issued me a warning about social media use and how I was 'interfering with the superintendent's orderly conduct of HVHS.' Then when I got to practice today . . ." He took a shaky breath, his bottom lip quivering. "Ez, I'm off the team. No state playoffs. Coach wouldn't even let me back in the locker room to get my shit. He met me at the door with it. Walked me to York's office to give me the news."

"They kicked you off the team?" I shook my head, trying to understand what had happened. "Because you came out?"

"York said it was punishment for violating the school policies." He stood up from the table and pushed his hair back. His breathing grew heavy as he paced, sniffling. "They told me I'd be a distraction to the team during playoffs. Moved me to fourth block agriculture instead of athletic training. None of the guys, my friends who I thought had my back, nobody cares, and . . ."

Rage lashed through me as tears cascaded down his cheeks. I reached out to pat his shoulder, to comfort him. He fell into me, burying his face in the crook of my neck. I wrapped my arms around him, and his breath was hot against my skin while he cried.

"A lot of people care about you, Jax," I said, rubbing his back. "I care about you."

The scruff along his jaw scratched my neck as he pulled back. My brain went fuzzy when he gazed down at me, recalibrating while my face heated with a scorching blush. Jackson F'ing Darcy with his bloodshot eyes and puffy face and snotty nose and tangled mess of hair. But there was more: a constellation of tiny freckles across his nose, the vein of blue striking through his green eyes, a scar under his bottom lip that stretched as he smiled.

He was real. Someone who risked everything to be himself.

"I knew this would happen," he whispered, our faces close.

"Then why did you do it?" I heard myself ask, head and heart battling for that proverbial puck. "Make the TikTok, I mean?"

"Because of you." He managed his signature crooked smile, and it caught me off guard. Caught me right in the feels before I realized it. "Because you made me feel like I deserve to stand up for myself."

I couldn't breathe, couldn't speak as he watched me intently. Guilt flooded me, and I was suffocating. *He doesn't realize what it could mean*—Presley's warning intermingled with Finley's dejected *Things aren't exactly easy for us, either*. Were they right? Maybe I'd been so caught up in getting attention that I overlooked how my actions would affect others.

Maybe this was all my fault.

"Ezra," Dad called from the sofa as I shut the front door. "Where have you been?"

"Sorry I'm late," I called, kicking my boots off. Jackson and I had talked way past the end of my shift. My guilt wouldn't let me leave him there alone. "There was this thing that happened at school. . . ." I went silent as I stepped around the corner. Dad was perched on the edge of the sofa, remote control in hand and anger wrinkling his brow.

"Why didn't you tell me what happened?" he asked, his simmering rage too much like my own.

"Tell you what?" I asked, shrinking back. *Does he know about the TikTok? How did he find out? Will he make me stop?* "A lot of things have happened. . . . Can you be more specific?"

My attempted laugh failed miserably under his glare. He pointed at the TV with the remote, and a recording of the *Birmingham News* began to play on the screen. The young reporter smiled cheerfully, and I wasn't sure what was happening. Then her ruby-red lips parted as she began to deliver the news update.

"A local high school principal in Harper Valley has been caught in an attack against a student."

She took a breath, and it seemed I'd forgotten how to breathe. *There's no fucking way this is happening.* My face appeared in front of rainbow flames onscreen. The weight of what my revenge campaign meant, of what York had done being called an attack, of the fight that had suddenly became very real instead of some TikTok blasting—all of it came crashing down. I collapsed onto the sofa, unable to speak as she continued.

"As you can see, Principal Joseph York was caught in a fit of rage over a campaign poster for Ezra Hayes identifying himself as LGBTQIA+. It appears to be filmed by anonymous TikTok user Last Boyfriends, who is suspected to be a student at Harper Valley High School. Special thanks to TikTok influencer Maeve Kimball for sending this tip in. We've reached out to the Acheron County Board of Education for a comment, but we have no update yet. We'll be following this story closely. Stay tuned."

Dad paused the recording and waited expectantly. I sat there, staring hard at the campaign poster on the screen. My stomach churned like I might throw up or crap myself. I tried to breathe through the facts of what this all meant. Maeve Kimball came through for me. Inhale. The news picked it up as a story, HVHS was getting called out, and not just on TikTok. Exhale. This was real life, actual *real life*. Inhale. There was nowhere to hide, not after that. Exhale.

Dad broke the silence that'd settled around us. He cleared his throat, startling me. "Imagine how I felt when I got home from work and turned the TV on. There was your principal ripping down that poster."

"I'm sorry," I said slowly, quietly as he shook his head.

"You have nothing to apologize for, bud." He put his arm around me, pulling me in close. He kissed my forehead and hugged me like I was a child. "Why didn't you tell me about any of this?"

"I thought I could handle it, but . . ." I breathed out slowly, trying to figure out how I could explain it and have him understand. "I thought it wouldn't, uh, matter. . . ." My eyes burned as everything Lucas and Finley had warned me about gurgled out in word vomit. "Seeing it on the news just now made it real. It's bigger than I could have ever thought, bigger than I think I can fight with some stupid campaign for Winter Formal."

"That's where you're wrong," he said, rubbing soothing circles on my back. "Don't let that asshole take it away from you because he ripped down your pride poster. You'll win this fight because you're not hiding who you are, and *I'm* proud of who you are."

"You're not . . . you're not mad at me?" I asked. *At this mess I've caused?*

"Hey." He shook me gently. "I could never be mad at you

because you're standing up for yourself. Who I am mad at, though, is Principal York. Maybe I should go down to the school tomorrow morning. Talk to him man to man—"

"That won't help," I cut him off with a small laugh. Shaking my head at the potential embarrassment of him popping off at school. "York is only a crony. It's the superintendent's Watch What You Say initiative that's affecting the entire school district."

His hand stilled, and he pulled back to look at me. "I'm your dad, and it's my job to protect you from this bullshit. Promise me you'll tell me if this happens again."

I nodded, unable to tell him that I'd caused it. If I told him what I'd done, the magnitude of what has happened with Jackson and now the news, there was a chance he'd make me stop. The thought of doing just that had crossed my mind on the drive home, but then I saw Jackson's face. He'd been so proud to be himself. It'd only left me more confused.

"Don't forget what I said," Dad added. "Believing in yourself is the best revenge. Your job is to keep existing and being you. This shouldn't have to be your fight."

"Right," I said, biting my lip. But how could I when it was growing increasingly difficult to believe in myself? Maybe making this bigger was only giving them a reason to target queer students. Maybe this *wasn't* meant to be my fight.

"That's my son," Dad said with a shoulder squeeze. "I texted Becca. Ms. Dion, I mean. She said she's got her eye on you at school."

"How do you know Ms. Dion?" I cautiously side-eyed him. *Will she tell him about me running the account?*

"She and I are old friends from our HVHS days in the Gay-Straight Alliance together," he explained over the growl of my stomach. Then a smile softened the lines around his eyes as he checked the time on his phone. "Hey, I'll throw us something together for dinner if you wanna go wash up."

"Maybe we could pick out a movie to watch too?" I suggested in hopes it'd make me feel better about lying to him (and myself). "Whatever you want."

"How about an episode of *Drag Race* instead?" he asked with a grin. "I'm getting pumped to see you on Saturday."

I nodded, a sadness swelling at the thought of disappointing him again with more bad news. *I'll tell him tomorrow that I'm not doing the competition,* I decided as he stood with a yawn. *One cataclysmic event at a time.* Nearing the end of a workweek always did him in, and he'd be asleep within a few minutes after eating dinner. That was another reason why I couldn't tell him what was really happening. He has done so much for me as a single father. The least I could do was not burden him with more worry.

The clank of a skillet hitting the burner sounded as I headed toward the stairs. I managed a weak laugh, already knowing what we were having for dinner, and dug my phone out of my back pocket. My heart somersaulted when I saw the new text notification, my feet stumbling over the bottom step.

Jackson: you're really awesome just so you know brah ☺

Ezra: as long as you know you are too ☺

Another text came through. He'd sent a picture of him smiling—the same exact crooked smile I'd envisioned on the drive home. I collapsed down on the edge of my bed, staring at his face. My knee bounced as I picked at my nail polish. As I picked at the raging war of emotions inside of me.

Guilt and shame collided with the pride I'd once felt. There was a chorus of memories all vying to be heard. Dad's *The best revenge is believing in yourself;* Finley's *Things aren't exactly easy for us;* Jackson's *You made me feel like I deserve to stand up for myself;* the reporter's *An attack against a student;* Ms. Dion's *You're doing something right;* Presley's *Think about what you're doing—*

"What the hell *am* I doing?" I asked the gray walls of my bedroom.

The Last Boyfriends Club had started because I'd wanted to prove to Presley that I was his equal. However, somewhere along the way I'd lost sight of myself. I had been Ezra the last boyfriend, Ezra the Lion King nominee, Ezra the anonymous TikTok celebrity . . . but that wasn't who I was. After what happened today with Jackson and now *Birmingham News,* I wasn't so sure who I had become.

"You're Ezra Hayes," I willed myself to remember. But all I could recall was how Jackson thanked me, that same smile that wouldn't leave my mind, the way he'd said I'd made him feel like he deserved to stand up for himself—and *that* was why all this mattered.

Jackson was the answer to the confusion I'd been feeling. He was proof there wasn't any pride at HVHS. They wanted students like us to be quiet. To sit back and accept the Watch What You Say initiative.

Finley and Lucas had been right—I'd been acting selfish, so focused on my own hurt that I'd forgotten how these bullshit rules affected all of us. But I'd been right too. By some miracle of the TikTok algorithm and Maeve Kimball, I'd gotten people to start paying attention. Then I became a threat.

Our existence—me, Lucas, Finley, Jackson, and every other queer student at HVHS—was a threat.

Unlocking my phone, I pulled up the group chat because Dad was also right. This wasn't my fight. It was *ours*. I'd spent so long focusing on me when it was about more than that. More than anything I could have ever thought possible when we set out to get revenge.

Last Boyfriends Club

Today 8:27 PM

> **Ezra:** Glitter bomb I've been a major dickhole

> **Ezra:** Can we have an emergency meeting so I can apologize?

A few minutes ticked by as I waited for a response, my heart sinking every time I checked for a new text, but then my phone finally dinged.

Lucas: Only if you promise to save me all your future red Sour Patch Kids

Finley: And the green ones for me

Ezra: Deal

Lucas: Come over to the back patio when you get a chance

Finley: 👠

Nineteen

The Riveras' heated pool steamed, vapor tendrils curling up from its softly lit surface. I sat beside it and let the warm ripples nip at my hand. Dad had fallen asleep as soon as he scarfed down his bacon sandwich, and then I'd snuck out without waking him. He'd only question where I was going, and it'd be too much to explain.

The cold from the stone patio seeped into my jeans as I waited for Lucas and Finley. As I mentally rehearsed what I needed to explain. *Birmingham News* reporting on my TikTok video was a shock. Jackson coming out and getting kicked off the team was too. None of this was going how I'd expected.

My breath fogged in the chilly night as I looked up at the stars. For a moment it felt like I was back on County Road 233, the cool metal of the truck bed against my back. The weight of the memory bore down on me as though Presley were straddling my hips. But we'd never really been alone. Jackson was always in the picture—he was still in the picture. He was the reason

Presley had played me, and he was also the reason why I now felt compelled to fight back.

And I couldn't do it without my best friends.

Through the open sliding glass door, I heard the clack of heels on the kitchen tiles. The sink ran and dishes clanked with Mrs. Rivera's voice muddled in the mix. "Si, Mamá," Lucas called back, and then he stuck his head out the door. "Mom wants to know if you want fresca con crema?"

I shook my head, the thought of strawberries and cream making my stomach churn. My appetite had been nonexistent since swallowing my nerves. Lucas disappeared back inside, and I exhaled slowly through the heaviness one more time. The stars were still twinkling above like they had all those summer nights, but everything had changed.

More footsteps clacked out onto the patio, and I watched as both my BFFs sashayed toward me in five-inch heels. Finley wobbled on the stones as he cleared his throat. "Take it you saw the news too," he said.

I didn't know how to form all my thoughts into words and have them make sense. So I nodded and braced for the inevitable *I told you so.*

"The *scream* my mom *scrumpt* when she saw your face on the TV," Lucas said instead, plopping down beside me. He slipped off the heels and dipped his toes in the pool.

"We were upstairs practicing," Finley added, sitting on my other side to do the same. "Damn near broke our ankles as we rushed down to see."

"Pretty sure my dad had the same reaction," I said, my voice a rough whisper. "He was waiting for me after work and was pissed AF that I didn't tell him what happened."

Lucas sighed, a puff into the cool night, and turned to me. "You need these," he said as he scrounged in his pocket.

He offered me a small bag, and I took it from him without question. Carefully, I opened it to find all blue Sour Patch Kids. The gesture of our longstanding friendship made my eyes tear up. "Luc," I said, voice thick with emotion. "You saved these for me?"

"Yep," he replied solemnly. "We never stopped being your friend . . . but it felt like you stopped being ours."

"No—" I tried to say, but Finley pointed out, "You've been so hung up on yourself it started to feel like you didn't care about what we were going through. . . ."

"That's not what I . . ." My voice fell as I looked from him to Lucas, clocking their downcast eyes. A shaky breath left from my chest. "No, you're right. I've been selfish. I'm sorry I haven't been here for y'all."

"Yeah, you should have been," Lucas started, not unkindly, as he reached for my hand, "but you're here now. That's what matters."

"Forgive me?" I asked, the question barely audible over my thumping heart.

"As long as you promise not to ice us out again," Finley replied.

I nodded as my eyes burned, the early November night blurring. The voices in my head grew louder with each heartbeat. The reporter's *A local high school principal in Harper Valley has been caught in an attack against a student.* Thump. Jackson's *It's more important than ever for us to show our pride.* Thump. *We'll be following this story closely.* Thump. *All because of Ezra.*

"As long as we're apologizing . . . ," Lucas started, interrupting my thoughts. "We should too. We were against you posting that video of York because we thought it would take us all down . . . but we were wrong."

"I don't blame you for being cautious," I said. "I've made so many mistakes."

"We're not denying that," Fin offered with a smirk. "But none of us can be expected to do everything right. There's no perfect way to respond to an imperfect system. Getting angry with you, it's exactly what HVHS wants. They'd rather we fight each other—or ourselves—than *them*."

"This is bigger than just us. It always has been," Lucas said.

"What happened to Jackson changes everything," Finley added solemnly.

"You heard about what happened?" I asked.

"I wanted to text you about it, but . . ." Lucas trailed off, motioning between us.

"I feel like it's my fault," I admitted. "Because I told him to be proud of himself. Because I posted *that* video. He decided to finally come out to everyone else and—"

"To everyone else?!" Lucas kicked at me, sending a wave of water across the legs of my jeans. "Ezra. Hayes. There's so much to unpack here. Spill the tea this instant."

My eyes darted between him and Finley, both of them demanding to know more. "I already knew Jackson was pan. He came out to me a while ago."

Neither one of them said anything for a moment, and then Lucas gasped. "Oh. My. God." He leaned over and gave Finley one of those silent looks they'd been sharing as of late. "You were right. Jackson *does* like him."

"What?" I asked in disbelief, ignoring the swell in my chest. *There's no way he still does.* "He's only a friend. We've been hanging out because he was lonely and . . . Don't give me that look."

Water gurgled around Lucas's legs as he scooted closer, patting my knee with a smirk. "He came out to *you*. For *you*. That's huge."

"He didn't come out *for me*. He did it *because* of me. Because of the stupid Lion King campaign. And look what it got him. He got kicked off the team."

"You can't blame yourself for that," Finley said. "It's not your fault Coach Carter sucks."

"It is, though. I didn't think of the consequences."

Lucas grabbed my hand again and gave a gentle squeeze. "Consequences mean you're doing *something*," he said. "Sure, it was because of your TikTok, but it's not your fault. He had to know what he was risking when he took a stand. And he still did it anyway."

"He might've known the risk, but he doesn't know the whole truth." I stared at the gently lapping pool. He didn't know about me and Presley or that I was behind the TikTok account. Would he blame me for everything if he found out? "He doesn't even know he's a last boyfriend, too."

"What do you mean?" Lucas squeezed his grip tighter in anticipation.

"Presley cheated on me with Jackson while we were . . . doing whatever it was we were doing." I waved my hand in the air, the universal WTF sign, and continued to tell them how Presley had been jealous and how it had been a manipulative ruse. "It makes sense, though," I concluded. "I knew there had to be an ulterior motive for why someone like him would want me."

Lucas blinked rapidly, processing what I'd said. His eyebrows rose in thought, and then he cocked his head to the side. "Ezra." That was all he said before he shoved me, and I splashed face-first into the pool.

Finley's surprised bark of laughter was cut off by the splash.

I clumsily kicked in my clunky jeans and propelled myself back up. When I broke the surface, the air was frigid but the water blanketed me in steam. "W-what the h-hell?" I sputtered.

"You know damn well," Lucas replied, kicking water at my face. "Don't put yourself down because someone like *Presley Daniels* did you dirty."

His assertion settled over me as I treaded water. Presley had once called me a fat-ass nobody, said people like him didn't date people like me. I hadn't realized how tightly I'd been hanging on to those words. How I'd gripped at them as though they were the only truth. How I couldn't stop comparing myself to Jackson.

"It's more than that, though." Ripples lapped as I floated on my back, gazing at the overhead constellations that reminded me of Jackson's little freckles. "None of this felt real, not until I posted that video of York."

"Dude, I was so sure that upload would backfire," Finley began, "but it's more than York ripping up your poster now.

HVHS, the whole freaking school district, they expect us to just follow Watch What You Say."

"And be afraid to fight back," Lucas added gravely.

I exhaled evenly, my breath clouding as I swam up to the side of the pool. "I'm tired of being scared and hiding on the sidelines and behind fake TikTok accounts. There are millions of followers watching the Last Boyfriends account. If *Birmingham News* has noticed, then maybe more people in real life are too. . . ."

Lucas and Finley looked at each other, another one of those secret exchanges between them. "What are you insinuating?" Finley asked, his expression unreadable.

"What you said, Luc, about how consequences mean I'm doing something." This was it. Now or never. I needed their help. "I want to stand up for Jackson. It isn't fair that he was kicked off the team. If we don't say something, then who will?"

"We?" Lucas asked, a slight edge to his voice. His laminated brows narrowed as he glanced at Finley.

My fingers ached as I tightened my grip on the pool's edge. The rough concrete bit into my palms while Jackson's smile flitted through my mind (again). His name had been removed from the football roster, no longer a Mighty Lion. They'd make it as though he'd never been there and would erase all the yearbook photos I'd taken of him in his jersey during Homecoming Spirit Week.

"I can't do this alone anymore," I said finally, recalling what Ms. Dion had said. "That video of York has lit a fire, and I want to fan the flames. It's about Jackson and the book bans and the attacks on student rights. But I need both of you. It's *our* fight."

Finley bit at his lip, nodding once at Lucas. "How could we even help?" he asked with caution.

"The Watch What You Say initiative wants us to be silent and accept things as they are," I explained. "I'm tired of being quiet, especially now that I know exactly how to fight back with my Winter Formal campaign. We keep putting them on blast like the poster video. With *Birmingham News* following the story, imagine what we could do now that people are listening."

Silence fell while they considered. I nervously watched an array of emotions flicker across their faces. Then I saw it, that same spark I'd seen in my own eyes back before everything spiraled out of control. They both knew what we could be capable of doing. Together.

"It's obvious they want to erase us," Lucas said with finality. "We can't accept it. We have to take Bett down before he takes us down." He shared a nod with Finley. "But if we agree to help you, we have some stipulations."

"Anything you need!" I promised in a rush.

"One, what the Last Boyfriends Club does will affect all of us, so we unanimously agree on what we do," Finley said, and I nodded.

"Two," Lucas continued. "We can't pull an Ezra and go on an ego trip."

"Harsh but fair," I agreed.

"Three, you have to *actually* tell us stuff, dude, instead of bottling it up."

"And four—"

"How *many* are there?" I cut Lucas off.

"Four," he repeated as a wide grin tugged at his pouty lips. "You have to get your ass out of that pool and dry off. We have forty-eight hours to get you ready for the drag competition, and then we make HVHS pay by doubling down on your queer-ass campaign."

"You mean it?" I asked, relieved they trusted me again.

"We've had pleeenty of time to think it over while waiting for you to get your head out of your ass," Finley said with a wink.

"*Excuse* me, but . . ." I trailed off as they both laughed at my shocked expression.

The conflicted weight on my chest dissolved as I joined in. The louder our laughs rang in the night—full of excitement over drag queens and the implications of what we were about to do—the more it felt right. Life might've been easier when all we had to do was hide. But this, all three of us teary-eyed with giggles and existing in plain sight, that was worth fighting for.

Twenty

The Regional Lyceum Theater was thirty minutes down the interstate, right off Exit 4 in Mountain Springs. It had been a new addition to Alabama Regional Community College when Dad had graduated a decade ago. I was seven years old at the time, and the building was so huge it'd felt magical to me. Like I was Percy Jackson walking into a Greek temple.

The theater had seemed so gigantic then, Dad so tiny when he walked across the stage. Not much had changed since except my perspective. Now it was less massive, less magical as I peeked out from behind the maroon curtains. It was a packed house, the *Harper Valley Tattler*'s coverage inciting curiosity. Those same navy seats I'd sat in years ago were so close to the stage that it made my heart jump in my throat. I clawed the neck of my white halter-top dress, my fake nails scratching skin as I tried to breathe through the stage fright.

Keep calm, keep fabulous, Lucas's voice reminded me, *and for the love of Jinkx Monsoon, keep your boobs even.*

I adjusted the rolled-up socks in my bra and searched the

front row. Finley's father was on one side of Mr. and Mrs. Rivera, my dad and Jackson on the other. Their heads were bent together, both of them laughing at something that'd probably embarrass me later. A smile pulled at my worry lines, though. Jackson had immediately said yes when I'd invited him yesterday in physics, and now he was here.

Everyone else realized it too.

Heads kept turning, fingers pointing in his direction. He had been the top story all over *Birmingham News* this morning. They'd reported on the TikTok the three of us had made after making up. It had been Finley's idea to take Jackson's coming out video and stitch it with yearbook photos of him in his football jersey, a voice effect narrating what HVHS had done to him. Since then, our exposé on his removal from the team had racked up millions of views. I still hadn't had a chance to talk to him about it. Prepping for the competition all day had been a whirlwind, but all I wanted was his perspective on a particular comment thread.

Did the dimples from his grin mean he'd seen what people were saying about me and him online, or that he hadn't had the chance to wade through the thousands of comments demanding justice? Were they as massive as they felt, or maybe they were tiny in comparison? I couldn't decide as his face filled with shadows from the dimming overhead lights.

"Welcome to the first annual So You Think You Can Lip Sync!" an announcement said over the speakers. "Proudly presented by Lewis Auto Sales!"

I forced myself to look away from the audience, letting the

curtain close, and fumbled for my phone. The screen flashed that it'd been recording in my cleavage for the second time today. I stopped the pocket (boob) video and checked the time: 7:00 p.m. Twenty minutes until we went on.

The Euphoria Gworls rushed by in flash of sequins and barely-there outfits. My heartbeat matched the staccato clack of stilettos as I thumbed my way to TikTok and pulled up *that* comment thread.

hey **@lastboyfriends** im over here hardcore shipping jackson and ezra <3

#jazra

omg he came out for ezra? 😍

that sucks but now **@jacksondarcy010507** can date his man

My thumb flexed on the side button, putting the phone to sleep. I hated how I kept reading those four comments as though they carried any real weight. As though they meant just as much as the others demanding explanations from HVHS and justice for Jackson. That was something the old me worried about. Who cared if he might still like me or not? I had to stay focused.

But I do care.

How I felt could be dealt with later (or not at all). I shoved the thought away and pushed the dressing room door open. My inner turmoil was immediately drowned out by a wave of heated voices.

With the added height of the five-inch heels, I could see straight back to our station. Finley was at the mirror, touching up the Taylor-red lipstick we'd picked for matching looks. LJM3 was reflected behind him with a sour expression. He was still in a wig cap and angrily tossing his hands up.

"I can't believe you!" he yelled as I rushed toward them.

Lucas turned at the sound of my heels, exhaling roughly around a mouthful of chewed up candy. "There you are," he murmured. He reached up to adjust my left boob. "This has turned into a shitshow."

"I have every right to be here," Finley said evenly as Logan paced behind his chair.

"Don't even," Logan spat. "You're only doing this to get me back, but I have news for you, *dude*. I don't want you—"

"Wrong," Finley cut him off. He turned around in his chair, a calculating arch to his overdrawn eyebrows. "Why would I want to get back together after all the bullshit you've pulled?"

"Should we . . ." I trailed off and motioned breaking them apart.

"This needs to happen," Lucas said, offering me the emergency Sour Patch Kids he'd stashed in his bra.

Someone slurped water from a straw, the gathering crowd wide-eyed as Logan reared back. "Me? How dare you come for me after the bullshit *you're* pulling!" He pointed a long-nailed finger. "You're hiding behind your toxic masculinity, just like your father—"

"Don't go there, Logan—"

"Now you're hiding behind that Party City look—"

"How dare you!" Lucas lashed out, and I held him back.

Logan laughed as Lucas flipped him off. "He's with you

now? Makes sense. Well, brav-fuckin'-o for getting him to finally commit to being ga—"

"You're problematic as fuck," Finley cut Logan off with an eerie calm in his voice. "I have never felt so confident as a bisexual man as I do right now, tucked and cinched for the gods. I'm reclaiming my identity, and it has nothing to do with who I'm dating. Unlike you, Lucas and Ezra are supportive of who I am as a person. *They* are the reason why I'm doing this. *They* didn't ask me to prove anything. *They* make me feel valid."

Logan opened his mouth for rebuttal, but the speakers crackled through the dressing room. "Now taking the stage, Blue Jean Louise," the announcer said. "Next up, The First Wives."

"Save it, Logan." Finley stood tall, confident and steady in his heels. "You don't own me. You couldn't make me feel like shit even if you tried. So, you might wanna wipe that shocked look off your half-beat mug and get ready."

Finley spun on his heel in a fanfare of rippling fabric, leaving Logan clench-jawed in anger. The halter-top dress he'd chosen billowed out behind him like he was a goddamn queen. He held his head high in a march toward the exit. Lucas and I rushed after him, nerves beginning to tangle in my stomach. It was time to prove Logan wrong. Prove to everyone out there watching that we would get up on that stage just because we could.

"Oh my god," Fin whispered, spinning around as the door shut behind us. "I cannot believe I just said that to him."

"You just told LJM3 where to shove his biphobia," I said with a proud grin. "And I am living for it."

"That was a serve. A swerve. A fucking skid, Fin," Lucas said in awe. He looked at Finley as though, despite the contour and makeup, it was the first time he was truly seeing him.

Fin laughed then, eyes darting between us. "I finally stood up to him," he said under his breath. "I dunno what I was nervous about. After that showdown, this lip sync is gonna be easy."

Maybe for him it would be. Nerves clawed their way through me as we waited in the wing. I tried to breathe and forget who was watching. But as we prepared to take the stage, I could see around the curtain to the front row. Dad and Jackson both had their phones poised to record.

You're not Ezra tonight, I reminded myself. *You're Brenda Morelli Cushman, a badass first wife.*

Blue Jean Louise finished her Billie Eilish routine, and applause followed her offstage. The speakers crackled through the auditorium, through the anxiety building in my chest. "Welcome to the stage . . . The First Wives!" the announcer introduced us.

This is it.

We marched out in single file as the spotlight shined down. It was sunshine cutting through the nerves. The beams turned everyone into silhouettes, hiding facial expressions as I hit my mark on the right. An eternity passed as Lucas wagged his elegantly drawn brows, and then the song finally began.

"Don't tell me what to do," Finley lip-synced, marching us down stage. Lucas and I shimmed on either side of him like we'd practiced. "And don't tell me what to say. . . ."

We hit our routine of hip swivels and sidesteps and spins. I could hear a wolf-whistle that sounded like my dad. "Ezra!" being called by a voice my brain refused to recognize or else I'd trip ass over boobs. *Step, slide, turn, one-two-three,* I kept repeating as the song led us through the marks. Until Finley gave me my cue, and it was my turn to take lead.

"I don't tell you what to say," I mouthed, pounding my chest.

Lucas spun forward with precision and stole the spotlight. "And I don't tell you what to do," he added, pointing a lavish fingernail for added effect.

Then Finley strutted around him, resuming his rightful place in center stage. "So just let me be myself!" he lipped with enthusiasm, shaking his bob with intense fervor.

Our steps brought us in a row facing the audience. Together as one, we held our hands up to stop our haters. "That's all I ask of you!" we sang, crossing our arms over our chests. One by one, we pointed to the darkness of the auditorium. To Harper Valley High School and Acheron County and beyond. To everyone who wanted to keep us silent.

They didn't own us.

"And that's all for So You Think You Can Lip Sync!"

The house lights came on as the announcement concluded, the auditorium buzzing with congratulations. Dad yelled and rushed toward the stage. He leaped up the side steps two at a time and wrapped me in a bear hug. "I'm so proud of you!" he exclaimed with so much excitement that it knocked my wig askew.

"Thanks, Dad," I said, clutching our third-place trophy. At least we placed higher than LJM3's Tracy Turnblad. "Not the best but—"

"But nothing," he cut me off, resting his hands on my shoulders to get a better look at me. "You were phe-nom-enal!"

We were eye level with my heels on. Being the same height let me see the crinkles around his eyes, the way he beamed, how maybe we weren't so different after all. "I was kinda fabulous, wasn't I?" I asked. He laughed, pulling me in for another hug.

"Without a doubt," called Jackson from behind us. How had I never realized just *how* smooth, *how* deep his voice sounded? Warm and gritty like driving with the windows down in the heat of hay-baling season.

"Mr. Popular is gracing you with an appearance," Dad teased, spinning me around.

"He's been calling me that all night," Jackson said with a sigh. He was no longer a silhouette. I could see him. He'd tucked a plaid button-up into his khakis, and he offered me a bouquet of wildflowers with a shy smile. "Didn't know what was appropriate for your first drag performance."

"T-thanks," I said, taking them from him. "I don't know what's appropriate either except maybe a wad of dollar bills, but then you'd have to shove them in my cleavage and whoa that would be awkward—"

Dad put his hand on my shoulder, giving it a squeeze. "How about I let you two . . . talk . . . and head on home. Don't stay out too late celebrating." He gave me his best stern fatherly expression, and then he turned to Jackson. "See you on Thursday for the big Slammers verses the Manatees showdown?"

"Yes, sir," Jackson said, and Dad gave him the same stern look. "I mean, Kevin."

Dad winked at him and dropped a kiss on the top of my wig. Awkward silence settled as we both watched him cross the stage, pausing briefly to congratulate Lucas and Finley. I wanted to break the quiet. To ask Jackson if he had seen the responses.

"About Tik—" I started.

"Hope it's cool I come watch the big game with you on Thursday . . . ," he said at the same time.

The question lingered between us as I searched his face. He was a little taller than me, even with my added height, but I could still see his dimples up close. Still no indication if he'd read those four comments, though.

"Of course." I gave an overdramatic *pfft* like I couldn't care less either way. *Why the actual F am I being so weird? It's just Jackson.*

"So," he said at the same time I said, "Yep." I motioned for him to continue. "Your dance moves were fire."

"It was all Finley and Lucas."

"They're to thank for you strutting like that?" He briefly glanced down at my hose-clad legs in a way that tested the strength of my tape.

"I was *not* strutting," I said, shoving him. Touching him. My hand on his upper arm. I let go quickly and gripped the bouquet with both hands.

"You're right." A playful look glistened off the emerald in his eyes. "It was more like shaking your ass."

"Whatever." The high-pitched laugh that, for some ungodly reason, decided to expel itself from my chest made me cringe. "You're so funny." Another cringe that made me start backing away. "I should probably go get out of this getup."

"Can I get a picture with you first?"

"Okay." Another squawk of laughter. *Get. Your. Shit. Together.*

Jackson draped his arm across my shoulder and pulled me in close. So close I could smell that citrus scent. "Perfect," he said, and snapped the picture. "You care if I post it on Insta?"

"Are you sure?" I asked with an even breath, taking the plunge. "People might assume something . . . like with those TikTok comments. . . ."

Another lingering question between us. He turned his gaze on me. I could feel his stare searching my face, beneath the foundation and the lashes and the lipstick. He cleared his throat again. "The ones demanding justice for me, or the ones about us?"

He said it so casually that I didn't realize it had unsettled me until I swallowed back a dry heave. "The last one," I managed, dying from anticipation.

"Doesn't bother me."

He shrugged with more casualness that made me teeter in my heels. I wanted to know what was going on in his mind, what the hell was happening in mine. If he even still liked me like *that* and why I'd become so invested in finding out. Then he ruffled his hair, smiling at me. It was just Jackson. He was same guy as before. Nothing had changed except for the fact that Lucas and Finley were convinced there was more.

But was there?

Twenty-One

@hockeyhayes9 is a hella sexy drag queen

He posted that photo of us yesterday while I was at work. We'd been in the middle of a text discussion about *Daredevil* when I saw the notification. I'd nearly knocked over the banned books display as I read the caption. It was typed out like a fact with no other explanation that I, Ezra Hayes, was associated with *that* adjective of choice. There were no context clues about what he meant, either.

Unable to refrain, I'd done something utterly stupid and commented on it (immediately regretting it). He'd liked my "i love when fans give me flowers" before I could delete it. The thousands of followers who'd spilled over from his TikTok blasted the photo with #jazra comments, but he hadn't liked any of them.

I kept checking every few minutes in search of a sign. Anything for proof that he did still like me. It was one thing to admit I had *maybe* caught feelings for him, but it was an entirely different endeavor to act on them. Not after everything that'd happened last summer.

Another refresh as I maneuvered through the crowded hallway. Another hundred likes tallied up. Another sigh from his lack of clarification.

"Duuuude," Finley said as he fell in line beside me. He bumped my shoulder with a grin as we headed to lunch. "How many times are you gonna keep checking that?"

"No clue what you're implying," I said, shoving the phone into my hoodie pocket. "But probably forever at this point."

"Why don't you just ask him?"

Someone called my name, and I gave them a nod before turning to him in horror. "Are you high or something?" I asked. "I can't *just ask him.*"

"There's no reason to be nervous, Ez." He held up a hand, counting off with his fingers. "One, you're smart. Two, you're funny. Three, you care enough to fight back. Four, you're so cute, and the fact you obviously don't think so makes you even cuter. Five, I've seen you naked. So why *wouldn't* he still like you?"

"Because." I returned another student's wave before mustering up my best WTF expression. "He's my *friend.* I don't wanna screw that up." We had been texting nonstop, and the thought of not having that sucked for some reason. "What if I did flat out ask him and he's like 'no thanks, brah' or 'you're just a fat-ass nobody'? Dunno if my mental health could rebound from another failure." *Another embarrassment.* "Or worse, what if we go on that date but he doesn't want to hurt my feelings because we *are* friends and he isn't attracted to me so he strings me along and—"

"Take a breath, dude." Finley patted my back. "You know none of that shit's true, especially you being 'a fat-ass nobody.'"

I realized my shoulders had risen up, and I forced them down. Forced a smile at someone else. Forced myself not to think about all the what-ifs and ignored Finley's encouragement.

"In conclusion," I finished with a deep breath, "I cannot *just ask him*."

"I get it," he said, rubbing a hand up the back of his head. He winced in thought and then shrugged. "Guess you're smart to think with your head instead of your—"

"Do *not* say what you're about to say."

Finley's laughter cut through the thought of compromising situations. It bounced around inside my head as we passed by the seniors on their way back from first lunch. Then it quickly died as a pair of blue eyes locked on mine. I held my breath, waiting for them to either pierce through me as they had countless times, or for him to avoid me out of fear.

Instead, Presley nodded once as he passed by. He continued laughing at whatever one of the dude-bros said like it was no big deal to acknowledge my existence. *Huh.*

"That's a first," Finley said, as if reading my mind. But when I turned to look at him, he was staring in the opposite direction. "Logan just waltzed right on by without making a scene."

"I'm shocked." I looked over my shoulder, and sure enough Logan was just a few paces behind Presley. "We could repost one of the TikToks from the lip sync," I said cautiously, not wanting to remind him of our fight. "I mean, if you want to maybe rub it in? Totally your call."

"I appreciate it, but nah," he said under his breath. "We have more important shit to do with the Last Boyfriends TikTok now, and I don't think taking my frustrations out on Logan is worth it."

"What do you mean?"

"I don't know how I feel." He cocked his head to the side in thought. "It's like . . . the hate I had for him left me gutted. Now I just feel nothing."

"I know that nothingness all too well." I glanced back again, understanding the weight of indifference. "How about your dad? He hasn't trashed your newfound fierceness, has he?"

"I keep expecting him to be like"—he scrunched his face up like his father—"*No son of mine will be going around wearing makeup,* but he's surprised me. Keeps saying he's proud of how brave I was."

"I'm proud of you too, Fin," I said with a gentle nudge. "Just so you know."

"That's what I'm focused on, being proud of myself." Then his face brightened with a grin. "That and how *great* it felt to beat Logan at the lip sync as myself. Might have to dust off the wigs and compete again next year."

"I'm soooo in," I said with a laugh. It died on the tip of my tongue when I saw Lucas, though. He beelined down the hall toward us with worry etched on his forehead.

"Presley is campaigning his dick off," he said quickly, sparing a smile at Finley.

"He is?" My nose wrinkled in confusion. Presley never worked hard for anything.

"Ex.Act.Ly," he huffed, blowing a silvered lock off his face. "If Golden Boy Daniels is worried enough to actually put effort into something . . ."

"Then you have a shot of winning Lion King," Finley surmised.

Winning? I didn't care if I won or not. All that mattered now was everyone seeing me as an out queer student despite Watch What You Say. But if Presley thought I was good enough to make it to the final ballot, then maybe others did too.

"Fiiiiine," I said, already striding toward the cafeteria. "I'll go kiss ass."

"You make it sound like work," Lucas called after me, "but I know it's your favorite."

I didn't bother commenting on his remark. The cafeteria door snapped shut behind me as Lucas and Finley chatted in the hallway, and then my feet hesitated. Campaigning was easy in theory when it was one person at a time. The packed lunch tables made my back sweat. I took a breath and began working my way toward the lunch line. Smiling, waving, introducing myself, answering questions. "I'm Ezra" and "Yes, that Ezra from TikTok," and "Gee, what's Jazra?"

Halfway through the cafeteria, I spotted Sam and her girlfriend Kasey. They were sitting at one of the middle tables with two others. She raised a hand, fervently waving at me to come over.

"Um, helloooo," Sam called, still motioning wildly. "We didn't know *you* would be competing in the drag competition!"

"O-oh," I stammered, caught off guard. "I didn't know y'all were there."

"Like there is any other culture in this butthole town," a girl with tousled red hair said.

"That's Aiden," Sam introduced us, and pointed to another girl who was wearing overalls, "and Shyla."

"Grateful, thankful, blessed I was recording it," Shyla commented, raising her hands in praise. "That was badass."

"We thought so too. . . ." I waved at a girl I had English with and turned my attention back to the table. Aiden's and Shyla's eyes were trained just past my shoulder. Before I could turn, citrusy warmth engulfed me.

"They're totally your number one fans now," Kasey was saying as Jackson draped an arm across my shoulder.

"Pretty sure I'm your number one fan, brah," he corrected wryly, pulling me close.

I hated how his use of *brah* had become endearing. And I hated how Aiden saw me slip up and go all heart eye emoji, how she yelled that damned hashtag out loud. I grimaced and took note of Jackson's reaction to see if it gave him as much grief as it had me.

I got nothing more than a lopsided grin that made me want to scream, and then he pointed at Kasey's jacket collar. "That's a cool pin," he said. "Where did you get it?"

"I've been making them for our friends," she said, her fingers brushing against the pride lion. Then I noticed the same one on Shyla's overalls and Aiden's sweater.

"Can I buy two of them?" Jackson asked, his grip on my arm squeezing so slightly that I wasn't sure if I'd imagined it.

"Pfft." She dug in her jacket pocket and pulled two loud and proud lions out. "You've both earned one after essentially starting the protest."

"Protest?" Jackson and I both asked simultaneously.

Sam nodded in earnest as Kasey dropped the pins in my palm. "Haven't you noticed?" she asked, motioning around the cafeteria.

Had I noticed? I scanned the tables and clocked one enamel pin after another. They were stuck to backpacks and sweatshirts, attached to necklaces and collars.

"It all started with that graffitied poster and the Last Boyfriends' TikToks," Aiden explained. "We're showing HVHS real pride like your campaign posters said."

I stared down at the two pins in my hand. Tiny lions in proud colors that stood for more than I could have ever imagined. More than I could have ever thought. "Now we are too," I said, holding one out to Jackson.

Instead of taking it, he puffed out his chest for me to pin him. "Don't poke me," he teased. I had to fight back hysteria (and a double entendre) as I attached it to his flannel shirt. My hands grazed a well-defined pec and Finley's voice reminded me of how good he looked—

"Okay," I said much too breathlessly, and quickly pinned mine on. "We should probably get in line for lunch and then eat lunch because we only have a little time left before lunch is over." I knew I'd said *lunch* too many times, and my face flushed as I backed away. "Thank you for the pins."

"You're welcome," Kasey said.

Shyla yelled, "And thank *you* for blessing us with Jazra content!"

I walked faster, not wanting to see Jackson's reaction. Trying to control my own. He caught up with me as we got in line, and I risked a glance at him. The tips of his ears were red, cheeks dimpled with a shy smile as he stared down at the cafeteria's tiled floor. Was he embarrassed, or . . .

Or maybe he does still like me?

Twenty-Two

Morning arrived with a flourish of frost coating Harper Valley. I'd slipped twice running up the Middlebury Hill but persisted. It'd been so long since I'd done this, and I could feel the weight of every new pound. Each lungful of arctic air was a painful reminder of my embarrassment. *You're just a fat-ass nobody* sounded in between each breath. It burned in my chest with every footfall. Burned with each drop of sweat rolling down my body.

The new Taylor album blasted as I pulled my earbuds out in frustration. The idea that Jackson might still like me only added to the wobbliness of my legs as I finished my run. My stomach grumbled in hunger with each step up to the front porch. *Why would he like me, though?* I thought, opening the front door. The answer was the lurking memory of Presley's voice as I kicked my shoes off.

My frustrated breaths disrupted the quiet darkness as I padded to the kitchen. The fridge's water dispenser was loud as I filled a glass, too loud to hear the footsteps coming down the stairs. The overhead lights flickered on with too-sudden brightness.

"Mornin'," Dad said sleepily, wiping at his eyes. He took in the layers I had on against the chill, the beanie pulled down over my ears. "You're running again?"

"Mmm-hmm," I said between gulps of water. "I need to get in shape."

"Something's off, bud." He eyed me as he scooped grounds into the coffee maker. "Everything okay with you?"

"It's fine." I set the glass in the sink, and he kept staring. "What?"

"It's too early for you to pretend you're fine." He pressed the on button, the switch beeping loudly. "Cut your old man some slack because we both know I'll pester you until you do, and I haven't had caffeine yet."

"Fine," I started, but he stopped me with an unamused scowl. "I mean, I do. Want to talk to you about it."

"Does 'it' happen to be north of six feet, have fluffy boy-band hair, and eyes only for you?" he asked over the sputtering coffee.

"Maybe." I clenched my hands into fists, leaning against the fridge.

"If you could have seen the way he was looking at you on Saturday." Dad reached for two mugs in the cabinet, tossing a grin my way. "Thought I'd have to have a little talk about treating you with respect and the importance of condoms—"

"Dad." My stomach gurgled with the water I'd chugged. "I don't think it's like that. We're friends. Only friends."

"Sounds like you want it to be more than that." The truth in his assessment made me shrug, unable to speak. He placed the mugs on the island and rounded the corner. "Why is that a bad thing?" he asked, pulling me into a hug.

"Because," I said into the stiff logo of his Hayes Railroad Construction sweatshirt, "why would he like me like that?"

"Ezra." He leaned back to look me square in the face. "Why *wouldn't* he?"

"Just look at me, Dad."

"I *am* looking at you, bud." His eyes sized me up for emphasis, and he gripped my shoulders. "And all I see is the wonderful, handsome young man you've become."

"But I'm fat—"

"So what?" he cut me off. "Weight isn't a bad thing! It doesn't change your value, you hear me? Because you're Ezra Hayes. Period. That's all that matters, not what *you* think is wrong with you. Who you are will always be enough."

I nodded, chewing on my lip. "You have to say that because you're my dad."

"That doesn't diminish what I said." He lowered his chin sternly and narrowed his eyes. "What I do have to say as your dad, however, is that you *have* to stop starving yourself and punishing your body with these runs, bud. I know you, and I know you're only doing it because you like someone." I started to refute him, but he held up a finger. "Listen to me, that way of thinking is harmful. You don't have to lose weight to keep someone's interest. If they do like you, then they like *all of you* without restrictions. Understand?"

"Yes, sir," I said weakly, embarrassed that he'd called me out. Embarrassed about how obvious it was that I was crushing hard. "I'll try to do better." His furrowed brow made me correct myself. "I *will* do better. Promise."

"That's more like it." His face softened into a smile. "So you and Jackson, huh?"

"Daaad," I groaned. "I don't even know if he likes me back."

"If you can be honest about how you feel, then you should let him have the chance to be honest about how he feels too. You'll never know someone's perspective until you give them a chance to share it."

Perspective. That's what I'd wanted from him since those stupid #jazra comments started. But I was apprehensive because the last time I'd gotten someone's honest perspective, it'd involved a darkened Magnolia and way too many tears.

"For what it's worth," he added, tugging the beanie off my head. "My money's on that boy liking you. You'll see what I mean when he comes over for the hockey game on Thursday."

I snatched my beanie from him, rolling my eyes. "I can't believe you've become besties with him."

"Everyone loves me." He winked then and ruffled my sweaty hair. "I'm a cool dad."

"You *really* shouldn't attempt humor before coffee." I smiled at him despite the sass, thankful he was my father. That he didn't care I was a hot mess. "Thanks, Dad."

"I'm here anytime you need me." He pushed me toward the door. "But your stinky ass seriously needs to shower, and I need coffee. Go get cleaned up while I get breakfast started."

"Yeah, yeah," I called back to him, trudging toward the stairs.

He was right, though. It'd taken me a while to be honest about my feelings for Jackson, and I needed to let him know before I lost my nerve. I owed that to the both of us. Maybe he'd do the same and tell me how he really feels. I could just text him and ask to talk. That's what friends did, right?

I felt my sweatpants pocket for my phone as I took the steps. The screen was already lit with a series of texts from Lucas. Another one came through as I hurriedly swiped to read them. If he was awake this early, something cataclysmic had happened.

Lucas: mom just woke me up bc of the news

Lucas: are you awake yet?

Lucas: turn on the local ABC stream

Lucas: they're doing a story about HVHS

Lucas: this is huge

Lucas: WAKE UP

Lucas: it's about to start stand by for live updates

I immediately rushed up to my room. It felt like all the air had been knocked out of me as I collapsed on the edge of the bed, as I reached for the remote on my nightstand, as the TV flickered to life. The streaming service loaded excruciatingly slow. I took a steadying breath and navigated to ABC.

A red van flickered on the screen, parked in front of HVHS. BIRMINGHAM NEWS was printed in big, bold letters on the side with their sunshine logo. A reporter with sleek, black hair held a microphone with gloved hands. The caption at the bottom of the screen read, *Vivian Singh on location at Harper Valley High School.*

I turned the volume up as she began speaking. "We're live with Principal Joseph York and Acheron County Superintendent Devon Bett." The camera zoomed in on her as she smiled broadly, and then the frame panned to York and Bett. Little puffs of breath slipped through their pursed lips as they faced the camera. "Could you comment on what's happening at your school?" Vivian asked, holding the microphone out to York.

Tension strained his brow, but he mustered his usual fake smile. "What's going on here is online harassment from an anonymous source that's disrupting the learning process," he delivered. Each word was slicked with oil like he'd rehearsed it too many times.

"You're referencing the Last Boyfriends TikTok account?" she asked.

Bett's jaw clenched roughly, mustache bristling, as his beady eyes cut to Vivian. "This perverse account is highlighting gross misconduct by students," he spat from the corner of his thin mouth.

Hunger glinted in the reporter's eyes, and she looked back at the camera. "Could you please elaborate on the quote 'misconduct' of students Ezra Hayes and Jackson Darcy?"

"It's merely an instance of students breaking rules—" York started, but Vivian jumped in.

"You mean, they went against the school district's Watch What You Say initiative, correct?" She didn't give them time to comment before pressing onward. "Based on the TikTok account's reporting, they've been targeted for being openly LGBTQIA+."

"That TikTok has done nothing but spread lies," York said gruffly. "Fake news for attention."

"Correct me if I'm wrong, Principal York, but how is it quote 'fake news' when there's footage of you ripping down a poster of Ezra Hayes in a fit of rage?"

"Well," he began, fingers anxiously flying over his lanyard, "that was taken out of context. He hung it up over a prominent school sign." He cut his eyes to Bett, sweat beading his forehead despite the cold. "It was my job to remove it, that's all. I was following the Watch What You Say guidelines."

"Could you tell our viewers exactly what this initiative stands for, then?"

"I don't know how you do things in Birmingham, ma'am, but Acheron County is family-oriented," Bett said, his strong Southern twang coating each syllable. "My initiative is to keep family values intact for a perversion-free environment."

"Student athlete Jackson Darcy was banned from representing the HVHS football team in your division at the state playoffs. This happened, as reported by Last Boyfriends, because he came out as pansexual. How does a student's innocuous identity go against family values?"

York took a deep breath and turned toward the camera. "Jackson Darcy is well aware he violated the social media policy. The consequences are of his own doing, and I had to enforce the punishment. That's my job as principal and why we agreed to this interview, to clear up this mess started by that TikTok account. The last thing we want is an absurd protest."

That hungry glint in Vivian's eyes swallowed his statement whole. A quick glance through the camera, through the TV, to me. Like she wanted everyone watching to know he was playing into her hand. "You're claiming Ezra Hayes and Jackson Darcy are responsible for their punishment?"

"They both broke the rules," he said. "Nothing less, nothing more."

"I beg to differ," she chirped in short, clipped words. "The banning of a student athlete from sports because he chose to use social media to come out, not to mention a rainbow-clad campaign met with rage, is *not* nothing. We've been digging through the documented minutes from your county's last school board meeting regarding Watch What You Say, and what we found is suggestive information directed toward the quiet suppression of students like Ezra and Jackson."

York's smile tensed on the edges, but he tried to save face. "Ms. Singh, I'm not sure where your wild accusations are coming from. All I do is make sure HVHS is run properly based on what I'm told by Superintendent Be—"

"No more comments," Bett cut him off aggressively, shoving the microphone away. "Remove yourself from this school campus at once before I call local law enforcement."

Vivian's eyebrows rose as she turned to the camera. "Now, *that* certainly doesn't sound like nothing. You heard it here first, Birmingham. Stay tuned for more updates."

The interview spot ended, and a commercial break for a lawn service began. I sat there, stunned and unable to process what I'd just watched. I was amazed by their audacity. Confused by their justifications. Frustrated over their use of "perversion-free environment."

Beyond all that, I burned.

One finger at a time, I released my tight grip on the remote. Lucas had blown up my phone with commentary on the broadcast, but I couldn't discuss it yet. Couldn't stomach regurgitating their piercing, glass-shard lies.

That TikTok account has done nothing but spread lies.

Last Boyfriends had only spread the truth, though. Bett was upset because he'd been keeping it quiet for so long, keeping his outright homophobia under the radar. The disappearance of the Gay-Straight Alliance club, library books, representation that differed from his picture-perfect idea of "family values." All of it was hidden behind Watch What You Say.

Fake news for attention.

He was wrong about it being fake, but he'd been right about wanting attention. If I was being honest with myself now, I no longer cared how many views our videos got or how many people liked them or the number of comments dissecting our identities. Those numbers still didn't add up to anything real. Yet.

The last thing we want is an absurd protest about this.

I looked at my nightstand, at the pride lion sitting there. Now that we had the attention of everyone behind those numbers, what mattered was action. Maybe it was time to give them the last thing they wanted.

Twenty-Three

PROTEST TO SHOW HVHS REAL PRIDE

The new TikTok was filmed in the HVHS lobby, but no one could tell it was me. It was a close-up of the lion pin on my jacket. Lucas had stealthily recorded it for me, making sure to showcase the HVHS logo on the floor. Using a voice modifier, Finley promised York and Bett and whoever was watching that Last Boyfriends wasn't a bystander. We weren't afraid to make a statement.

It had been viewed 5 million times since Tuesday with comments still pouring in. No one was theorizing about who was behind Last Boyfriends anymore or calling out everyone who wore a basic, gray fleece. Instead, all the comments repeated a simple hashtag created by students at HVHS: #IStandWithEzraAndJackson.

Most of them had watched the news interview, finally waking up to the extent of Watch What You Say. More people came up to me, asked me where I got my pin, asked me about why

I was running for Lion King. It seemed like the whole school wanted to talk to me—

Except for the person I shared that hashtag with.

Something was up with Jackson. I'd texted him in physics after posting the video, asking if we could talk like I'd planned. He'd made up an excuse and sent a funny meme instead. Aside from those random texts, he hadn't bothered to actually engage in a conversation. It was a simple hello and goodbye at work the last two nights. At least he still cared what Last Boyfriends had to say. He'd uploaded a TikTok with his signature smile and the pride lion pinned to his jean jacket.

Now I'd have to watch him hide behind a grin when he showed up for the game. Maybe we could talk again on the front porch afterward like last time. If he was even coming. He still hadn't replied back to my text asking about tonight.

I leaned back in the side chair, swiping out of our message thread as the vacuum shut off. Dad had been intensely cleaning since I'd gotten home. He'd nagged at me nonstop while we counted down to the game. *Febreze the sofa, bud. Dust off the TV, bud. Set out the real plates, bud. You call that polishing the coffee table? Put some elbow grease in it, bud.*

"Why are we cleaning?" I asked again, watching him roll up the Bissell's cord. "I don't know if Jackson's coming." I woke my phone screen. Still no message from him, and I hated how much that bothered me.

"He'll be here," Dad said with a huff. How he knew for sure, I had no clue. "The game starts in ten."

"If you say so," I started, but then the doorbell sounded. "Guess you said so."

"Let him in while I put this away." He rolled the vacuum cleaner by me, pausing to run his hands over my hair. "Okay, you look nice."

"Stop being weird," I begged, but he only grinned.

I tossed him a WTF expression and made my way to the door. *It's just Jackson,* Lucas's earlier pep talk reassured me. *He's your friend now, and you can talk to him.* Finley chimed in as I shuffled into the foyer. *If he doesn't like you like that, dude, that's his loss because you're the shit.*

The doorbell rang again.

With a deep breath, I gripped the knob and opened. My knees went weak when I saw the same Nyberg jersey he'd worn to Hallo-Weird. His hair was a tangle from where he'd obviously been running his hands through it, his face on the cusp of a full flush.

Dad came up behind me and opened the door wider before I could say anything. "Jackson!" he greeted, motioning for him to come inside.

"Hi, Mr. . . . Kevin," Jackson said. His eyes darted over to me, and I tried to smile like I wasn't worried something was wrong. The look on my face must not have relayed the message because his brow pinched together. "Are you sure it's still okay that I watch? I could totally go home—"

"Nonsense," Dad said for me, ushering us toward the sofa. "It's more than okay. I'll be right back, but you two have a seat. The game's about to start."

The fact he would rather go home was a red flag. Maybe he didn't like me. I'd find out after the game. As I watched Dad disappear into the kitchen, I tried not to think about having *that* conversation with him. "Excited to see the Slammers take down the Manatees," I said awkwardly, turning on the TV.

"Same," he replied stiffly from beside me. In my periphery, I watched his hand reach up and tangle itself in his hair. Then he exhaled slowly before turning toward me. "Hey."

"Hi?"

"You said you want to talk." He checked the time on his phone, looked at the TV. "Sorry I've been avoiding it. I was nervous because, well, I've been waiting for the game and yeah."

We were doing this now. *I wish Dad would hurry up with the wings and rings,* I thought as nerves sloshed inside me. *Save me from having to go through with this.* "It's all good and def not a big deal and tonight's game is huge and—"

"Remember when I came out to you and asked if we were friends?" he asked, cutting off my rambling. I nodded as he licked his lips, as he cut his eyes to the TV. "If I'm mistaken . . . promise me we'll still be friends after this."

"After what?" I asked, forcing a laugh. Pretending he wasn't about to drop some bad news on me.

He pointed toward the screen as the players were announced on the ice. *"Slammer Nation, theeeeey are your 2024–2025 Bama Slammmmmers!"* the commentator yelled as a horn sounded. *What the hell is he talking about?* I glanced over at him. His face was fully blushed now, his leg bouncing.

"Barry, before we get started tonight," one of the commentators said. "We have a special message going out from our Sweet Home Alabama Arena here in Birmingham."

"What's happening . . ." I trailed off as Rolf Nyberg skated out to the middle of the ice. He was holding a sign over his head as the camera zoomed in.

"Iceberg received a sweet request from a fan in Harper Valley where things aren't so great, from what I've heard," the commentator continued. I looked back at Jackson (he'd gotten even redder) and saw Dad hovering in the doorway with his phone raised. "Ezra, if you're watching, and I do hope you are, our very own queer hockey hero has a message for you." Cheers and applause from the crowd, frantic hysteria from me as I leaned forward to read the sign. "Iceberg, and all of us here in Slammer Nation, want to know if you'll do Jackson the honor of attending Winter Formal as his date?"

An ache detonated in my chest as Nyberg skated toward the camera with the sign that read WINTER FORMAL, EZRA? I clutched at my exploding heart, unable to form words or thoughts as I breathed heavily.

"Ez?" Jackson asked cautiously, his voice barely audible. My face was hot, my eyes burning. "It's okay if you don't like me like that. Tickets don't go on sale until tomorrow and—"

"Yes," I said quickly.

Somewhere Dad yipped with joy. It sounded far off, blood rushing to my ears, and I glanced once more at Nyberg on the screen to make sure I wasn't hallucinating. Then back to

Jackson who *wasn't* embarrassed of me. Who had just made a grand declaration with a capital M Moment. Who looked at me doe-eyed with that damned lopsided smile.

"Yes, I'll go to Winter Formal with you."

"Ezra Hayes!" Lucas laid into me the moment my Jeep door opened.

He and Finley had been waiting in the school parking lot when I pulled in. That was my first clue something was up—Finley was *never* here this early. The second was Lucas's perfect-sister eyebrows set in dangerous slopes. The pride lion pin on his sweater glimmered in the early light as he squared his shoulders.

"How *dare* you not tell us what happened last night?"

I startled, confusion etching itself in my smile. "I was waiting to tell y'all in person . . . Wait, did y'all *finally* decide to watch one of the hockey games?"

"Ew." With a steely glare, he shoved his phone in my face. "The first thing I saw when I woke up was Jackson's form-posal on TikTok." My eyes searched his screen, where I saw our living room on full display with 1.5 million likes.

"Dude, even the Slammers dueted it with Nyberg holding that sign and—"

"Oh my god!" Lucas cut Finley off with a squeal. "It was so romantic. In a dude-bro type of way."

He threw himself at me. The hug rocked me side to side, sending thoughts clashing together. *Fuck me, the Bama Slammers*

234

have me crying on their TikTok and *Jackson posted it for the world to see.*

"Yeah," I said into his swept-back silver hair. "Still in shock, TBH."

"Obviously need all the details on what happened after you said yes," he ordered, releasing me.

"Did you make out with him?" Finley yawned and offered a sleepy grin. "That definitely warranted tongue."

"N-no!" I stammered, tossing my backpack over my shoulder. "*Nothing* like that."

In fact, nothing major had changed after the form-posal. It'd been like any other game night, except for small moments here and there that I mentally replayed with a smile. How he'd kept finding innocent ways to touch me: gripping my shoulder to balance himself as we hopped and spun around with each goal, wiping wing sauce off my nose, letting his knee rest against mine, giving me two very long goodbye hugs that made me feel some type of way.

"Fin, he's grinning. Something happened." Lucas snapped his fingers at me. "Out with it before I combust in anticipation!"

"Okay," I began as we walked toward the school, "so we were sitting on the sofa when Connor got the Slammers their first goal with an assist by Nilsson—"

"Maybe not *all* the details."

"Fiiine," I huffed as we took the steps. "After the game, I walked him out and we talked, god, for like an hour sitting in his car. He's been acting weird all week because he thought I didn't like him. He and Dad, who are *apparently* besties now, had been planning the whole form-posal."

"I told you he liked you," Finley said through another yawn.

"And we *love* a romantic king." Lucas smirked as we reached the door, tossing a chuckle toward me. "Both him and Zaddy Kevin."

"I'll let that slide." I pushed past him into the school, their snickers following behind me. "Because it *was* romantic, and my dad came through . . ."

My voice died in my throat.

Jackson was leaning against the wall beside the PTA table. His hands were fisted in the pockets of his North Face jacket, the brown floof of hair bobbing as he talked to Presley. I looked between them and fought the overwhelming urge to freak out. *Presley knows too many of my secrets. What is he saying to Jackson?*

"You don't think," Finley began, and Lucas finished, "that he's trying to sabotage you and Jackson again?"

I gulped as Presley noticed me watching. His eyes briefly locked with mine, lips saying my name. I stopped walking, my feet dead weights, unable to move forward as Jackson turned his head and saw me.

"Ez!" he yelled, and crossed over to us.

He wrapped his arms around me, and I was caught in a rush of sporty deodorant mixed with minty toothpaste. His chest was warm and rumbling against mine. "I've been waiting for you."

"You were being awfully friendly with Daniels," Finley pointed out as Presley disappeared down the hall.

"It was so weird," Jackson said, pulling back to look at me. "Do you know him?"

"Uh." I didn't want to lie but couldn't quite bring myself to tell him the truth. That I knew more about Presley Daniels (and him) than I should.

"Why?" Finley asked for me.

"'Cause he said Ezra was a good guy."

That wasn't what I was expecting. Presley Daniels had admitted he knew me, after all the shit he'd put me through. How he'd pretended I hadn't existed. *What's gotten into him?* I wondered as Jackson draped his arm around my shoulders.

"Told me he was happy we were going to formal together and I could be myself," he added, smiling down at me. "Apologized for how the team treated me. And stuff."

"That was nice of him," I said carefully.

By "stuff," I knew he meant how Presley had tried to manipulate him and play with his emotions like he had with mine. He couldn't know I knew that, though. Then he'd find out what Presley and I were over the summer. How stupid I'd been. What if that changed the way he thought of me?

"More like shocking," Lucas muttered as we got in line at the PTA table, and then he raised his voice to Jackson. "Ezra *is* a good guy, though. Don't play with his heart."

"I'll treat Ez here with respect, brah." He put his arm around my shoulders again. "Promise."

Lucas pointed a finger. "Don't get crazy. Disrespect him a little. Please. Smother him with your as—"

"That's enough of that," I cut him off without looking at Jackson, wanting to evaporate on the spot.

"Yeah, yeah," he said, rolling his eyes as Finley snickered. "Now that our future Lion King has a date, we need to discuss tuxedos."

Lucas launched into a detailed discussion about color patterns, and Jackson's arm tightened around me. He pulled me next to him as the line moved forward, his eyes sharp as people stared. It was obvious they'd seen the TikTok he'd posted.

For a second, I worried someone would be rude about two guys going to formal. Then I noticed the pride lions. They were boldly displayed on jackets and bags, right there in plain sight as people smiled and waved at me.

"Next," called a high-pitched voice in a thick Southern accent, and the line moved forward.

It was our turn, and I smiled at the woman behind the table. She was wearing a PTA name badge with Karlynn scribbled in flowery cursive. "Couple's ticket please, ma'am," I said as Jackson dropped his arm and reached into his back pocket.

"I'm paying," he said.

"Excuse me?" Karlynn asked, her eyes narrowing.

"He's my date." Jackson smiled at me, and I felt my face grow warm. "I finally worked up the nerve to ask him out last night so we could get tickets today—"

"I can't sell *y'all* a couple's ticket." She gave a stern shake of her head, the bleached blond curls dancing. The way she said it made my stomach drop. "Couple's tickets are for one boy and one girl. You can buy individual tickets only."

"Since when?" Finley asked behind me.

Lucas added, "Homecoming wasn't like that."

"Wait your turn," she ordered, turning back to us. "So two individual tickets, then?"

"No," Jackson said slowly. "We're going together. Why can't we buy a couple's ticket?"

"Because," she stressed through clenched teeth as she eyed our pride lion pins, "couples take part in the promenade. As PTA chair, it's my job to make sure our children adhere to Watch What You Say. What kind of message would it send if *y'all* were seen together? We don't want any more scenes like that TikTok." She made a face, counting off two individual tickets. "That'll be fifty dollars each."

I opened my mouth to tell her off. Tell her how it wasn't fair. How I'd been so happy about Winter Formal until she crapped all over it with her hoity-toity righteousness. Jackson nudged me with his elbow before I could say a word, and I met his gaze. That vein of blue mixed in his green eyes, promising me he wouldn't let formal be ruined.

"It'll be okay, Ez," he said as he pulled money from his wallet. "We can still go together. This changes nothing."

He was wrong, though. It changed everything.

Twenty-Four

What kind of message would it send if y'all were seen together? Karlynn's voice replayed all through first block. Every time I looked at Jackson, he'd smile or make a silly face. Anything to show me it would be okay. But all I could hear were her words. Feel as they sliced through me. Ache from the thousand cuts they'd slowly been forcing us to not only endure but also to accept.

Realization rang inside my head with the bell for second block. The reporter on *Birmingham News* had been right. The entire point of Watch What You Say was to quietly suppress students like us. The PTA table was proof enough as we walked into the lobby. The people in power were keeping us from having an identity, prioritizing the so-called good students, not giving a damn how the rest of us felt, robbing us of what voice we had.

Now they weren't pretending any longer.

"Forget Karlynn," Jackson said with yet another smile of reassurance. "At least we'll be there together. That's what I wanted."

"Me too," I said, my lips twitching to match his. It *was* what I wanted, but not like this.

He winked, giving me two thumbs-up as he backed down the hallway. I waited for him to disappear into his classroom before turning toward the front office with determination. York had once told me he was on my side, told Vivian Singh that he was making sure the school was run properly. Maybe I could just talk to him. Maybe everything we've done with Last Boyfriends has helped him understand how it wasn't fair.

The administrator glanced up at me as I stepped inside. "Good morning!" she beamed. "How can I help you?"

"Can I talk to Principal York?" I asked. "It's an emergency."

Her cheeriness never faltered as she picked up the phone and dialed. "Yes, sir," she said into the receiver. "You have a student here to see you. Ezra Hayes. Says it's an emergen— Mmm-hmm." The handset clicked into its cradle, and she looked back up at me. "You can go on back."

"Thank you, ma'am."

The doorway loomed ahead as I shuffled toward it. Not bothering to knock, I turned the handle. York's fingers stilled over the keyboard, but he didn't look up at me. "What's the emergency?" he asked absently.

"It's about the PTA," I said, hovering just inside the door.

York sighed. "I don't have time for this."

A scowl contorted his face as he resumed typing. The clack of keys punctuated his dismissal, signaling for me to leave. I squared my shoulders and cleared my throat. "The PTA is refusing to sell tickets to same-sex couples for the dance."

"That's simply not true," he corrected without bothering to look up. "You were sold two individual tickets."

"That's not the same."

"Ezra," he began, twisting in his chair, "you get to go to the dance. Why are you making it an issue?"

"It's *already* an issue." I forced my voice to stay even, firm. "The woman from the PTA said she's upholding Watch What You Sa—"

"Ezra." He stood, crossing out from behind the desk. "HVHS has allowed you and Darcy to buy tickets. What more do you want me to do?"

"Let us be in the promenade."

"The Winter Formal is sponsored by the PTA; therefore you'll have to talk to them about it." He motioned for me to leave with a rushed wave. "I don't have time for this melodrama. I have enough to do as it is keeping this school orderly while this TikTok fiasco blows over."

"But—"

"No buts. The Mighty Lions made it to state playoff semi-finals, and I must prepare a press release on the strong likelihood we'll host the championship game." He herded me toward the door. "Some things are *more* important than you."

With that, he forced me from his office, slamming the door in my wake. His shameless gaslighting confirmed everything I already knew: York understood what was happening, but it wasn't his job to care. He did what he was told without question, and that made him just as bad as the superintendent.

Last Boyfriends had landed two spots on the *Birmingham News* and created a protest with the students at HVHS with our latest videos. But it wasn't enough—using my Winter Formal campaign to fight back didn't feel like enough. Not anymore. Not if York and Bett thought we were a minor inconvenience that would "blow over" and be forgotten about.

I slipped back into the hallway with determination, already typing a text to the group chat. They weren't playing fair, and neither would we.

Some things are more *important than you.*

York's words pulled at me as I gripped the red marker in my hand tighter. Their implications tugged at my shoulders, pulling me underwater like they had all weekend. None of them cared how this affected us. How our lungs ached to just breathe and exist. How much we had to fight to keep our heads above the surface.

I inhaled deeply and faced the dry-erase board. Nearly two months had passed since we'd first set foot in this office display and dreamed up the rules for revenge. Our club of last boyfriends had all begun with want: Lucas wanting to sabotage the HalloWeird party, Finley wanting to enter the drag competition, me wanting to run for Winter Lion King.

Our priorities had changed since then.

It wasn't about what we wanted anymore. Now there was only *need.* The need to breathe and exist, the need to prove no one was allowed to treat us this way, the need to hold all the twisted school board members, and administrators, and politicians accountable for their actions.

They can fuck all the way off, I thought, and uncapped the red marker. A loud squeak emitted as I struck a line through our first two rules. "Y'all have been successful," I pointed out, turning around.

Lucas leaned back in the desk chair. A smirk twisted his grin, a giggle under his breath, as he swiveled from side to side. "It does give me life that the seniors are *still* talking about Cass's party," he commented. "And I feel even better knowing I didn't let him walk all over me again."

Finley nodded, swallowing a mouthful of Bubba's pizza special. "The drag turned into more than getting back at Logan," he added. "It was about confidence and being validated. Drag definitely made me feel that."

"Is it kinda ironic how what we thought we wanted turned into something else?" I asked with a parting smile, looking back to the board. "Not sure how Winter Lion King fits into this now."

"You don't want to be on the court, booboo?" Lucas asked.

"I did, but . . ." I shrugged, reading the words I'd written what felt like forever ago.

"You'll make the final ballot, dude." I glanced back at Finley, and he nodded with assurance. "Everyone knows your campaign is about something bigger than formal."

Lucas pointed to the lion on his chest. "So many people are showing their support with these pins," he said.

"I know, but . . . when this started, all I wanted was to prove I was good enough to beat Presley."

It wouldn't matter if I was elected, though. No amount of campaigning would cause change at HVHS or with that stupid initiative, even if I won the crown. They'd just find another way to drown us, to silence us. We had to put a stop to it.

"I need to do something else now."

A silent rage tore through me once again as I crossed out my rule, as I wrote a new one on the dry-erase board. It was different this time around because now I knew that the best revenge was believing in yourself. No matter how hard they pushed me down, I'd keep trying. They couldn't take that away from me.

RULES FOR REVENGE

~~SABOTAGE HALLOWEIRD PARTY~~

~~ENTER DRAG COMPETITION~~

~~RUN FOR WINTER LION KING~~

TAKE DOWN WATCH WHAT YOU SAY

Those six words lifted me above the water. If the PTA and York and Bett were worried about causing a scene, then that's exactly what I'd give them—keep giving them until one of them finally fucking listened and cared what was happening to students like us.

"If they're gonna pretend like we don't exist," I began, plunking into a chair, "then we have to remind them we're here."

"Aren't we already doing that?" Lucas asked. "It's starting to work."

"Not fast enough," Finley said, wiping pizza grease on a napkin.

"Exactly." I tapped the marker against the table in thought. "We need to go bigger . . . starting with the PTA."

"Miss ma'am has another thing coming if she thinks she can suddenly police same-sex couples." Lucas said, glancing nervously at Finley, his lashes fluttering. "I was thinking. For TikTok, of course. What if Finley and I tried to buy a couple's ticket tomorrow? You could record it."

Finley cleared his throat. "That could work," he said, ears reddening. "If you don't mind pretending to be my date."

"I don't mind." Lucas absently twirled a strand of hair and stared straight ahead. "That's settled. Finley and I will get Winter Formal tickets. Together. For the sake of this video."

"Then I'll post it tomorrow. Tag the school and put the PTA's enforcement of Watch What You Say on blast." I nodded, happy they were willing to go to extremes for this. "That'll get people talking on TikTok, but we'd need to do something bigger. Something that'd get us news coverage. Something that will prove once and for all Watch What You Say is Bett's personal homophobic agenda."

I rubbed a hand across my face and tried to think. *What made Last Boyfriends blow up at school?* It'd been right after that upload of me falling in the hallway. Someone had graffitied the football poster with my words. *There is no pride here.* That had set York off because he'd prided himself on our football team. The team of "good students" representing HVHS. The team that Jackson was once a part of until he'd come out. The team that had a chance of hosting the state championship game next week.

It all came down to football.

"What if . . ." I trailed off, recalling those sprayed words over Lions Pride. "What if we painted another message over something York loves as much as that poster?"

"Like what?" Finley asked with a snort. "I don't think we could get away with graffitiing the superintendent's ass."

"He loves kissing it, but—" Laughter bubbled inside me as all of it began to make sense—Bett and York and football. "Think *bigger*."

"Dude, that's what she—"

"Now isn't the time for a dick joke, Fin." Lucas sat back, his eyes widening. "Whoa. Never thought I'd say that. But for real . . . how big?"

"The football field." A laugh escaped my throat at the sight of their shocked faces. "We tag it like the poster. Stitch a video of it with the news interview of York and Bett saying they don't want an absurd protest."

"We couldn't . . ." Finley hesitated and tilted his head. "Wait, the playoff semifinal is Friday in Huntsville. Nobody will be paying any attention to the home field while they're away. If they win . . ."

"Then the field will be ruined before their championship game." I wasn't sure how York or Bett would react, but whatever it was we'd take it. Make another post. Keep luring them into reacting until we had unquestionable proof that the initiative targets queer students.

"They'll be so pisssssed," Lucas said in awe. "I love this so much." I could see the gears turning as he thought it through. "One, we're gonna need a shit ton of paint, and two, won't the gates be locked?"

I breathed out nervously. "Do either of you happen to know the code?"

"*One-Thirsty PM!*" Finley cut his eyes toward me. "Any of the dude-bros on the team would know it. They use the field for athletic training."

All those times we'd watched our favorite show replayed in my mind. How the Mighty Lions marched out led by Presley. How he'd horsed around with Jackson as they unlocked the gate.

"Jackson knows the code," I said quietly, already realizing what it meant. "I could ask him to help."

"Hold up." Lucas snapped forward in his seat. "Did you tell him we're Last Boyfriends?"

"No, I haven't," I said, scratching at my thumbnail.

If I told him, then he'd put two and two together. Figure out that I'd burned Presley's jacket, that I was the person he'd played over the summer, that I was the person Presley had called a lame nobody not worth his time. Would he change his mind about me?

"You *could* tell him, you know." Lucas's eyes softened as he reached out, covering my fidgeting hand. "It'd be okay. Like you said, he's a Last Boyfriend too."

"I know, but I can't deal with him finding out right now." I managed a tight smile. "I could just pretend we're trying to get the attention of the Last Boyfriends TikTok. Do something big so they'll boost it. Use the pride protest at school as cover."

"If that's what you want," he said with a comforting squeeze before pulling away. "You just worry about getting the code, then."

"Lucas and I will figure out the paint." Fin smiled.

I nodded, reassuring myself. I had just a few days to convince Jackson to help us, and then once all this was over, I'd tell him the truth. Maybe then he'd still feel the same way about me.

Twenty-Five

"My name is Vivian Singh with *Birmingham News*," the DM read. "Our ABC affiliate network would love to interview you for the evolving story on Harper Valley High School and the Acheron County Board of Education."

I reread the message yet again. She'd sent it moments after I uploaded Lucas and Finley's ticket setup. They'd received the same treatment as Jackson and I had, and I'd recorded the whole thing from my jacket pocket. *As PTA chair, it's my job to make sure our children adhere to our school's family values and follow Watch What You Say.* It had been as though she was reading from a script, and everyone had a lot of thoughts on it.

Harper Valley Tattler had posted about Last Boyfriends on their Facebook page, causing a war in the comments. Customers who drifted through Magnolia would pause when they recognized me or Jackson from TikTok. Some offered their apologies while others whispered quietly to one another, less friendly. That whispering was a constant shadow following me around town, down the hallways of HVHS even as more pride lions popped up. It felt like the entire town was on high alert, and our TikTok was proof enough.

More than two thousand comments piled in calling out HVHS and the PTA for discrimination. Once verified queen Maeve Kimball dueted her reaction, the plays hit 5 million overnight. All these numbers were adding up online and in real life, and now the news wanted us to forgo our anonymity for an interview.

We can't, I'd replied. If we did, our identities would be weaponized against us. They'd make Last Boyfriends go away like they did with Jackson and the football team.

I glanced up from my phone and watched as Jackson restocked the fiction section. Seven o'clock had come and gone, but I hadn't left yet. Hadn't talked to him about the field. Lucas and Finley had come through on their end, and now it was my turn.

My throat bobbed with a gulp. I knew I couldn't keep prolonging it. Every time I tried to talk to Jackson, though, I kept hearing him in the lobby last week. Him telling me it was okay, that we didn't have to make a scene. I didn't know how to make him understand without telling him everything.

He reached up to shelve a book while I worked up the nerve. His sweater rose, exposing the happy trail leading into his jeans. It inched even higher, until I saw those three moles forming a constellation by his belly button. Suddenly, I was standing in the same spot, only it was dark outside while I clutched Presley's phone. *You're just a fat-ass nobody,* the memory reminded me.

"Brah?" Jackson asked with a laugh. "Are you checking me out?"

"What? No," I said, my face flaming. "Don't know what you're talking about."

"Oh. Well. This is way awkward," he admitted with a wince. "I was totally checking you out."

I didn't know it was possible for my face to get any hotter. "You're right," I managed to say despite the pull of a grin. "This *is* way awkward."

He laughed and crossed over to me. I quickly swiped out of TikTok before he could see the Last Boyfriends account. Quickly tapped the web browser as he leaned against my back.

"What have you been staring at all evening, then?" he asked, peering over my shoulder.

We both looked down at the tuxedo Google search on the screen. "Just thinking. About Formal." My brain misfired over the heat radiating from him. Any moment now I'd spontaneously combust (in more ways than one) from his touch.

"I like this suit," he said, reaching around me to point at the screen. "You'd look handsome in maroon. Not that you aren't already handsome. I mean, you'd only be more handsome. In maroon."

"You said 'handsome' a lot," I told him, watching in my periphery. A blush creeped up his neck, to the tiny scar under his mouth.

"*Definitely* making this awkward," he said with a deep breath. "But you are. Handsome."

My heartbeat stuttered with nervous energy and want, palms sweaty and yearning to feel him. The desire made me blink more than normal while I stared at his face. At the vein of blue in his green eyes. At the tiny freckles. "You're . . . you're beautiful."

"No one has called me beautiful before." He leaned in slightly, and we were closer. Too close. Close enough I could hear the soft pop as his lips parted.

"WhatareyoudoingFriday?" I blurted, standing up from the stool. In my head, I heard Presley telling him I was a lame nobody not worth his time.

He backed up a step, instantly tangling a hand in the floof of his hair. "Sorry, what?"

"What are you doing Friday?" I repeated, slower this time.

"You mean other than voting for you as Lion King?" he asked, and I nodded. "Nothing. Why? Aaare you asking me out?"

"If asking you to help me paint the HVHS football field is a date . . ." I trailed off nervously, and he shook his head like he hadn't heard me correctly. "Then, yes?"

"Why are you painting the field?"

"To get back at HVHS about the dance," I said, holding my breath. Waiting for him to tell me it wasn't worth it as he studied me intently. "I just wanted to have the perfect night with you, and I want to get the attention of Last Boyfriends and get back at the school for what they're doing to us and what happened to you on the team and . . . Why are you grinning like that?"

"You're so damn cute," he said with a shake of his head. "No one has ever defended me."

If only you knew what I've done, I thought, but said, "You had my back, and I've got yours."

"Thank you, Ez." His voice was wobbly as he stepped forward, as he pulled me into a tight hug. "Yes, I'll help, but only on one condition. . . ."

His touch was electric, and I was stricken with yearning again. "W-what's that?" I managed to ask, voice too breathy.

"You let me take you on a *real* date."

"Deal."

He sighed, and I leaned into him as we stood there in Magnolia. The soft rise and fall of his chest took me further and further away from that night with Presley. The tiny constellation under his shirt navigating me somewhere entirely new.

Everything about today was criminal. It was early. Too early for a Friday. Lucas had said I should greet people as they arrived. He'd not only made me wear a button-up but also tuck it into my khakis. *York doesn't know we got something else planned*, he'd texted our group chat last night. *Play the part, booboo! Winter Formal is in two weeks!*

"Easy for him to say," I whined, and climbed out of my Jeep.

The HVHS student parking lot was deserted, the sky fuzzy with morning light. I hugged my jacket against the cold and headed to the steps. The first Winter Formal election would be in the lobby today. The votes cast would determine the final two candidates for King and Queen who would make up the court. All I had to do was go through the motions. Smile and wave as though I still gave a damn about wanting that crown. Pretend

I was excited to see my name listed on that ballot with Presley Daniels, Jesse Saros, and Filip Peterson.

I was more excited about what would come later.

The TikTok of Karlynn had kept us relevant. *Birmingham News* featured it, and more people were watching what Last Boyfriends were doing. Once we painted the football field, there would be no going back. No more passively reacting to whatever fresh hell Watch What You Say brought. We'd force them to react to *us*. It'd be a shift in power—an act of war against York and Bett and anyone else who mistakenly thought we didn't have a voice. The anticipation made me shiver as I pushed into the lobby.

Then I shivered again as fumes immediately smacked me in the face. A chemical smell made my eyes water, and I searched for the source. Someone in a black jacket, hood pulled over their head, was squatted in front of the PTA table. They held a spray-paint can, a cloud of blue mist evaporating to reveal what they'd written on the Winter Formal tickets sign.

THERE IS NO PRIDE HERE

It was the same message that'd been tagged on the Lions Pride poster. I hesitated as they looked up, their face hidden by their hood and the shadows. The spray-paint can dropped with an echoing clatter. Whoever it was jumped up and grabbed their bag, making a run for it down the hallway.

"Wait!" I called out, wanting to know who they were. To know who had taken my words and turned them into the catalyst that'd started this fight.

They stilled, considering me for a moment. "It's just you," called a voice I couldn't quite place. "You scared me. Why the hell are you dressed like Principal Numb Nuts?"

"Sam?" I stepped closer, ignoring the question as I searched the shroud around her face. "What're you doing?"

She pulled the hood back and flashed a smile before inspecting her work. "Making a point," she said.

"It was you who tagged the poster."

She bent to pick up the discarded can, holding my gaze. "Kasey if we're being technical," she corrected. "It's all of us, though."

"All of you?"

"Me, Kasey, Shyla, Aiden." She unzipped her bag and shoved the can inside. "Last Boyfriends started this, and now we're here too."

"What do you mean?"

"It's like we're all part of Last Boyfriends. We have no choice but to fight too." She let out a deep breath, scoping out the hallway. "All of us. Every single person who wears a pride lion pin. Everyone you united by running for Winter Formal. If we don't do anything, what happens then?"

"We become nothing."

My words came out wavering, afraid of what would happen. Afraid of their truth. They'd removed books, stopped us from being seen in the promenade, gaslighted us into believing we were nothing. If we gave up now, that's exactly what we'd become.

Nothing.

"Whoever's running that TikTok, they aren't alone. We're here." A car door slammed outside, and she startled. "Shit, Numb Nuts can't see me with these cans. Good luck today!"

"Wait," I called out again as she backed down the hall.

She turned back, looking over her shoulder. I wanted to tell her that I didn't care about whether I got enough votes to move on to the final election. That I didn't want to stand here and campaign and smile and wave like it'd make any difference. That I was doing everything I could with Last Boyfriends to fight. That we were striking tonight and waging war.

But all I could manage was "I'm here too."

Twenty-Six

A chilly wind bit at my face while Jackson and I trekked along the road. The football stadium was up ahead, its towering lights dark as midnight approached. They'd loomed over us since we'd parked back in the shadows.

"I can't believe we're doing this," he said, a breath clouding around us. He'd helped me sneak out after the hockey game ended, leaving my dad asleep on the sofa.

"If you're worried about getting caught," I told him, "you can open the gate and let us handle the rest."

He laughed, a fogged ha-ha, and cocked his head. I could barely make out his face but knew he was grinning. "I'm *not* worried," he said. "Just excited that Last Boyfriends might post it. Knowing I helped do something."

"Yeah . . ."

I looked down at my boots, the crunch of chipped asphalt under their soles. We'd told Jackson that Lucas was going to record our message and send it to Last Boyfriends. He didn't know I had a draft already set to be uploaded.

"Besides, I can't miss out on helping the future Lion King pull off a major FU to the school," he added with another laugh. It echoed deeply into the night, running ahead of us toward the field.

"Not sure about that." I inhaled, filling my lungs with icy air. "We won't get the results until after Thanksgiving anyway."

The first vote to narrow down the contenders for Lion King had been interesting to say the least. Many people had stopped to tell me they'd chosen me. Even Filip Peterson told me he was an ally, proudly pointing to his lion pin. He'd used his vote for me instead of himself (I'd voted for him on principle).

"Whatever the final election results are"—our hands brushed together, and he grabbed mine—"you're still my Lion King."

My blood pulsed in the spaces between our laced fingers. I opened my mouth to joke about his cheesy lines, but I was speechless at the sight of him. I traced his arm up to his shoulder. Across to his neck where his head tilted to the side and the stars reflected in his eyes.

"Thanks for believing in me," I managed to say, my voice rough. As rough as his calloused palms from football. "In all of this."

He didn't say anything, only tightened his grip. It sent my brain into a hectic state. *He's holding my hand!* and *Oh my god!* and *Jackson F'ing Darcy likes me!* sparked through my thoughts as we reached the HVHS campus.

I was enjoying this moment so much that I half wished Finley and Lucas would be late. They were right on time, unfortunately, waiting by the gate with the paint and brushes. The flashlights on their phones bobbed while they huddled together.

"Are you ready?" I asked Jackson as we crossed to them.

He nodded. "We get in. Write the message on the field as big as we can. I'll turn the lights on long enough for Lucas to record a video of it."

"Then we get the hell out of here before anyone notices."

"Not sure our first date can top this, but I'll try."

I laughed, and he tightened his grip again. He didn't let go, not even when Lucas shined his light on our conjoined hands as we neared. Then he pointed it in our faces and demanded, "What took you so long? Were you two making out?"

"Please tell me you were," Finley said, picking up two giant cans of paint. "Because if you weren't, then I owe him twenty bucks."

"B-brah," Jackson stammered. "Y'all were betting on us?"

My heart beat even faster. The thought of kissing Jackson had been on the forefront of my mind ever since Wednesday. Since he'd leaned in close enough for me to hear the soft pop of his parting lips.

"Something like that," Lucas replied, his breath clouding in the cold. "Now stop holding hands like you're on a date and help me with these."

We unlaced our fingers and grabbed the other cans. The label on top was faded, the color name illegible. The smudge along the lid was the same glittery gold as his bedroom stars. I knew it was the leftover from when we'd painted his ceiling.

If there was ever a reason for a Glitter Bomb, tonight was it.

"This is perfect," I said as we carried them toward the gate.

"Thought it was appropriate." Lucas's smile was easy enough to spot in the moonlight. He nudged me while Jackson entered the code. "Do you have everything ready?"

"Yes," I said, patting my pocket for emphasis. I'd started the new upload, stitching together the news interview where York said he didn't want an absurd protest. All that was left to do was add Lucas's recording.

"Speaking of Glitter Bombs," he whispered with a nod toward Jackson, "you owe us tea."

"There's nothing to spill," I whispered back as the gate swung open. My face burned with the memory of Jackson's palm against mine. I wanted there to be something spill-worthy.

The lights began to flicker to life one by one. A soft glow cut through the 1:00 a.m. darkness while Jackson and I huddled together in the press box. Despite the cold, sweat rolled down my back. Painting hadn't been easy, especially with only our phones to see. Sprinting up the bleachers hadn't helped either.

"They have to warm up," Jackson explained, looking up at the towers. "It'll be a few minutes before it's bright enough to see anything."

"Oh," I breathed out heavily, and leaned against the announcer's table.

The last waves of adrenaline crashed through me. Crashed against the halting wait. It made me light-headed as I stared through the windows. Halfway down the bleachers, Lucas's phone was at the ready for our message to materialize across the 50-yard line.

"What made you want to write that?" Jackson asked, and I glanced over at him.

Soft light spilled on his face. It caught the thick lines of his eyebrows and the errant swipe of gold across his cheek. I wanted to tell him what Sam had said this morning. How we were all being forced to fight back. How Last Boyfriends had started this, and now I had to see it through. How I wanted everyone who was wearing a pride lion to know they weren't alone.

"It's the only message I could think of that meant something," I said instead, staring down at the field.

Each paint stroke had only provided more fuel for my fire. York's dismissive *Some things are more important than you* rang in my ears as we'd started the *W. What kind of message would that say if y'all were seen together?* asked Karlynn in her Southern twang with each of the *E*s. The *H* and the *R*s told me to watch what I said.

WE'RE HERE

Those two words were now scrawled out on the green turf. They were a whisper in the night that would soon turn into a battle cry. This was more important than football. A reminder yelled at the top of our lungs.

"I'm really glad you asked me to help tonight," he said, draping an arm around my shoulders.

I was very, *very* aware of his body up against mine. Aware of how he'd gone so easily from annoying me to making me crave his attention. Too aware of us alone in the press box and the nagging worry of whether I'd forgotten to wear deodorant.

"For what it's worth," I said, cutting my eyes up to his, "I'm glad you're here."

"I see what you did there."

He laughed, and his minty breath rolled across my face. The soft pop of his parting lips made my stomach lurch. "Ishouldletthemknowitllbeafewminutes," I blurted, pulling my phone from my jacket pocket before he could lean in. Before that voice popped up to remind me how much of a lame nobody I was.

My fingers fumbled as I typed in the passcode, and the glow of the screen dropped down to the floor in a noisy clatter between his feet. "Sorry," I groaned, wishing I could get off this feels trip.

The warmth of his arm fell away, and he bent to help me pick up my phone. "Ez, are you . . . Is everything okay with me and—" He stopped short, staring down at my phone.

The apology lodged itself in my throat as he looked up me. His eyebrows climbed high in a nonplussed expression, lit by the glow of my phone. I followed his confused gaze back to the screen, to where the TikTok draft was pulled up for Last Boyfriends' new upload.

"Jax, I . . . I'm so—" I said quickly, reaching for my phone.

He didn't let go, and my hand encased his. I saw the understanding unfold with the rise and fall of his brows. "It's you," he said quietly as though he were whispering to himself. "You're Last Boyfriends."

"Yes," I breathed out, unable to deny it.

"You're the one who stood up for me. Who got the *Birmingham News* involved after what'd happened with the team. Who's fighting Watch What You Say. Who started all this."

Our eyes locked in the growing light. I knew there was no getting out of it. No lying or stretching the truth. The realization made me want to throw up and run away.

"Yes."

I braced for him to put two and two together. For him to remember how Last Boyfriends had started with the burning varsity jacket. For him to realize Presley had rejected me. For him to wake up to why. *Fat-ass nobody.*

"Ezra."

He said my name like I was a stranger. He finally understood what it meant for me to be Last Boyfriends. He knew.

"I can explain all of it," I said, taking a step back. "I thought he and I . . . that we were . . . I was wrong and please don't think less of me. I can explain what happened during the summer and with Pres—"

"Stop."

He grabbed my arm to keep me from backing away. "You don't have to explain," he said, holding my gaze. "You're so incredible, and my god, Ez . . ."

"Jax—"

My voice broke as I looked out the window. Everything I hated about myself rushed to remind me why he was wrong. But all I could focus on was the field down below. The message we'd written was bold and loud. A reminder that I was here, too, so far from who I thought I was. And I *liked* who I'd become.

I'm not a fat-ass nobody.

I looked back at Jackson. In the growing light of the stadium, I could see each of his tiny freckles and the vein of blue in his green eyes. Then there was that tiny scar stretching with a smile. This boy knew me, knew the person I was all along.

Now I knew it too.

Slowly, I reached out and touched his arm, sliding my hand up to his shoulder. His neck. I cupped his jaw, pulling him closer. Closer until I heard that soft parting once again.

My lips met his with intensity, a ragged breath escaping as he exhaled roughly against my mouth. I pushed forward to close the distance between us. Our bodies pressed up against one another as the kiss deepened. In between our thunderous heartbeats, I heard the door open. Heard Lucas's "We got the video!" and Finley's "You owe me twenty bucks, dude!"

I didn't care, though. I was kissing Jackson F'ing Darcy with glittery, gold-stained hands tangled in his floofy hair. And he was kissing me back like I was *somebody.*

Because I was.

Twenty-Seven

"Have you seen this yet?"

I looked up from loading our breakfast plates into the dishwasher. *GMA* went silent as Dad tapped his phone, and he stood from the island. I dried my hands off with a dishtowel while he held the screen toward me. The stream was minimized in the corner, and the Facebook feed was open to the *Harper Valley Tattler*'s post shared by Becca Dion. One glance at the image of Vivian Singh told me everything I needed to know. Jackson had sent a link to the same story along with a good morning text. I'd watched it before (and after) I'd taken a long shower with the memory of our kiss in my slick grip.

The news had spread fast around town Saturday. People were upset over us destroying the field, and I was living for their anger in the comments. It meant we'd done something right if they were taking note of what was happening at HVHS. Then by Sunday, the TikTok we'd posted had gained millions of views and the immediate attention of *Birmingham News*.

"What's that?" I asked, feigning ignorance.

"It's a story about the vandalized field," Dad said, and tapped to play the video.

I fidgeted with the dishtowel as Vivian began the all-too-familiar introduction of the segment. "'We're here. We didn't choose this fight. We won't back down until Watch What You Say is gone,' the anonymous account claims in a new TikTok post," she delivered to the camera, eyes boring directly into mine.

Our video played, and it still felt bizarre to see it headlined as breaking news. Surreal that our plan was working. Surreal that the news wanted a statement from Last Boyfriends. Surreal that at the same exact time Lucas had recorded the footage I'd been kissing Jackson Darcy.

The most recent DM from Vivian weighed heavily in my back pocket while their drone footage aired. Someone had tried to clean it up, but it was as though the words had been burned into the grass—our message refusing to be erased.

"We have reached out to the anonymous account regarding what some locals are calling a horrific turn of events, but still no comment," she concluded. "The vandalization took place Friday night while Harper Valley High School's football team won the state playoff semifinals in Huntsville. With the school set to host the championship game this coming Tuesday, it's anyone's guess what will happen next if the Acheron County Board of Education doesn't address the student rebellion spreading like wildfire."

The screen went black, and the sudden silence prodded at me. I turned to the sink. *They called us a student rebellion. Dad can't find out it's us. Does he suspect anything?*

"They're saying it's that, uh, that Last Boyfriend account,

is that it?" he asked, voice pitching. "The one who posted that video of your poster."

"Oh. *Woooow.* I had no idea."

The fake surprise in my voice was too detectible, and I quickly turned on the faucet to rinse the rest of the dishes. Lying to him twisted my stomach into a knot. There wasn't any other choice, though. I couldn't risk him stopping us.

His gaze pricked the back of my neck, and then he cleared his throat. "This student rebellion they're talking about," he began, "are you part of it?"

The plate nearly slipped from my grip. I inhaled sharply, hoping the running water masked my surprise. *Don't lie,* I reminded myself. *He knows all your tells.*

"I'm protesting." My words were measured as I turned toward him, pointing to the lion on my fleece pullover. "Showing HVHS real pride. For my campaign."

His responsible father expression gauged my words.

"What do you think?" I asked, changing tactics. "About them calling it a rebellion?"

His eyes lingered over the rainbow pin before moving up to my face. Part of me wondered what he saw, if he could see how messy this was getting. Then he nodded once, resolutely. "You know I think for good things to happen, ya gotta raise a little hell. . . ."

"But?"

He breathed out a sigh, leaning against the counter. "You're just like me at your age. Becca—Ms. Dion I mean—and I started the Gay-Straight Alliance back in our day. It was an uphill battle, and I get it. It's something you have to fight yourself, and I'm proud you're protesting." With a steady grip on my shoulder, he looked me straight on. "Just be careful, okay? Whoever's running that anonymous account will get found out eventually."

I swallowed roughly, pulling away to continue loading the dishwasher. To push away the fact that he was right. I'd been denying it ever since Friday night. Jackson not only knew who we were now, but he'd also figured out everything we'd done. Why we'd done it. He wouldn't be the last to figure it out. How much longer could we keep up the anonymity? Keep protesting and fighting this newly declared rebellion from the shadows?

WE'RE HERE.

There were seven shirts with those two words—our words—painted across them. My heartbeat thumped in my throat as I scanned around the crowd outside the gym. There'd been a notice on the lobby doors for the mandatory assembly instead of first block, and I was on edge. HVHS had been silent despite the news coverage and the outcry on both sides from our town.

"Dying to see how ballistic York is gonna be," Lucas muttered under his breath.

"On a scale of one to an *Untucked* fight, how bad do you think he'll go off?" Finley asked as the doors opened.

"At least a solid eight-level," I offered, glancing over my

shoulder as we shuffled forward. *Eight, nine, ten . . .* "There are now eleven shirts with 'We're Here' on them. It's actually working."

"We *are* leading a rebellion after all, booboo."

"Still shocked the news called it that." Finley let out a nervous laugh. "That makes it sound, I dunno, so—"

"Fabulously resisting the so-called authority of ignorant homophobes?" Lucas offered.

"Something like that," Fin said, lowering his voice. "It makes what we're doing as Last Boyfriends sound official, and, like, we could be walking to our doom right now, dudes. I'm having flashbacks to the spring musical. What if York calls us out in front of everyone?"

"He doesn't know," I said quickly, making sure no one was nearby. "We'd already be in trouble if he did. Whatever this is, it's all for show."

Though my smile might've been reassuring, Dad's warning from earlier echoed in its hollowness. *Whoever's running that anonymous account will get found out eventually.* If we were to be found out, we'd lose the upper hand. They'd find a way to silence us if they knew.

Between the crowding thoughts and the crowd pushing to get through the doors, I was pulled into the chaos of the gym lobby. There was a steady roar from a hundred voices gossiping loud, but Coach Carter was louder.

"Keep moving!" he yelled gruffly. "Find a seat! Phones away! If I see you on it, it's mine!"

"It gives me so much satisfaction seeing him bent out of shape," Finley said, and then his gaze landed over my shoulder. "Make that twelve shirts . . . and his man tits really make those words pop."

I'd thought I was prepared to see him, but then I turned around. Jackson's varsity football shirt was stretched tight over his sweater. He'd scribbled "WE'RE HERE" in white over the Lion. The sight of him sent my stomach fluttering. Our eyes locked, and his slow smile took me back to yesterday, when we were decking the shelves for Magnolia's Black Friday sale. He'd confessed he had been played by Presley, too, and I'd confessed how I had known. That it changed nothing. Then, right there underneath the twinkling lights of the front window, he'd kissed me again. I had been so stunned—*I can't believe I get to tongue Jackson F'ing Darcy now!*—that I'd thanked him like an idiot.

Now he leaned in and pressed his lips against mine. The kiss was quick and minty, sending a misfire of thoughts down to my jeans. "Thank you," he whispered, not caring that everyone saw it.

"You're welcome anytime," I repeated his words from last night.

For the briefest of moments, I forgot about the lobby and the crowd around us. All I could focus on was his eyes sparkling, reflecting the rising sun. Then someone cleared their throat and brought me back to a very embarrassing reality.

"PDA so early in the morning," Ms. Dion said with a tsk. Her tone was playful, but her usually warm eyes were strained.

"Ezra, I hate to steal you away from your boyfriend, but can I speak to you for a moment before the assembly starts?"

"Um." My face was on fire, my voice lilting. "Okay?"

She motioned for me to follow her, and I hesitated. "Don't worry," Lucas teased, grinning. "We'll watch after your *boyfriend* and save you a seat."

"Sorry for whatever hell you're about to endure," I told Jackson.

He winked and bumped me with his shoulder. "Don't worry. I can handle them."

"That's what you think, dude," Fin started. "If you're gonna take Ezra out on a date . . ."

I walked away quickly before I could witness the humiliation. Ms. Dion had stepped off to the side while everyone filed into the gym. She anxiously checked her smart watch, her quick taps on its screen synching with my racing heart.

Something was wrong.

"Is everything okay, Ms. D?" I asked carefully.

Her attention snapped to me. "Other than having our principal call me on a Sunday to help organize an assembly," she began, blinking slowly with a sigh, "because some students trashed our football field and got the town in an uproar?"

"I feel like I should say I'm sor—"

"Don't you dare." She checked to make sure no one was near before stepping closer, nodding toward Lucas, Finley, and Jackson. "You mean to tell me your club of Last Boyfriends painted the football field, made headline news, forced the citizens of this town to pay attention to the injustice, *and* overshadowed the HVHS football team's semifinals win all in the course of one weekend?"

"You're smiling. . . . Am I not in trouble?"

Her grin grew wider, and she patted me on the arm. "Not with me. I'm impressed by what you're doing, Ezra. Students in other high schools in Acheron County are noticing." She nodded toward the gym. "Principal York and Superintendent Bett are on the warpath now. HVHS is the biggest school in the district, and they want to put an end to this before it gets out of their control."

"We're on the warpath too," I said, each word steady and brimming with rage. "I hope *all the schools* in this county make a scene."

"As do I, but please be careful. You might want to leave your phone in your car. They're looking for any excuse to take them and find out who's running the account. I can't protect you if you get caught. Ever since Watch What You Say dissolved the GSA, I'm not allowed to get involved in queer student matters."

Her mouth tilted downward with a frown as she looked into the gym. I followed her gaze to where the front desk administrator was setting up a microphone. Bett had a scowl on his face, and tension cracked the facade of York's signature fake smile.

"Ms. D, what do I need to do?"

"Keep preparing for Winter Formal. You being in the running is a sign of hope. It's inspiring everyone to make their own voices heard, and the powers that be don't want any other student to do what you did. That's why they're announcing a revision to the school's social media policies. Students will be banned from using phones at school and engaging with Last Boyfriends."

"That doesn't sound so bad," I said, attempting to rationalize it. "They can't catch us. We can still do what we're doing."

She shook her head sadly, apologetically. "Ezra," she began, "you're running on borrowed time now. Superintendent Bett is about to announce a reward to anyone who comes forward with the identity of those hiding behind the TikTok account."

Whoever's running that anonymous account will get found out eventually, Dad's voice reminded me as static crinkled over the speakers. Nausea thrashed inside me once the realization hit. Outside of Lucas, Finley, and Jackson, only one other person knew the truth about Last Boyfriends.

Presley could take us down if he wanted.

Twenty-Eight

The whispers of student protests had turned into a foghorn.

Elmore High School, Sulfur Springs High School, Mountaintop High School—all of their football fields had been painted last night. HVHS wasn't the only school that Watch What You Say was affecting. I'd woken up to duets from more anonymous TikTok accounts, each new post a reminder to Acheron County: WE'RE HERE TOO.

At first, I'd been excited. The people behind our view counts were taking action. They were fighting back too. Then I realized whatever they did, it would be because of us. Because we'd started Last Boyfriends. If this rebellion went off the rails, if it got too messy, if Presley ratted me out . . .

Everything that's happened would be my fault.

Each new notification made my heart leap into my throat. They'd pile up during school while I was waiting for the final bell to ring. The moment I got back to my Jeep, I'd check my phone. Every time I refreshed the page, there were more and more comments from students in other schools rallying behind our message. But there was one that I kept coming back to, one that had racked up 3,000 likes.

"Listen to this comment," I called to Lucas. An orange shirt went sailing across my bedroom as he poked his head out of my closet. He'd been rummaging through my clothes since I'd gotten out of the shower, trying to find something for me to wear on my official date with Jackson. " 'How can y'all demand visibility while hiding behind an anonymous account? Does anyone know who they are?' "

"Sound like something Vivian Singh would say," he said as he met my gaze in the mirror. "We've talked about this before—don't let it get to you."

"I'm not," I said quickly. "But what if they're right? Someone could spill for the reward?"

"Don't worry." He turned around with a button-up shirt in his hand. He'd said the same thing when I'd told him and Fin how Ms. D had found out. "Everyone who knows our identity are people who care about our fight—"

"You're forgetting about Presley."

His mouth formed a silent *Oh,* and a line formed between his perfect brows. "Shit, do you think he'll tell?" he asked, voice on the brink of wavering.

"I don't know." I'd played out every worst-case scenario since yesterday. "He could easily get me back. All it would take would be him anonymously tipping off York. Then it'd all end before we could take down Watch What You Say."

"Would he do that?"

I shrugged, picking at my thumbnail. The truth was I didn't

know. Didn't know who Presley was anymore. I wasn't sure I ever knew.

"Stop ruining your polish." Lucas tossed the button-up at me and snapped his fingers. "Hand over the phone and put this on over that hockey shirt you insist on wearing."

"Why?" I asked, hesitantly passing it over.

"Because you don't need to worry about this. Plus, since Fin's at work, it all comes down on me to use my bestie powers and make sure you don't look, well . . ." He glanced back at my closet. "You do know you only have hoodies, hockey shirts, and for some unknown reason a ton of plaid. This is the least offensive option."

"Very funny," I deadpanned. He had chosen a green plaid mixed with blue, and it reminded me of Jackson's eyes. I picked it up as he unlocked my phone. "Excuse me, but what do you think you're doing?"

"Like I said, don't worry about it." I watched his thumbs fly across the screen in quick succession. He paused, attention snapping back to me. "Don't just stand there either. Put that on before your *boyfriend* gets here."

I pulled the button-up on over my shirt, begging the universe for a break. He hadn't let it go since Ms. Dion had called Jackson that. Now Dad was downstairs waiting to take pictures and embarrass me in front of someone who was very much *not* my boyfriend. Sweat beaded on my brow at the thought, and I wiped it with a plaid sleeve.

"Crisis averted," he announced, handing the phone back.

"What does that mean?"

He shrugged nonchalantly, and I keyed in my passcode. The screen went straight to Snapchat, to the messages he'd sent elvislion0007. *"Can we trust you?"* I read in disbelief, my voice squeaking. *"Also, good luck on the championship game tonight!"*

"Don't give me that look, Ezra." He winked. "I thought buttering him up would help."

"What the actual fuck, Lucas!"

I glanced back down at the messages. At the relic of a thread where the Snaps we'd sent and received brought back sour memories. Nausea crashed inside me. If he hadn't thought about turning us in, he would now.

"This is all I'm gonna think about." I swiped out of Snapchat, putting my phone to sleep. "What if he does plan to turn us in and he's just waiting and now he knows we're sweating—"

"I love you, booboo, but calm down. The last thing you need is *another* reason to sweat. Seriously. You did put on deodorant, right?"

"Yes," I muttered, sniffing to make sure it was doing its job.

"Good." He reached out and began fastening my shirt buttons. "You were worried, and we both know you'd say you were fine despite letting it bother you tonight. You can deal with it when he replies instead of worrying about 'what if?' The ball is in his court . . . or is it his end zone? I dunno. He'll be busy with the game, so you don't have anything to worry about tonight."

I knew he was right, but that still didn't stop the panic when my phone lit up with a notification. My heart raced through those what-ifs in the few seconds it took for me to see the text.

"Jackson's almost here," I said, smiling at the heart eye emoji he'd used.

"Let me get a look at you." He stood back, an analytical glare in his dark eyes. From the boots and jeans to the plaid shirt and the sour expression on my face. He smiled softly then, pushing hair off my face. "All we need is a spritz of cologne and you'll be ready to go," he announced. "Oh, did you shave?"

"Listen, Snapping my ex was one thing, but we both know I can't grow a beard. It's a sore subject—"

"Not your face." His eyes traveled south, and my face heated.

"My dad can hear you!" I covered his mouth, lowering my voice. "Plus, it's not like that." The night of HalloWeird came rushing back. How Jackson had said Presley was pressuring him and that he wasn't ready for sex.

"The way he looks at you, things could most def get spicy."

I tried really (really) hard not to think about what that would entail. In between the rapid blinking away of thoughts, I imagined enough that made my pulse quicken. "I . . . uh . . ." I cleared my throat. "I wanna take it slow this time."

The sudden ring of the doorbell made me gulp, and I nervously wiped my palms on my jeans. Lucas grabbed my shoulders to level his gaze on me. "Don't be nervous. Your first date will be magical," he promised in a trust-me-I-know-these-things tone. "Fin and I will be hanging at the store, just a text away if you need a pep talk."

Your first date. Presley and I had never gone out, not like tonight. Jackson was taking me to Bubba's for burgers and then the movies. We'd be seen in public. Together. That fact alone made me immediately sweat profusely, pitting out the under-arms of my lucky Nyberg shirt.

The warmth of Jackson's hand in mine untangled the anxiety inside me. I held on tightly as he led us through the Twinkle Lights lobby. My first official date had been three hours filled with explosions and chaos of the newest Marvel movie. It was perfect. Between the surround sound and the steady trace of his thumb on my palm, nothing else had mattered.

"After you, Mr. Hayes," he said, unlacing our fingers to open the exit door.

"Why, thank you, Mr. Darcy," I replied with exaggerated awe at his chivalry.

It had been our polite game all night, him being the roman-tic gentleman and me acting comedically shocked. He'd brought flowers, held the doors, snuck a kiss on my cheek when the the-ater lights had dimmed—everything that made me feel like the main character of the rom-coms I'd once watched.

I stepped out on the sidewalk, and the cold promise of December gusted through my jacket. His warmth was imme-diately missed as I glanced up at the marquee above. Past the large red letters, even farther past the end of Main Street, to the HVHS stadium lights still glowing in the distance.

Whether those Mighty Lions won or lost, we'd been on that field with them. Our message had been under their cleats, a reminder we were here too. A reminder that Presley Daniels could turn us in if he wanted, that he could—

Nimble fingers laced with mine again and pulled me away from my tangled thoughts. Jackson nudged me with his shoulder as we walked, the lights dancing across his smile. "I wish that movie had been longer," he said softly, "so our first date wouldn't have to end."

I squeezed his hand, nudging him back. "It has to end, Mr. Darcy. That's the only way you get a second date."

"Correct me if I'm wrong, but . . ." He spun me around to face him, and I fought the urge to kiss that tiny scar as he grinned. "What I'm hearing is that you want me to take you on another one."

"Nope," I said nonchalantly, and his smile tremored. "I want to take you." Relief eased the furrow of his brow, and he exhaled deeply. His buttery popcorn breath made me want to kiss him even more, to relive this night all over again.

"You nearly got me there," he said with a laugh. "Thought I was misreading the signs. This is new to me, the whole first date thing."

"This is your first date too?"

"With a guy." His cheeks blushed as he squeezed my hand. "A *real* first date with me being out, and someone knowing me fully. Like you do. There's no one else I'd rather be with, Ez. I just hope I'm doing everything right so I can kiss you good night."

"Jax . . ."

Words left me, my palm going sweaty in his grip. When

York had threatened me for wearing the very same shirt I was still pitting out, when Jackson had been pestering me in the hallway, when he'd heard what I'd said about believing in yourself—I never imagined it would lead me here. To him finding the confidence to come out and me finding the confidence to believe in myself.

"You know me too," I finally said, leaning toward him.

Our lips touched softly at first. His rough palm caressed the nape of my neck, and his tongue pushed up against mine in a deepened kiss. It caused an electric shock through my body. Right down to my jeans.

"For the record," I began, pulling back so he couldn't feel the effect he had on me, "you can kiss me anytime you want."

"Definitely won't hear me complain."

His lips brushed against mine once more, and then we slowly began drifting toward his hatchback. Our feet shuffled along the sidewalk, our smiles bashful. Neither one of us wanted this night to end.

Up ahead, the lights of Linda Sue's glowed softly in the night. "Who says our first date has to end now?" I asked, pulling him toward the diner.

The polite game continued with him holding the door, but I couldn't pretend to be shocked anymore. His hand felt natural in my mine while I led us to the corner. The vinyl booth seats crackled underneath us, our legs weaving together as the waitress brought menus over. She said something in a sugarcoated twang, but I was too focused on Jackson sitting across from me. We'd spent the last six months working together. Six months of crossing paths, him crushing and me oblivious. I was fully aware now. He'd been in front of me all along.

"Ezra?" he said, nudging my knee.

"Oh. Uh." I felt the blush at the same time Jackson saw it, and his eyes went soft with a smile. Like he knew what I'd just realized. "I'll have whatever he's having."

"That'll be two slices of our Thanksgiving sweet potato pie, two coffees, and two orders of waffle fries," she said, jotting it down on her pad. "I take it y'all aren't ready to say good night just yet."

"No, ma'am," we both said at the same time, grinning at one another.

"Good. You boys both deserve a little happiness with that mess going on at the school."

She winked, letting us both know she (like everyone else in this town) had been following along with the Last Boyfriends drama. I watched her put in our order as Jackson watched me. His leg nudged mine again, and then his hand found my knee under the table.

"You're famous," he said with a squeeze.

"No," I replied, wishing I could kiss him again. "*We* are."

He smiled bashfully, his thumb rubbing the inside of my thigh. "I was, um, thinking, maybe I could take you to dinner somewhere nice before Formal next Friday? Maybe over in Gadsden? We should celebrate before you're crowned Lion King."

"That's so very kind, Mr. Darcy," I said, nagging thoughts pulling at me. "I doubt I'll even make the court, though."

"Regardless of the court announcement Monday"—he squeezed my knee again—"you're still my Lion King."

His palm sent another flutter in my stomach, but it was short-lived. I knew that at any moment all of this could come crashing down. It could be over before Winter Formal. They'd find a way to stop us.

"Thanks, Jax," I managed as the waitress dropped off our coffees.

He continued rubbing his thumb along my thigh, reaching for the sugar with his other hand. I took the moment of distraction to slip my phone out. What I needed was a quick pep talk from Lucas. It felt like the weight of Formal kept crushing down on me. When I woke the screen, the pressure bore down even harder as I read the new Snapchat notifications.

elvislion0007:
| don't worry i won't tell
elvislion0007:
| you didn't out me so i won't out you
elvislion0007:
| Jackson's a good guy don't let him go down for this when
| you get caught

Twenty-Nine

Don't let him go down for this when you get caught.

The thought was kudzu vines overtaking my mind. Presley's message had creeped through Thanksgiving, spreading guilt during the Black Friday sale at Magnolia. Slowly suffocating me with the fact that we were on borrowed time until someone discovered our identities. Presley was right: even if he kept quiet, it was just a matter of time before someone discovered who we were.

And then what?

I glanced up at Jackson as we approached the entrance of Rivera Furniture. We were meeting to discuss our game plan for next week. I'd spent all day debating whether or not to include him, but I couldn't leave him out of it. This was as much his fight as it was ours.

He smiled at me, and I saw all the different versions of him I'd come to know. The guy who'd cried on my shoulder when he'd gotten kicked off the team. Found the confidence to come out. Risked everything to be himself. *I won't let you get in trouble over something I started,* I silently promised him, pulling open the double doors.

"Why, thank you, Mr. Hayes," he said, stepping inside.

"Anything for you, Mr. Darcy," I replied in earnest, and his returning grin only drove home the fact. It was as warm and cozy as the sitting room entrance.

A fire danced under the mantel full of family portraits, gently welcoming us inside from the cold. Jackson eyed the oversized chairs, the soft glow of the television. "Totally not what I was expecting for your evil lair," he said, shaking his head.

"Not this exact display room." I laughed, leading him down the red carpet. "There's an office setup where we've been planning *slightly* evil things for the right reasons."

"I had envisioned something more like your bedroom, and you'd be wearing those black and gold flannel pants you had on for Pajama Friday."

"You remember what I wore during Spirit Week?"

"I remember everything." His voice was soft, dropping down to a whisper. "Especially all the times I've tried flirting, and you never picked up on it."

"Likely story."

My words were steeped in disbelief, and he tugged me to a stop. "Literally any time I tried to talk to you in the hallway. Or that time I asked you to tutor me. And how about that time—"

I cut him off with a kiss. Everything about him made me feel like a main character who deserved the romantic lead. And it was him.

Our clasped hands fell only to hold each other. His lips worked against mine slowly at first. He traced his fingers up my arm, my shoulder, my jaw. The roughness of his palm cupped my face so gently, his tongue pulling me in deeper.

He moaned into my mouth, pushing up against me. The effect of the kiss was a hard truth between us. I gasped. Then he inhaled deeply and broke the kiss.

"S-sorry," he breathed, resting his forehead against mine.

"Don't be," I managed with a shaky laugh, and worry pooled in his eyes. "Hold up, what's wrong?"

He took a deep breath. "I'm not trying to be . . . uh . . . a tease."

"I don't think that," I said quickly.

"I've been called that . . . before."

"A tease?"

"It's just that, yeah, my body may be reacting to this mad hot guy in front of me right now, but I'm not ready to have sex. If that's a deal breaker, I underst—"

"Most definitely not a deal breaker," I told him. "I don't want to have sex with you. I mean, *obviously* I'm attracted to you. Hello, you're the mad hot one here. But I don't want to do anything you aren't ready to do."

"You sure?"

The waver in his voice made me want to protect him even more, prove to him he could trust me. "I'm more than sure. I like you just as you are, Mr. Darcy."

He pulled me into a hug then, resting his chin on my shoulder. I could only sigh as I held on to him, as he held on to me.

This was the romantic moment I'd been wishing for. No sleazy lines to get my pants off. It was us, being real.

"We should get going," I whispered. "They're waiting on us."

"Lead the way, Mr. Hayes."

Silence fell between us, but it was comfortable. He didn't need words for me to understand him. Each shoulder bump and soft smile crinkling the corners of his eyes told me all I needed to know.

I was so wrapped up in him that it took me a few seconds to realize something was amiss. The office cubicle was dark. I flipped the light switch, and the fluorescents flared to life above the empty conference table.

"Lucas and Finley are supposed to be here," I said, feeling for my phone in my pocket. There were no new messages. *Where are they?* I looked back into the hallway, but there was no sign of them.

"So *this* is the slightly evil lair."

"The one and only." I laughed as he took in the dry-erase board. "This is where Last Boyfriends was created."

"Hmmm." He chewed on his bottom lip while he eyed the rules for revenge. "What if, say, you got a new boyfriend . . . what would happen to these residual feelings?"

"Like for our exes?"

"Love and hate have a lot in common," he hedged.

"Oh. Ew, Jackson. No. There are absolutely no residual feelings." He arched one of those bushy brows, and I pointed toward the fourth rule. "See? I moved on from him a while ago. Now it's all about getting back at the school."

"I've moved on, too, just so you know," he added in haste. "Besides, I can't get over my crush on this amazing guy I know."

The blush that simmered across his face was adorable, and I wanted to tell him how hard I was crushing on him. How he took up a majority of my thoughts now. How I liked him so much that I felt guilty for getting him involved. However, the sound of padded footsteps stopped me before I could say anything.

"Sorry!" Lucas said, exploding into the office with Finley on his heels. He smoothed his hair down hurriedly. "We were at the reception desk when—"

"Huh?" I eyed him in confusion. "I didn't see y'all."

"That's beside the point." He waved a hand in dismissal. A red flush had crept up his neck, his lip gloss oddly smudged. "*Birmingham News* came on the sitting room TV, and, Ezra, they just did a breaking news story on what they're calling 'the Last Boyfriends Student Rebellion.'"

"They *what*? What did they say?"

"As of today," Finley said, adjusting his shirt, "twelve schools in Acheron County have had their football fields tagged by queer students."

"Twelve?" My mouth went dry, and Ms. Dion's voice echoed in my head. *They don't want any other student to do what you did.*

Jackson gaped, wide-eyed. "Holy shit, brahs, we caused that!"

"Everyone most def understood the assignment." Lucas shot Finley a glance, a tiny smile. "And the best part? We're the reason why there's a petition for Devon Bett to resign as superintendent."

"We're actually fucking doing it, Ezra." Finley held his fist out for bump, and I stared at it, seeing something else entirely. "Are you okay, dude?"

We. They all said *we*. We were running on borrowed time until they'd eventually find out who we were. Those warnings from Dad, Ms. Dion, Presley ensnared me with their vines of doubt. They pulled me down onto a rolling chair, and I braced myself against the table.

"Ez, what's wrong?"

The warmth of Jackson's palm found my shoulder, and I tilted back to look at him. At Lucas and Finley. I couldn't let any of them go down for this.

"It's only a matter of time," I said in a hollow voice, "before we get caught. Before one of us slips up and someone figures it out. It's getting too big. I won't let y'all get in trouble for this. It's my fault."

Lucas rolled out a chair beside me. "Listen," he said, pointing a finger at me. "If you think I'm gonna let you be a martyr and take the fall, then you have another thing coming."

"What he said," Finley added as he claimed a seat. "I won't let you go through what I did. It's not fun being singled out in front of a crowd, dude."

Jackson rolled up on my other side, spinning to face me. "I know I'm new to this," he said, and I didn't know if he meant Last Boyfriends or us. "But we're in this together now."

"Exactly." Lucas nodded as he scrounged in a pocket for his emergency Sour Patch Kids, and I grabbed the bag from him. "Do you remember what you said about the aftermath of our disaster relationships?"

"Honestly, no," I said, popping a blue raspberry in my mouth.

"You said they'd define us either way. That we should grow from it instead of letting it drag us down." He searched my face as I chewed. "We're so close to actually doing something for queer students in Acheron County. We need to keep growing this instead of worrying about how it might drag us down."

I ate another one, and Jackson motioned for me to pass the bag. "What do we do next, then?"

"We were discussing"—Finley's ears went pink as he shared another smile with Lucas—"that we need to bait York again."

"He won't fall for it like with my campaign poster."

"No," Lucas agreed. "He isn't that dumb, but he *is* stubborn. We have to keep prodding until he explodes."

Jackson coughed, choking on a mouthful of candy. "Just had a *very* disturbing image of him that I can't unsee," he said, eyes watering.

"I bet York's get-off face looks like his rage face." I snorted at their disgusted grimaces.

"Focus." Lucas snapped his fingers. "Get your minds out of the gutter and . . . Oh my god, I just saw it."

We sat there for a beat, staring down at the tabletop in silence. "Anyway," I said, cringing away from the joke. "What should we do?"

Lucas took a deep, cleansing breath and cocked his head to the side. "We're gonna show up at school Monday and go full *reputation* era Taylor every day until Winter Formal. Make those 'We're Here' shirts and wear our pride lions. Campaign like crazy before Thursday's final vote and really rub it in that a queer student could represent HVHS. When you win that crown, it'll send him over the edge."

"Brah, that would like for real piss him off."

"Ex. Act. Ly." A slightly evil arch appeared in Lucas's eyebrows.

"Then we'll record his reaction at Formal," Finley concluded. "It'd be all the proof *Birmingham News* needs."

"That could work . . . but there's no guarantee I've gotten enough votes to make the final ballot."

Jackson's leg nudged mine under the table, and his lips quirked in a smile. "C'mon, Ez. Believe in yourself."

"Listen to your boyfriend, booboo. Your campaign sparked the fire, and now we just need to keep fanning the flames."

Underneath the strangling vines of doubt, I heard my dad. *You're Ezra Hayes* and *There is one thing they can't ever stop you from doing, and that's trying* and *Believing in yourself is the best revenge.* He'd been right then, and it still held true.

I smiled. "Let's burn it all down, then."

Thirty

For me, growing up queer meant learning how to fold into the smallest version of myself possible. Hide away and hope my existence bothered no one. It was a survival instinct I'd learned long ago on my grandparents' farm. Back before we were the Last Boyfriends with our ex drama, before we all became best friends, before I knew what it felt like to be a part of something.

That was the problem with only surviving.

All the ways we'd been forced to hide parts of ourselves— only speaking up behind anonymous accounts and making hushed promises to get out of this small town—kept us isolated. That was the real motive behind Watch What You Say. Behind the growing number of state legislations across the South. If they erased us, they kept us alone. If they kept us alone, they made sure our focus was only ever on *survival*.

But when a group of survivors join forces, they become fighters.

That was how it felt pulling into the HVHS parking lot on Monday morning. Students in shirts with battle cries of "WE'RE

HERE" and "ALLIES ARE HERE TOO" crowded the steps up to the lobby. My own was written in rainbow, matching the three others waiting as I parked.

A gust of wind swirled around me when I opened the door, summer long forgotten in its chill. December had arrived over the weekend and brought a cold sense of finality: final court for Winter Formal, final month of the semester, and what might be the Last Boyfriends' final stand against Acheron County.

"Good morning, future Lion King," Jackson said as I climbed out of my Jeep.

He pulled me to him and dropped a kiss on my lips. "We'll see about that," I said, his minty toothpaste and citrusy cologne as familiar as home. "When will we know the final court?"

"It should already be announced in the lobby," Lucas said while I grabbed my backpack. "And as your campaign managers, we think you're polling in the top percentile."

"And annoying the fuck out of York," Finley added.

"Then what are we waiting for?" I laced my fingers with Jackson's and pulled him toward the school. "Let's go find out if I made it . . . or if we need to make a plan B."

"Whatever happens, we're gonna celebrate regardless." Lucas huddled up close to Finley as we made our way toward the steps. "Takeout, sweatpants, *Drag Race,* and as many emergency Sour Patch Kids as needed."

"Can't wait to see the looks tonight," Finley said to him. "Bet *both* of my nuts that Rubi Tusson takes the crown."

"Hate to break it to you, but Miss Ferrera Rocher has this in the bag," Lucas corrected.

I bumped against Jackson as they compared the queens, grinning as he nudged me back. "You're still coming over to watch the finale with us, right?" I asked.

He nodded and leaned close, breath warming my ear. "For the record," he began, "as the guy dating you, I *know* we'll be celebrating you making it on the court."

I squeezed his hand and kept a firm grip while we walked, all four of us side by side. The Last Boyfriends. Like the strong women in *The First Wives Club,* we had come together to do something bigger than getting revenge on our exes.

If we are successful this week . . .

Apprehension prickled with each step up to the lobby. There was still a good chance I hadn't received enough votes. That we'd get caught before Friday, even if I left my phone in the Jeep.

"Let's get this over with," I breathed out.

"After you, Mr. Hayes." Jackson held the door open with a wink.

"Jackson, you tryna make this the New Boyfriends Club?" Lucas asked, sending a rush of heat across my face. "Because if y'all are gonna make it official, you'll need a background check and at least three letters of ref—"

His words were lost in applause. Heads began turning our direction, battle cry after battle cry on shirts in a rainbow of colors. The doubt I'd been hiding behind dwindled. Even if they tried to silence us, they wouldn't be able to stop this fight.

We weren't alone anymore.

"Ezra!" My name came from every direction all at once as we pushed through the gathered crowd. Smiles and waves, fist bumps and pats on the back. It was a slow motion of cheers and smiling faces—Sam and her friends, even Logan and Cass—in between each thunderous heartbeat. And then I saw the banner for the 2024 Winter Formal Court: Yasmin Spencer, Ashley Gonzales, Presley Daniels, and Ezra Hayes.

"I knew you'd make it!" Lucas and Finley yelled.

"Told you so, Ez," Jackson said, draping an arm around my neck.

Equal parts shock and relief coursed through me every time I read and immediately reread the banner. The whole point of running for Lion King had been to prove that I was just as good as anyone else. Seeing my name up there, I knew this meant so much more than that now. I wasn't just doing this for me—but for every queer student.

I'm Ezra Hayes, I reminded myself. *And now they're not gonna forget who I am.*

"You can't win Lion King."

Superintendent Bett's twang was molasses thick. His declaration slowly rolled across York's desk as his mustache danced under pursed lips. Both of them had been waiting for me in the lobby after third block, and the high I'd been riding nose-dived as I was ushered into York's office.

"What the superintendent means is," York began curtly from his position by the door, "is how did you rig the election?"

"Who says I *rigged* it?" I countered, offended.

York leveled his gaze at me. Those wiry, gray eyebrows drooped in exasperation. "I'm not in the mood. It has been a long day of fielding PTA complaints about you, so let's cut to the chase."

Bett leaned toward me, haughtily pointing a finger. "How did *someone like you* get a landslide of votes if it wasn't rigged?" he demanded.

"Maybe because the students wanted someone fabulous as their Lion King," I said, dialing up the sarcasm. "Or because I had the guts to say everything Watch What You Say didn't want—"

"I will not tolerate any further indiscretion," Bett cut me off, his nostrils flaring.

"I didn't do anything wrong," I explained to them through gritted teeth. It felt like that was all we ever did, explain ourselves.

York stayed silent, like the doormat that he was, as Bett persisted. "Didn't you?" His jaw clenched in anger. "That is the question. Ezra, given the perverse posters you've hung up—"

"Wrong. You're wrong," I cut him off.

Bett's beady eyes studied me intently. I felt the pressure to cave under his glare, to look down at my boots and pick at my nails and hide myself. But I wouldn't, not anymore. Not when he was the embodiment of a cartoon villain come to life. No one thought someone so vile could *actually* be real. That was how he'd gotten away with Watch What You Say so far. I had to push forward with our plan to uncover the hatred in it.

"I haven't done anything *perverse*," I continued, egging them both on.

"Ezra," York attempted, holding his hands out in a calming gesture. "We find it highly suspicious that you've paraded around promoting *your agenda*. Especially given that someone has been terrorizing my school and hiding like a coward behind an anonymous account—"

"Let's cut to the chase," Bett interrupted. "Have you been acting as Last Boyfriends this entire time?"

Words threatened to leave me as they both leaned forward in anticipation, waiting for me to slip up. My heart skidded at the accusation and dropped heavy into my stomach. "I wish," I made myself say calmly, "I was the person running that account this entire time. Someone who saw through the bullsh—crap you've been putting us through."

It was the most truthful thing I'd ever said. Because I did wish I'd been this version of me sooner. A fighter who was tired of hiding.

"I should have known it wasn't him," York said to Bett, tugging at his lanyard. "He's merely a kid who thinks winning a popularity contest means something; that's all this is."

I gripped the chairs, refusing to feel insecure under their scrutiny. "What does that even mean?"

Bett eyed me carefully and stood. "It means that you are too stupid and immature to realize no one cares if 'you're here.' As long as you're in *my* school district, you'll do best to keep quiet and stay out of my way—"

A quick knock pounded on the door before it swung open with force. "Principal York," Ms. Dion said, striding into the room, "Superintendent Bett, what's the meaning of this?"

"How dare you just storm into the principal's office—"

"How dare *you* harass a *student*?" she pressed, cutting through Bett's outcry. Her gaze was calculating as she stared them both down. "Jackson Darcy alerted me when you both dragged Ezra away. Watch What You Say might ban me from being involved in LGBTQIA+ issues, but it is my right as a teacher to both intervene and report harassment of any student who is *here*."

"Let's not get hasty," York replied in panic. "There was no harassment."

"Are you okay, Ezra?" she asked, ignoring him.

Her warm, brown eyes searched mine. At first, I felt the urge to tuck myself away so I wouldn't be a bother. Then Bett rolled his eyes.

Fuck them.

After everything he'd done, everything York had allowed to happen at HVHS, they both deserved to be called out for what this really was—what Watch What You Say was doing to students. "They were threatening me, Ms. D," I said evenly, locking eyes with Bett as I did. "It's the third time this semester Principal York has harassed me for being queer."

"That's certainly not true." York held his hands up as though I were attacking him. "I've merely done my job as principal to protect the students at this school."

"Your idea of protecting students is questionable," she scoffed at York, standing between us, and then turned toward Bett. "And you, sir, are a matter for the teachers' union to discuss with the school board."

"You're speaking out of line," Bett warned.

Ms. Dion ignored him. "Ezra," she said, resting a hand on my shoulder. "I'm sorry you've experienced this gross misuse of power. Head on down to the Media Center where you can wait for me safely."

I stood and gave them both one last look before slamming the door, prodding them with a shit-eating grin. Tension radiated off York. He was on the verge of exploding again, and now the teachers' union had caught Bett harassing a queer student too. The plan was working better than expected, and come Friday we'd get all the proof we needed.

Thirty-One

The rain had started Monday night and hadn't let up since. By Wednesday, what was left of autumn's leaves had fallen to a soggy pile in the backyard. It was too wet to do anything other than sit back and watch pensively.

I tried to shake York and Bett from my mind, but they'd pretended like nothing had happened. There was no reaction from York when I hung up more posters or had my photo taken for the yearbook. No reaction when I passed him in the hallway. No reaction when I'd argued with PTA Karlynn in the lobby about who'd escort me in the court if I won. It was as though I didn't exist. That was the problem. He would keep on pretending like none of us mattered, and then it'd all blow over after the school board meeting this coming Monday.

Will it ever stop raining? I wondered, turning from the window.

Our kitchen was darkened from the overcast morning, and I flipped on the light to start breakfast. Anything to give my mind a reprieve before Dad came downstairs with more worry.

He'd been on edge since Ms. Dion had texted him right after the incident in York's office, and I didn't know how to make him believe that I had it under control.

Percolating coffee and sizzling bacon soon filled the silence between the pitter-patter of rain. When the toaster dinged, the creak of floorboards overhead joined the cacophony. I stared hard at the bubbling grease in the skillet while Dad's footsteps thudded closer and closer until . . .

"Everything all right?" he asked through a yawn, cutting straight to the point. There wasn't a *Mornin'!* or *You're cooking breakfast again?* or *Who are you and what have you done with my son?*

"For the millionth time, yesss," I said with a forced smile. He eyed me blearily as I flipped the bacon.

"You know you can talk to me about anything, right?"

"Everything's okay, Dad."

"Are you sure?" he asked, pouring a cup of coffee. "Becca said the teachers' union is gonna take Bett and York to the wringer over that whole initiative thing. Maybe I should go down there Monday afternoon. It's at three-thirty, right? I'll give them a piece of my mind—"

"Don't make me swear on the Slammers making it to the playoffs again."

His eyes went wide, and we both crossed our fingers. It was worth nearly jinxing the Stanley Cup to get a few minutes of normalcy. For him to sit down at the island and stream *Good Morning America* like nothing was wrong.

The correspondents' voices joined the drone of rain, and I blissfully tuned everything out. Until Dad couldn't take the silence any longer. "Ezra, listen," he said with a sharp inhale.

"Dad, I keep telling you," I began, forcefully spreading mayo on the toast, "I'm fine—"

"No, you're on *GMA*."

The knife stilled as I spun toward him. He turned the volume up, and I dropped it against the counter when my name slipped from the speakers. ". . . Ezra Hayes. This is the third known instance of harassment against an openly LGBTQIA+ student by Principal Joseph York on the orders of Superintendent Devon Bett, a representative for Acheron County's teachers' union has confirmed to our affiliates in Birmingham."

I crossed over to Dad, bracing myself against the island to watch. An image of my campaign poster filled the screen, and then it was ripped down by York. "This footage comes from the TikTok account leading a student rebellion against Acheron County Board of Education's Watch What You Say initiative. These anonymous students calling themselves 'Last Boyfriends' have taken an inspirational stand against their school system. Though they are choosing to remain anonymous, their efforts have inspired thousands of students to take action. Last Boyfriends, if you're watching, all of us here want to say thank you for being a bright light of hope and refusing to be bystanders. You are what this world needs. Stick around after the break for a more detailed look at the petition for the district's superintendent to resign and how this movement has spread across the country."

A video preview of students in Texas flashed across the screen. They were picketing the football field, painting our battle cry in broad daylight for everyone to see. Then the stream cut to an ad for a once-a-day pill for heartburn.

I blinked rapidly as the reality of what was happening settled in. We weren't just reaching students in Acheron County. More high schools had noticed our fight, and they'd joined in.

"Holy shit," I said, gripping the edge of the counter, my eyes burning.

"Definitely letting 'shit' slide," Dad said in awe. "Because holy *shit,* you were on *Good Morning America.* . . . Ezra, are you crying?"

I wiped at the hot tears spilling down my cheeks. *When had that happened?* Dad stood from the stool and pulled me to him.

"Bud," he said, rubbing my back, "can I ask if you're okay again?"

I opened my mouth to swear that I was fine, but I couldn't. The stress of Last Boyfriends, the campaign, having to fight every day to be a fucking human being with thoughts and feelings and an identity—all of it came crashing down with the resounding *You are what this world needs.* I was too tired to keep hiding.

"I started it." My voice was rough with the blur of emotions spinning through me. "Lucas, Finley, Jackson, me . . . we're Last Boyfriends."

"I know," Dad said, holding me tighter.

"Y-you do?" I asked against his construction sweatshirt.

"Your old man isn't dumb." He laughed then, and his chuckle reverberated into me. "I figured it out a while back."

"When?" I asked, pulling back to look at him.

"Back when *Birmingham News* first reported on it."

"Why didn't you say anything?"

"Because you came to life. You looked me in the eye and I could see that you believed in yourself. You were finally acting like the Ezra I've always known. That's how I knew you'd be okay. I'm so proud of you, son."

I felt the tears coming again.

"I can't believe it's over."

Jackson popped a waffle fry into his mouth, melted cheese dribbling down his chin. I watched as he wiped it off with a thumb and licked it clean. The sight of his tongue sent tingles through me, and I refocused my sights on the shelf behind him. We'd been sitting in an aisle at Magnolia since closing. Neither of us had been ready to go home.

"And all the votes are in," he continued with another fry. Another lick. "Tomorrow we'll find out if you're the Lion King."

"Didn't you say I was already *yours*?" I teased, reading the spines of the books on the shelves around us.

"Well, um . . ." He ran his hand through his floof of hair, leg bouncing the takeout container from Linda Sue's. "I meant that, um, when you're crowned, we'll find out if York will explode. If we will get what we need to finish this."

"I know." All the votes for Winter Formal Court were in, and there was nothing else we could do about it now. "It all comes down to me winning."

He startled when I reached for a fry and readjusted the container over his lap. "I'm glad that, um," he began, clearing his throat, "that your dad didn't get mad and make us stop . . . or make you stop hanging out with me because of it."

I swallowed the fry roughly and tore my gaze from the shelf. A blush had creeped across his face, caressing each and every one of those tiny freckles. "At this point, I wouldn't let that stop me from fighting back," I said, and then I nudged him with my foot. "Or from seeing you."

"Good." His deep voice was full of so much relief as he smiled, as he dropped a hand to steady my own jittering leg. The warmth of his palm sent me searching the spines again. "Because I don't think *this* will be over anytime soon," he added suggestively. "It's just beginning."

I knew he was referring to us, but he was right on multiple accounts. Our fight was only just beginning. After *Good Morning America,* more schools were seeing their own student-led rebellions. More TikTok uploads of graffitied football fields. More mentions thanking Last Boyfriends. More likes on the comment asking how we could demand visibility while hiding behind an anonymous account.

It was so much that I wasn't sure how *much* more I could handle.

"Vivian Singh DM'd me again this morning about the ABC affiliate network interview," I admitted softly, staring hard at the book spines to the right of his pink-tipped ear. "It's *Good Morning America,* Jax. *GM*-freaking-*A* wants her to interview Last Boyfriends for another story about the petition and the rebellion."

"Holy hell—wait, why aren't you excited?" he asked, studying me. "You turned her down again, didn't you?"

"I haven't replied to her yet."

"So you're considering it?"

His thumb traced along my calf, and I focused on those calming circles. *Though they are choosing to remain anonymous,* the correspondent's voice resounded. *Their efforts have inspired thousands of students to take a stand.*

"I don't know," I finally said. "This has turned into something I never could've imagined. It's more than getting back at HVHS or Acheron County. Like those students in Texas who openly painted their football field . . . they really are here and not afraid to show it. How can we keep fighting to be heard if they can't see who we are? I think . . . I have to come forward before I can even let myself consider that interview."

"I won't let you do it alone," he said with that same deep certainty. "You can't take the fall for this."

"That's the problem," I said with a shake of my head. "It

drags you *and* Lucas *and* Finley into it. I might've started the Last Boyfriends account, but it's all of us now. I can't make the decision by myself."

"You don't have to." He set the takeout container to the side, scooting closer. Close enough I could see the bits of blue in his green eyes. "If you want to come forward or give that interview or burn down the fucking school, I'm with you. We can talk to Lucas and Finley together."

"The amount of trouble we'd be in—"

"I don't care about any of that. This is more important."

"There's no going back if we come forward," I warned him. "You wouldn't be able to swoop in and save me again."

"You don't need saving. You're not some damsel in distress in some cheesy rom-com." He reached out and laced our fingers together, bit his lip, and raised his gaze. "I want to be by your side while we fight this. That's what boyfriends do, if you'll let me."

I nodded fervently, the revelation making my heart beat in rapid-fire. A grin spread on his face, and I pulled him toward me. All I thought of were meet-cutes, capital M Moments, grand declarations—everything that I'd dreamed of—as I kissed Jackson F'ing Darcy between the bookcases. For so long, I'd been waiting to be swept off my feet by a dashing prince or a football jock or the most popular guy in school. Those rom-coms had it wrong, though.

You have to take control of your own story.

Ever since that day in October, I'd been telling my story

my way. Since I'd set that jacket on fire and kept going, burning down everything that tried to make me a bystander. I might've made a few mistakes along the way, but at least I kept trying.

This *was* my story.

Thirty-Two

My reflection stared back at me in the mirrored closet door. I braced myself for something to be wrong. For the maroon tux to make me hideous or for a voice in my head to tell me I was too fat to pull it off. However, it had been tailored to fit perfectly.

My gray fingernail polish stood out as I ran my hands down the jacket's lapel, over the white dress shirt I'd tucked in. I turned to the side to scope out my profile. The longer I looked, the more my queasy smile shifted into one of confidence. The wonky Hayes nose actually suited me, and the messy wave of hair had been tamed back with product. Even the hazel of my eyes popped with the dark maroon of the suit.

A light knock sounded on the door, and Dad's wide grin reflected in the mirror. "How long have you been standing there?" I asked him.

"Long enough to know you're feelin' yourself," he said with an appreciative nod. "Long enough to have an existential crisis because I don't look nearly old enough to have a son who's so grown up."

"Daaad," I said as he came up behind me.

"Look at yourself. The spittin' image of me at your age, if I do say so myself." He put his hands on my shoulders and gave a wink. "My little boy is turning into a brave young man, and a handsome one at that."

"You think I'm brave?" I asked, my mouth going dry.

"I know so."

"So . . . what if I wanted to stop hiding behind Last Boyfriends? Is that brave or stupid?"

He studied me for a moment in the mirror, concentration lines furrowing his brow. Then he gently turned me to face him. Up this close, his responsible father expression only reminded me of how alike we were. How the determined set of his mouth, his analytical gaze was so much like my own.

"You want to do that interview for *GMA*." Not a question but a statement. "Which would mean your principal, that superintendent, all of Acheron County, *and* whoever is watching you on TikTok would know your identity. Everything y'all have done."

"Yes," I said, my voice unwavering. "Jackson and I want to come forward . . . only if Lucas and Finley agree, though. It's all of us or nothing."

"Why?"

I flexed my hands, refusing to pick at the polish. "I'm tired of hiding, Dad. These are our identities they're trying to erase. I want them to see me, for anyone watching to see us, and know we are people too. That we exist and won't back down."

"It sounds like you've already decided."

"Is it stupid?"

"No," he said, shaking his head. "Being brave is doing what's right when you know the consequences. That's the opposite of stupid. All I need to know is . . . do you believe it's the right thing to do?"

"Yes," I said without a shred of doubt.

"Then as long as you believe in yourself, that's what matters," he said. "Promise me one thing, though."

"What's that?" I asked nervously. Worried he'd tell me to think through those consequences again. Worried he'd tell me it wouldn't be worth the trouble it'd cause.

He smiled, his eyes crinkling. "Promise me you'll go to Winter Formal tonight and enjoy yourself. Dance with your new boyfriend and be in the moment. You're still my kid, no matter how grown you are, and I want you to have fun. Worry about this rebellion after you win that crown." He paused and considered me for a moment. "And wear a rubber if you're gonna have sex."

"Oh god, Dad," I groaned, heat scalding my face.

"I'm just saying." He held his hands up, laughing. "Now hand me that bow tie, and I'll show you how to put it on."

"Good luck," I started, grabbing it from the closet doorknob, "because it won't stop fighting me."

I tossed the intimidating scrap of fabric to him. It was the same gray as Jackson's tux. He and I were really attending Winter Formal as a couple. That fact alone made me nervous in the best possible way, so much so that the slick satin bow tie had slipped through my fingers too many times. However, Dad handled it with ease as he looped it around my neck.

"Don't be afraid of a fight," he said, holding my gaze. And we both knew he wasn't talking about the bow tie.

From the window of Longleaf Farm's main ballroom, the holiday lights along the winding drive twinkled in the night. I watched their glow over Jackson's shoulder while we swayed in a slow dance to Beyoncé. Everything about this moment I committed to memory: the weight of his hands clasped around my shoulders, mine around his waist; the smokiness of crackling fires; Lucas and Finley spinning next to us; Jackson's warm voice against my ear.

"I'm having the best time tonight, Ez," he whispered, his words curling with a smile.

I murmured in agreement, pulling him closer. We'd gone to dinner in Gadsden, a little place by the river (after Dad made us pose for way too many pictures). He'd opened the door for me and held my hand and knew I existed. There wasn't the need to remind him, to worry if he was thinking about me. The affirmation was in that tiny scar along his lip, the vein of blue in his eyes, each tiny freckle across his nose.

He was here with me.

Beyoncé's final note vibrated through the ballroom. We stopped swaying but kept ahold of each other as the next song began. He laughed, the soft chuckles like kisses against my ear, when a fast beat dropped through the speakers.

"I love this one," he said, hips already moving with the rhythm. Each shake sent my thoughts into a tailspin.

"Don't just stand there!" Lucas yelled, bumping against us in his fuchsia tux.

"You have to *dance* to Ariana, dudes!" Finley chimed in.

Jackson's hands fell, and he gripped my waist. "C'mon, Ez!" he encouraged, pulling my hips in sync with his. "The last dance before you get the crown!"

I laughed, throwing my head back. It was another moment I wanted to remember. How the strobe lights flashed and the music was so loud it vibrated in my chest and we all moved together. We weren't the last boyfriends of anyone—we were weightless, floating higher and higher along with Ariana Grande's whistle-tone.

By the time the song ended, I was breathless and sweaty and happy. "I need more punch. . . ." My words fell away when I saw Finley. His chest was rising and falling in exertion as he gazed down at Lucas. Slowly, he brought his hand up to cup his face. Lucas grabbed a fistful of Finley's smoky gray jacket and hauled him into a kiss too intimate to watch.

I blinked, rubbing my eyes to make sure I wasn't hallucinating. *Did someone spike the punch?* "What the actual fu—"

"Finally," Jackson cut me off, draping an arm around me. "I was wondering when that'd happen. The sexual tension was unbearable."

I looked up at him, at his crooked smile as my two best friends made out on the dance floor. Then I turned my attention back to Lucas and Finley. Braced myself for the jealousy and the jarring realization that they'd definitely leave me on the sidelines now, but it never came. All I could think was, *This makes sense.*

"I think . . . I already knew this was a thing," I said, leaning my head on Jackson's shoulder.

In hindsight, there had been so many signs: Luc's embarrassment while helping Fin tuck, them hanging out without me, the other night at the furniture store. They weren't bad friends who had forced me to be a third wheel. They had been growing closer like I had with Jackson. I could see that now, and I couldn't fault them for it.

"I'm happy they have each other," I added. "After all the shit they've been through with their exes, they both deserve someone good."

"Guess this really is gonna be the New Boyfriends Club, huh?"

Jackson grinned down at me then, kissing my cheek as a spotlight lit up the stage. The way he made me feel was something else I wouldn't forget about tonight. Taking a stand like Nyberg, fighting for what was right, telling our story—all of it had led me here. No matter what was about to happen with the announcement, I'd still feel proud whether or not that crown was mine.

"Are you ready?" Lucas asked, appearing by my side with puffy lips. "Go ahead and start recording. There's no way you didn't win. Everyone voted for you."

"Excuse me, but we're *not* not gonna talk about you and Fin," I whispered, grabbing my phone from my slacks. "You two are perfect together, and I'm here for it."

"You think so?"

I gave him a pointed look before tapping the screen to record, slipping it in my front jacket pocket.

His smile was dazzling despite the smudged gloss. "At first I wasn't sure what we were doing, and I was worried what you'd think . . . but . . . yeah, feelings have been caught. I like him."

"I like him for you, that's what I think."

I reached for his hand and gave it a squeeze. Instead of a trademark cheeky remark, he smiled shyly as Finley slipped beside him with two cups of punch. They shared one of their secret eye conversations, but I understood what they were saying now.

We stood like that, Jackson with an arm around me and Finley on Lucas's other side, while York took the stage. He tapped the microphone. The loud thumps rattled through me as I braced myself again. Whatever happened next, we were in it together.

"Can I have your attention, please?" York's voice slithered through the speakers. "Tonight is such a special occasion that our very own Superintendent Bett is here to do the honors."

He clapped as Bett stepped out from the right wing of the stage, two gold envelopes in hand. Jackson tightened his grip on my shoulders as silence filled the ballroom, Lucas squeezing my hand. This wasn't good. If the superintendent was here, that meant they'd planned something of their own too.

Bett took the microphone from York, who stepped back into the shadows where he'd been all along. "Thank you for having me here tonight. I know you've been waiting for the results. Trust me, we have too," his drawl announced, mustache twisting with his own shit-eating grin. "The time has finally come to crown your 2024 Winter Lion Queen and King. You cast your votes, and I'm eager to see the *good* students you've chosen to represent HVHS." He made a show of opening an envelope with a flourish. "Your Lion Queen is . . . Yasmin Spencer!"

A round of applause followed Yasmin up the stage steps. York reappeared in the spotlight with a sparking tiara. Her eyes were teary as he placed it on top of her dark curls.

"And now the moment we have all been waiting for," Bett continued before Yasmin could have a chance to soak up her win. His rushed tone made my stomach turn. "Your Lion King this year is . . ." He opened the other envelope, pausing until his beady eyes found me in the crowd. "Presley Daniels!"

Heads snapped toward me in surprise, everyone hesitant to clap. I remembered what he'd said in York's office. *How did someone like you get a landslide of votes if it wasn't rigged?* I should have known this was how it'd end. How it was always going to end. They'd never allow a queer student to take the spotlight and represent HVHS. The election had been rigged, and judging by Bett's grin, he wanted me to know it.

I didn't give in to his antagonizing gaze. Instead, I smiled and clapped for Presley. There was nothing I could do. The fight was far from over, and we'd have to figure out another way to take down Watch What You Say. Not right now, though. Tonight was about having fun, not being soldiers in the war they'd forced us into.

"You're still my Lion King," Jackson said, holding me close.

Lucas shook his head, his perfect brows steep slopes of anger. "There's no way in hell you didn't win."

"Dude, that ain't right. Everyone voted for you. I *know* they voted for you," Fin added.

"It's okay," I promised them while Presley made his way onstage. "We'll figure something else out."

York's grin was too wide, too fake as he bestowed the golden crown onto Presley's golden mane. The perfect Lion King to represent HVHS. They'd finally gotten what they wanted.

"Now, your King and Queen will lead the promenade—"

Presley cut Bett off, pulling the microphone stand toward him. "Thank you to everyone who voted," he said into it. York shot him a questioning glare, but Presley gave one of those charming smiles that always got him his way. "It's a great honor to be your Lion King, but if a pack of lions is called a pride . . . I think someone else deserves this crown." He removed it from his head, holding it up to the audience. "This belongs to Last Boyfriends because they're the true leaders—"

"Enough!" Bett screeched over the burst of applause, his outrage skidding through the sound system.

He jerked the microphone away, and Presley stumbled to the side. The crown dropped to the stage by York's feet with a clank. Presley looked directly at me and mouthed, "I'm sorry." He may have been the absolute worst, but I didn't blame him anymore—I understood him better now. Understood how when someone was scared, like he had been in the bathroom, all they could do was react.

"Last Boyfriends are *not* leaders," Bett ranted. "They're cowards hiding behind anonymity, making outlandish claims to groom others into following their perverted agenda. Stupid, immature, unnatural, that's what they are." Boos erupted around us, and I swallowed roughly as he went wild-eyed. "Watch What You Say will put a stop to this nonsense, mark my words, and when I find out who they are, they *will* be sorry."

I breathed in deeply as Bett shoved Presley to the right wing of the stage, and York let it happen. Worry over his threat should have been eating away at me. But Dad's voice bolstered my courage—*Don't be afraid of a fight*—as I reached for my still-recording phone. We finally had the proof we needed.

But I was tired of hiding and reacting out of fear.

"We need to talk," I said, stopping the pocket recording.

The last time I'd been in the service corridor of Longleaf Farm, I'd been nervous. Nervous about following the plan. Nervous about revenge. Nervous about getting caught.

Tonight, it was different. There weren't any more nerves left.

"Legit cannot believe Presley just did that," Lucas said as he leaned back against the wall. He crossed his arms over his fuchsia tux. It'd seemed like a lifetime ago since he'd first worn it. Back in his bedroom underneath those stars we painted. When

I'd desperately wanted to tell him about Presley so I wouldn't be alone.

"Brah, I'm a little shocked."

"Dude—"

"Glitter Bomb," I said, finding my voice.

Finley's eyebrows shot up as he joined Lucas. "It's a thing we do," he told Jackson. "Glitter bombing with a secret."

"This must be juicy too." Lucas smirked, and his gaze darted from me to Jackson. "Did you suffocate him—"

"No," I interrupted. "It's . . . I can't . . . I can't do this anymore."

"Can't do what?" He briefly glanced at Finley, apprehension passing between them.

"Do you remember that comment about demanding visibility while hiding?" Both of them nodded, and I took a deep breath. "It got me thinking, and . . . I can't stay hidden anymore."

We now had the footage to make a new TikTok, but it didn't feel like enough. York was using our identity against us. Threatening us to keep quiet. And I refused to allow him to have that kind of control over me.

"With the school board meeting on Monday about all this, I want them to know who I am. For everyone to know Last Boyfriends are people too. That we're valid. That queer students matter, and they can't pretend we don't exist."

"Are you sure?" Lucas steadily held my gaze, and I nodded. "You know what'll happen, right?"

"Suspension, detention, expulsion. Whatever they try, I'm not scared."

Jackson slipped his hand into mine and squeezed reassuringly. "It can't get worse than it already is," he said. "This is all new to me, but the superintendent just called all of us cowards, perverts, and . . . I can't hide anymore either."

"We won't let y'all get dragged down with us," I added.

"I told you, booboo. You aren't taking the fall for this. Neither of you."

Finley shared a quick glance with Lucas, and they intertwined their own fingers. "Ezra," he began, "back when Logan outed me to the entire school, I had never felt so alone. That moment when he stopped the musical and everyone was looking at me, it had been terrifying. We won't let that happen to either of you. We're *all* Last Boyfriends, and we all go down together."

"Are you saying what I think you're saying?" I asked.

"That you're right. I know, don't get used to me admitting that," Lucas said with a teasing grin. "They need to see who the hell we are—that we're their students—before the school board meeting. That's the only way we're gonna win this, and I can't hide anymore either."

"I'm done hiding, too," Finley added. "Watch What You Say won't force me back in the closet."

"We're all coming forward as Last Boyfriends, then." It wasn't a question but a fact. All of us believed this was the right thing. Believed in ourselves. Believed *we* were the best revenge.

"The question is," Lucas began, arching one elegantly shaded brow, "when are we gonna go public?"

"Tomorrow." I tightened my grip on Jackson's hand, turning toward the ballroom. "Tonight, we deserve to go back in there and dance. They can't control how we react, not anymore."

Thirty-Three

"What you just watched is proof Acheron County's Watch What You Say initiative is based in hate." My face filled the screen, early morning sunlight flickering in my bedroom. I stared directly into the lens and spoke steadily without nerves. "My name is Ezra Hayes, and I'm no coward. I'm a Last Boyfriend."

The frame switched to Lucas at his vanity. Soft lighting caressed his golden-brown skin as he leaned into the camera. "My name is Lucas Rivera," he said, swiping mascara on his lashes. "I'm not stupid or immature. I'm a Last Boyfriend."

Another switch, this time Finley standing in front of Lewis Auto Sales. "My name is Finley Lewis, and I'm not unnatural." He smiled, shrugging once. "I am a Last Boyfriend."

Jackson was next, sitting on our sofa in his Nyberg jersey. "My name is Jackson Darcy, and . . ." His eyes looked off to the side to where I'd been encouraging him. "And I'm not sorry. I'm a Last Boyfriend."

I joined him, a glob of wing sauce on my lucky shirt. He

draped an arm around me and kissed my cheek. "We're coming forward because they need to know we're their students," I said, and then Jackson added, "We're human beings, and Watch What You Say is endangering our lives."

"They cannot pretend we don't exist anymore," Lucas said, both he and Finley in the office display cubicle.

"We refuse to be erased," Finley added.

The video finished with the footage we'd filmed last night at the formal—a simple "We're here!" all said together, all of us still in tuxes with tired smiles from dancing. Then it began to loop back to Bett's rant onstage in the ballroom. My thumb hovered over the upload button, too anxious to tap. Too anxious to think.

The soft trace of fingertips along my neck made me look up from the TikTok draft. Jackson was leaning back against the headboard, my head on his chest. It'd been too cold to talk outside after the game, and now we were on my bed—*my bed!*—and surrounded by the pressure of what we could do.

"Your heart's racing," he murmured, a soft laugh rumbling through him and into me. "You nervous?"

The way he asked, his words slipping out sharp, was the epitome of a loaded question. Because yes, we were about to reveal our secret identities to the world. It was more than that, though. *And the fact he's on my bed lookin' like a whole-ass snack.*

"Just a little," I admitted, listening for Dad's snores downstairs. He wouldn't be mad if he caught me with a boy in my room. It'd be much worse. Like a safe sex talk that'd teleport me onto a new plane of embarrassment.

"It's gonna be okay, Ez." He wrapped his arms around me in a cuddle of warmth. "Whatever happens, it'll be okay."

I sighed as he held me, his heartbeat matching my own, and looked up at him. "Everything could change, Jax."

"Except us." He leaned down, kissing the top of my head.

"Except us," I agreed as the curve of my smile dipped. "Unless your parents are gonna be mad and force you to stay away from me . . ."

His soft laughter made my head bounce against his chest. "They'll do the opposite," he said with certainty. "They're all for me standing up for my rights and everything you've done at school. I was given explicit orders to invite you for dinner so they can finally meet you."

"They might change their mind after I post the TikTok." I shrugged, and he scooted down so we were both stretched out on the bed. "We're for sure facing suspension and then maybe expulsion."

"Let's say we do get in trouble," he began, snuggling closer, "so what happens after that?"

"Depends on the school board meeting. Either they've heard us, or . . ." I swallowed roughly with sudden awareness of our bodies touching.

"Or?"

"Or we have to keep fighting until someone listens."

"See? No reason to be nervous, Ez. It's no different than what you've been doing all along."

"We shouldn't have to keep fighting this. It isn't fair. None of this is fair."

"I know." He buried his face in the crook of my shoulder, the soft tickle of his breath against my ear as he held me close. "Listen, no matter what happens Monday, it'll be okay."

"How can you be so sure?"

"Because a very"—he kissed my neck—"very smart guy once said that our favorite queer hockey hero believed in himself enough to come out and take a stand for queer rights. And I believe in you."

"Jax." My voice broke with his name, with his lips trailing along my ear.

"Yeah?" he whispered.

"Thank you for being incredible."

His mouth stilled, and he hitched a leg over my waist. Then the mattress squeaked suggestively as he straddled me. As he looked down at me in a way that made it hard to think.

Too hard. I panicked, but he smirked.

"No, thank you for what you've been doing, Ez."

My hands settled on his thighs, the shifting weight jolting through me. Our lips met in a tender kiss, our tongues brushing before I broke it off to look up at him. At the constellation of freckles and the tiny scar and blue mixed with the green of his stare. At all the ways he made me feel real and alive within these gray walls.

"I don't care what happens," I whispered urgently. "It doesn't stop what we're doing. We'll have dinner with your parents and watch more hockey games and double-date with Lucas and Finley and keep existing. That's what matters. What we have to do."

"I'm happy to exist with you."

He kissed me again, stars filling my vision as his hips ground down. I forgot about the worry and the draft waiting to be uploaded to TikTok. Forgot the world was about to crash down around us. Forgot everything as I committed this moment to memory.

He leaned back, a flush of red creeping up from the scruff of his jaw. His floof of hair was stuck to his forehead with sweat as he looked up above my bed. "Wait, is that a limited-edition Nyberg jersey from his first year on the Slammers?"

My hungry eyes raced up his body, up the arch of his neck to his mouth open in awe. "Yeah," I breathed out heavily.

"And he continues to impress," he declared with his lopsided grin that reminded me I was anything but boring and average.

That made me feel at ease with tapping that upload button.

Everything changed overnight.

There were no more conspiracy theories. Everyone now knew we were Last Boyfriends. *Harper Valley Tattler* posted us on Facebook as the "delinquents" who trashed the field, and my dad fought for us in the comments. Our TikTok upload skyrocketed to 10 million views in less than twelve hours, the whole world watching. Despite the millions of likes and thousands of encouraging messages and even Maeve Kimball's duet—despite all that, it didn't feel like real life.

None of it would feel real until we faced the consequences. Then I'd know we'd done *something*.

While I braced for HVHS's reaction, there was an odd sense of normalcy outside the bubble of notifications. I still had to get up and clean my room. Study for finals. Hide the hickey on my neck. Pretend like nothing was wrong and decorate for Christmas. Talk Dad down from the "I have the mind to kick that superintendent's ass" ledge. Come to work and pretend not to hear the whispers when customers recognized me.

The Sunday-afternoon crowd was setting me on edge, though. Every time the door's three-ring chime sounded, my heart sprouted wings and tried to fly the coop. As though York or Bett would burst through the door, and I'd have to make a run for it.

Those three little rings ricocheted through me yet again, and I sprang up from the stool. "W-welcome to M-Magnolia," I managed, slumping against the counter. It was just Ms. Dion, though.

Ms. Dion?

I blinked several times, unsure if I was imagining her. She was severely out of place without the backdrop of a classroom. She nodded appreciatively at the banned book display, her lips tilting in a grin when she saw me.

"Kevin said I'd find you here," she said, crossing over to the front counter.

"My dad?" I asked as my brain caught up.

"I called to speak to you but thought it might be best if I came down to tell you in person."

"York's gonna kill me, isn't he?" I gripped my phone, and her eyes softened.

"He won't harass you again, that I can assure you." I forgot how to breathe as she paused in thought. "However, let's just say it may be best for you all to avoid school tomorrow. He'll make an effort to regain control and have you escorted off the premises."

"So we're expelled, then?"

"I'd lean more toward suspension until a disciplinary meeting is set, but that's not why I'm here."

"More bad news?" I asked with an unsteady breath.

She shook her head, fingers drumming against the countertop as she leveled her gaze. "Ezra, I've been a teacher for nearly eleven years, and what you boys did is by far the bravest thing I've ever witnessed."

"You don't think we were dumb?"

Contemplation etched itself across her forehead. "Fighting for what's right is never stupid. Well, maybe breaking the law to vandalize a football field wasn't the brightest, but that's beside the point. I saw your video this morning on my For You Page—"

"You have TikTok?"

"I'm not ancient." She rolled her eyes. "I've been following all the media attention you've gotten. The outpouring of support in this school district alone is incredible. Now that you're not hiding anymore, and as a representative for the teachers' union, I'm here to formally invite Last Boyfriends to the meeting tomorrow."

"The school board meeting?"

She nodded encouragingly.

"What can we do?"

"What can't you do? You've incited a student rebellion, rallied a protest in the hallways of HVHS, and"—she glanced around before lowering her voice—"you have blown the goddamn lid off this thing. You, Lucas, Finley, and now Jackson."

"We haven't done anything yet."

She pointed a finger at me. "You've found your voice despite Watch What You Say, and now we need Last Boyfriends to speak to the school board. They're discussing the petition for Superintendent Bett's resignation and the complaints against Principal York."

"Will it be enough?"

"Everything you've done is more than enough."

This is real life, I thought. York had harassed me multiple times because of Bett, and I wouldn't let them do it again. I wouldn't stop fighting until they were the ones who were sorry. *This is something. A chance to take control.*

"Okay," I said. "I'll make sure we're there."

"Three-thirty tomorrow," she added. "At the Acheron County Board of Education over in Sulfur Springs . . ."

I was already texting a new message to the group chat before she could finish talking. If the teachers' union wanted us to speak out against Watch What You Say, then we needed a game plan. And the best way to organize revenge tactics involved a dry-erase board and a red marker.

Thirty-Four

YOU AREN'T ALONE. WE ARE ALL LAST BOY-
FRIENDS.

♡ 1.2M

Maeve Kimball's top comment had inspired thousands more like
it, but I kept scrolling to hers. *You aren't alone.* A little over two
months ago we had been, though. The background was blurry
in that perfect picture schools had painted all across the South.
Out of focus and lonely. Our voices had been silenced before
we'd learned how to speak, our feelings buried as we learned to
tolerate it.

But not anymore.

We weren't the same people as before. This wasn't some
revenge scheme against ex-boyfriends. This was something more
than accepting the way we were treated, more than allowing ourselves to be erased or pushed to the background. We were Last
Boyfriends, Lucas and Finley and Jackson and me and everyone
else screaming until we were heard.

When we'd first walked through those double doors of

Rivera Furniture, we'd been on a broken-hearted, broken-spirit vendetta. Unaware of where that red zigzag of carpet would lead us. More than two months had passed since the three of us sat down and wrote what we'd thought we wanted on the dry-erase board. Now, millions were with us as we tackled the last rule for revenge.

Take down Watch What You Say.

"Ms. Dion came to see me earlier at work," I announced, swiveling the chair back around.

"How screwed are we?" Lucas asked from across the table. He had rolled closer to Finley, closer than they'd sat the last time we'd been here. "They're gonna ruin us, aren't they?"

"We aren't gonna give them the chance," I said, looking to Jackson. We'd talked it through when he'd come in for his shift. He nodded in encouragement, pulling the hoodie over the bite mark on his neck. "We're gonna skip school so they can't cause a scene."

"And do what?" Finley asked, scooting even closer.

"Prepare for the school board meeting tomorrow." One of Lucas's wordless expressions raised a question. "The teachers' union wants us all to speak on Watch What You Say as Last Boyfriends."

"Holy shit," Lucas gasped.

"Ditto," Jackson agreed. He'd been nervous when I'd told him, worried about what to say. That was the reason we were here.

"We have to figure out how to present our case," I explained. "Make them understand the bullshit they've put us through."

"We'd literally have to write a book." Lucas shook his head in disbelief. "How would we even begin to explain it?"

I nodded once and stood, crossing over to the dry-erase board. A familiar thrill ran up my spine as the new reality set in. We were finally doing this, finally being heard.

"Lucas," I began, reading his loopy handwriting, "why did you write down 'Sabotage HalloWeird Party'?"

"To ruin Cass's ego and show everyone how big of an ass he is."

"Why?"

"Because he was so obsessed with his perfect image."

"Exactly." I turned toward him. "York is one of Bett's puppets. He's focused on keeping 'family values' intact through the initiative, and that's where we begin. Ruin the perfect image they've been peddling by addressing what they've really done to students."

"I see where you're going with this." Lucas held up a hand, counting off. "Banning books, targeting students with intersectional identities, eliminating support for mental health in school, not allowing same-sex couples to buy tickets to formal . . . god, I could go all night."

"I know," Finley said under his breath, and Lucas's ears went pink.

"Brah," Jackson groaned.

"Hey, at least we're not the ones with hickeys, dude."

Lucas shook his head and mouthed, "Not where you can see at least." I nodded in appreciation. That was a definite Glitter Bomb that'd require extensive details later.

I got us back on topic, clearing my throat. "Finley, why did you want to enter the drag competition?"

"Because I wanted to show Logan I'm not ashamed to be who I am." He gave a sharp nod as he caught on. "We can tell them how they've made us feel."

"Watch What You Say has deliberately tried to invalidate our identities."

They nodded in agreement, and Jackson waved toward the board. "What about yours?" he asked. "You wanted to run for Winter Lion King for a reason."

I followed his line of sight to my handwriting from so long ago. "I wanted to be seen as Presley's equal."

"For the record," he said, "you're so much more than he'll ever be."

"Speaking of equal"—I spun around to the board, cheesy grin in place, and tried to focus—"they haven't been treating us like we are."

Run for Winter Lion King was an echo of the past. I wasn't the same person who'd written it. That version of me had no voice, hid in plain sight, and did his best not to exist.

Taking a deep breath, I turned back to the table. "Last Boyfriends has showed them the consequences of treating us like we're less than," I said. "We need to remind them of that."

Jackson smiled weakly and shrugged. "I don't have anything up there, but—"

"Yes, you do," I said, waving toward him. "You're the reason I wrote 'Take down Watch What You Say.'"

"I was?"

"Everything you've done, coming out and supporting me and being proud of who you are—that's why I wrote it. You inspired me to fight back."

He didn't say anything as he swallowed roughly, as we met each other's gaze. A memory of him, bloodshot eyes and snotty nose, came to mind. How he'd just been kicked off the football team and I'd finally saw the real him. Underneath it all, he'd been someone who risked everything to be himself.

"And we have to do the same tomorrow."

"Will it be enough?" Lucas asked. "Will the school board even listen to us or that petition or the complaints about York?"

Everything you've done is more than enough, Ms. Dion had said. The attention we'd gained on TikTok and the news and the support of other schools in Acheron County and . . .

I grabbed my phone from the table. Our account was still pulled up when I unlocked the screen. Clicking the comment section, I scrolled until I saw Maeve Kimball's username.

"They might not listen to us, but there are millions of Last Boyfriends now."

"What do you mean?" Finley asked, leaning forward.

"That we don't have to do this alone." I glanced back at my phone, at the TikTok account with millions of followers. That was the answer. If we wanted to be seen, we had to make a scene. "What if we made a post about the meeting tomorrow—"

"Then everyone who can will show up," Lucas said with a slap to the table.

"Dude, just think about all the protesters in Acheron County alone."

"Exactly." The news coverage of the protests in Texas flickered through my mind. Students picketing and chanting our battle cry. The cry we'd started at HVHS with the shirts and the pride lions. "If we ask people to join us, we can fight this. We can make damn sure they know who the hell they're dealing with."

"What are we waiting for?" Jackson asked, already out of his seat.

I nodded, feeling more and more sure by the second. Lucas and Finley followed suit and crowded around me. All we had to do was record a message and call on the millions to stand as Last Boyfriends. If they did, we'd have a shot of making Watch What You Say go away. Maybe the news would pick it up, too, and—

"Oh my god!" I yelled too loudly, nearly dropping my phone with shaky hands.

"What?!" Lucas shrieked, stumbling backward into Finley.

"The news!" I waved my phone and turned to Jackson. "Remember? Vivian Singh wanted to interview us for *GMA*?"

His eyes widened in understanding while Lucas gripped my arm. "Ezra Hayes, you mean to tell me we could be on *Good Morning America*?"

"We could if I message her back." I blinked rapidly as my

brain raced to catch up. "If she'd be willing to come to the meeting tomorrow, then we could do the interview there. Go big or go home."

Lucas nodded, glancing at Finley. They shared a silent exchange that had somehow become their thing. "I do like to go big," he said with a mischievous glint in his eye. "Let's do it."

Thirty-Five

Growing up in a small town is a game of hide-and-seek. You're waiting to be found or waiting to find something better. Either way, you're waiting for life to happen.

For seventeen years, I'd waited.

I'd thought Presley found me last summer, but he'd forced me to hide until I forgot who I was. Letting myself disappear in what I thought love was supposed to feel like and everything everyone else forced me to be. All this time, I should have been seeking. There was something better beyond all the hiding spots. Beyond the long hallway of HVHS and the fields racing out of town.

The best revenge, I thought as farmland flashed by.

Dad's work truck jostled along the county road. He raised a finger in a wave each time a car passed in the opposite direction. Though everything would change when we reached the GPS's destination, he had no sense of urgency—only the soft humming of the tires on asphalt and the ease with which he steered. His confident grip of one hand on the wheel, the other on the gearshift, was calming. He knew where we were headed. We'd get there no matter how many potholes he had to navigate around.

The late-afternoon light flickered across his MY SON IS HERE shirt as he drove around the final bend to Sulfur Springs. I thought of everything that'd happened since I'd come out in seventh grade, since that classic movie night at Twinkle Lights. And yet, he was still proud of who I am.

He smiled over at me, slowing down at the four-way stop. *You're Ezra Hayes. Don't forget that.* "Thanks, Dad," I told him, told the memory. "I couldn't do this without you."

The signal blink-blinked as he laughed. "This was all you," he said, turning right. "Good things happened because you raised a little hell."

"Because you raised me to be a hellion," I pointed out.

"Then my job as a dad has officially been successful."

"You say that now, but . . ."

We passed the Sulfur Springs town limits sign, and he glanced over again. "Are you nervous?"

"Not really." I leaned back against the headrest, breathing deep. Watching how he steered so easily. Counting down until we'd be there. "I'm ready to do this."

"Listen to me, okay?" He locked eyes with me for a second, and I nodded as he regarded the road ahead. "Whatever happens today, happens. The school board might listen to y'all, or they may choose to ignore you. That doesn't make what you're doing any less important. When you stand up for what's right, there will be people who try to make you sit down. You have to keep getting right back up."

"I will, Dad."

He was right. There wasn't a guarantee we'd be successful in having Watch What You Say removed, but we could try. Fight until we won. Keep fighting in the Last Boyfriends Student Rebellion.

"Good." He clapped me on the knee and then shifted gears, picking up speed. "You aren't alone. I'll always be here anytime you get knocked down."

Sunshine beamed across his face. I catalogued the wonky Hayes nose, the charming smile, the beard with more gray than I remembered—everything that made him my dad. If it wasn't for him, I don't think I would have ever learned how to believe in myself.

"Everything all right?" he asked, noticing my stare.

"Everything's fine." For once I meant it. Everything would be fine because I'd keep fighting for something better.

He nodded in understanding, following the GPS onto Lake Drive. His foot eased on the brake as flickering red lights filled the cab. The road was blocked by a truck with VOLUNTEER FIRE DEPARTMENT emblazoned on the driver's door. A woman in a baseball hat reading the same stepped out, motioning for Dad to roll his window down.

"Howdy," she called with a slight nod. The flashing lights washed over her dark brown skin as she drew near. "You folks'll have to go around. Lake Drive has been closed."

"Appreciate it, ma'am," Dad said, checking the dash clock. It was nearly three o'clock already. "We're supposed to be up at the town square."

She laughed, bracing an arm on the windowsill. She took a

look at Dad's shirt and pointed over her shoulder with a thumb. "You and thousands of others. That's why I'm here, for crowd control."

Thousands? I craned my neck to see around her, and my heart slingshotted. Lake Drive was a sea of protesters flowing three blocks up the hill. The sight of picket signs with our battle cry, the bright rainbow flags, the support blurred my vision.

"It worked," I said hoarsely.

The woman considered me for a moment. "You're Ezra," she said with a kind smile, recognition in her eyes. I nodded at her through the tears. "My so—I mean, daughter. Sorry, this is new to me, but I'm learning." She patted the windowsill and stood upright. I caught sight of a tiny pride flag pinned to her jacket collar. "I dropped her off to protest. She's up there now, waiting on you with everybody else."

"Is there another way around?" Dad asked.

"I'm 'fraid not." She shook her head, looking back over her shoulder. "There's too many people. All roads to the square are blocked. The only way from here is on foot."

I checked my phone. It was 2:50 p.m., and there were no new messages. "The reporter will be set up in front of the building in ten minutes," I said, checking our group chat. My last message still hadn't gone through.

Dad nodded once at the woman and turned to me. "Why don't you run on ahead? I'll find a place to park and will be right behind you."

"Are you sure?" I glanced nervously at the crowd migrating up the hill.

"Bud, I have never been more sure." He leaned across the console and pulled me into a quick hug. "This is your moment, okay?"

"I got this." My grip was sweaty on the door handle. I wiped it on my jeans and looked back at him. "I got this, right?"

"You're Ezra Hayes," he answered.

Every bit of advice he'd ever given me was wrapped up in those three words. I breathed roughly, leaning back across to give him another hug. "Love you, Dad."

"Love you too, son." He patted my back. "Remember, whatever happens—"

"Keep getting back up."

And that's what I planned to do.

I opened the truck door and climbed out, standing tall. A wave of voices from the crowd rolled on the cold December wind. Breathing it in, I waited for Dad to pull forward. He nodded at me, and I did the same, taking off.

My footfalls slapped the sidewalk, and I gulped in the chilly air. Each breath brought with it a memory as my mind darted around every WE'RE HERE shirt. I could feel that metal lighter in my hand, hear the clink as the flame ignited. Still smell the scorching smoke of the burning HVHS logo that started this fire.

"Down with Watch What You Say!" someone yelled.

Another cried, "We are all Last Boyfriends!"

"Ezra!"

"That's Ezra!"

"Move out of his way!"

The sea parted, clearing a path for me. Their yells matched

the pounding heartbeat in my ears. I hit the incline up to the town square. It was like the hill in our Middlebury subdivision. I'd run up it too many times for other people, never for myself. Running away from everything that I'd thought was wrong about me. Now I was running toward something right. Something that truly mattered.

This time, I was running for me.

When the sidewalk leveled out at the top, I saw the red van. *Birmingham News* had already set up to record their partner interview for tomorrow's *Good Morning America*. My three best friends were huddled together near it, scanning the crowd.

I pushed harder, and my calves joined the screams of protest. As though he could hear my frantic heartbeats, Jackson found me in the crowd. Never would I get used to seeing him smile at me like that.

"H-hey," I called through heavy breaths, running toward them. "I wasn't . . . I didn't expect . . . so many . . ."

"There you are!" Lucas yelled in relief. "We've been trying to text you about all this." He waved his hand frantically toward the protestors. "There's no cell service with this many people."

Jackson collided against my chest, wrapping his arms around me. "Hey," he whispered. "I was worried you wouldn't make it."

"And miss this?" I asked, holding on to him. Hanging on for everything.

Over his shoulder, I looked out at the crowd I'd just run through. There were so many faces I didn't recognize, but the few I did filled me with pride—Sam and Kasey, their friends Aiden and Shyla, Filip, our ex-boyfriends, and— *Wait, Presley's here?* He was wearing a shirt with his own message of I'M HERE and cheering loudly with everyone else.

We made brief eye contact, and he nodded. I could still smell his jacket, the scorching smoke. Every picket sign, every shout, every proudly waving rainbow flag fanned the flames. Our fire had spread. There was no putting it out.

"You ready?" I asked, pulling away from the hug.

"I'm ready," Jackson said, and laced our fingers together. "For a lot of things." He squeezed, and I knew we'd keep on existing together no matter what happened next.

"As ready as I'll ever be, dude," Finley added. "I've memorized everything to say to the school board—"

"Think he meant the *GMA* interview, Fin," Lucas whispered with an endearing laugh.

"Oh, the interview will be easy," he said. "We've been preparing for it ever since we watched *The First Wives Club*."

Jackson gave me a puzzled look. "We'll have a movie night this weekend," I promised him.

"Who would've thought me getting dumped would lead us here?" Lucas asked as Vivian Singh climbed out of the news van. "I wouldn't change anything. Okay, maybe a few things. Like, hello, I would've called him Cass the Ass a hell of a lot sooner."

I snorted, watching the shine of light against her sleek hair. Watching the ripple of the crowd turn toward us. As the ripples of everything we'd done began to overlap.

"Whatever happens," I began, smiling as Vivian approached us, "they don't own us."

"They can't tell us what to do," Lucas added.

"Or tell us what to say," Finley concluded, grabbing Lucas's hand.

Vivian grinned a pearly white smile, and the crew member on her heels flipped a switch on his camera. I blinked away the brightness. "Finally!" She beamed, clutching her microphone. "It's truly an honor to meet the Last Boyfriends."

"Thank you for agreeing to do this under our terms, Ms. Singh," I said. "We appreciate your coverage of our battle against Watch What You Say."

"It has been so inspiring watching what you've done, and hey! I appreciate the chance to be on *Good Morning America*!" She laughed, its chime easing the last remnants of tension. "Do you mind if we start recording?"

The time had come for us to be heard, to say everything they didn't want us to. As the red light blinked on the camera, I heard York in my mind. *Ezra, you used to be a quiet student,* he'd told me once.

And now it was time to show him how loud I really was. How loud we could be.

"I'm Vivian Singh reporting on location in Acheron County with some very special young leaders for an inside story on the Last Boyfriends Student Rebellion."

The cameraman panned toward the crowd, a loud chant rising. "We're here! We're here. We're here!" I gripped Jackson's hand and felt his calloused palm against mine. Dad told me to be in the moment, and now I knew what he meant. What he had been telling me all along. It was amazing what you could accomplish when someone believed in you—when you believed in yourself.

Vivian held out the microphone and asked us to introduce ourselves. I cleared my throat, finding Lucas's other hand. The four of us were a united front. We existed in this moment, and we'd keep right on existing after the interview and the school board meeting and the decisions people forced on us. Keep standing back up instead of shrinking down. This was only the beginning, and there were more students out there who needed a voice.

"We're Last Boyfriends," I said, staring directly into the camera. The spotlight was on us, and there was nowhere to hide as everyone watched. Nothing could hurt me, not anymore.

We were here. And we were fighters.

Acknowledgments

"We're here" is a powerful reminder that we—the queer community who has never once stopped fighting—exist. It became my battle cry when I wrote *The Last Boyfriends Rules for Revenge*. As the story was taking shape in my mind, Florida House Bill 1557 began targeting queer students. I watched in horror as events unfolded, and I felt helpless. So I did the only thing I could control and started typing.

It took me eleven years and five manuscripts to get here. I didn't know writing *The Last Boyfriends Rules for Revenge* would lead to my first book deal—all I knew was the rage I felt. And I had to write it. During early mornings and late nights, my anger strengthened into resilience right along with Ezra's, Lucas's, and Finley's. The result is my fight back, and to have this story make my lifelong dream a reality fills me with such great pride.

None of this would have been possible if it weren't for my literary agent, Katie Shea Boutillier, who believed in my words when I needed it most. Thank you, Katie, for everything you've done to get me here and for representing the stories I want to tell. I still remember pitching you *The Last Boyfriends Rules for Revenge* with one single line, and you immediately *knew*. The direction you gave me made all the difference. You nurtured my idea every step of the way, and I'm a better writer because of it.

When I first spoke with my editor, Alison Romig at Delacorte Press, I *knew*. She understood my story, my characters, and my mission. To have someone both in my corner and fighting alongside me made editing a joyful experience. Ali, you took *The Last Boyfriends Rules for Revenge* to the next level with your genius insight. Working together was like the spark Ezra ignited by burning that jacket—but both of us *knew* what it meant. Thank you for believing in my story (and loving *The First Wives Club*).

Can we take a moment for this book cover's rainbow flames? Because c'mon! It was designed by Casey Moses and illustrated by Jess Vosseteig—thank you both for giving *The Last Boyfriends Rules for Revenge* the most perfect dream cover. Furthermore, working with the fabulous publishing crew has been a dream. Thank you to my marketing team of Megan Mitchell, Jasmine Ferrufino, and Michael Caiati; publicist Kim Small; managing editor Tamar Schwartz; copy editor Colleen Fellingham; interior designer Megan Shortt; production manager Shameiza Ally; and everyone else at Delacorte Press, Underlined, and Random House Children's Books for treating this story with such care and understanding.

Writing is a vulnerable experience, and I almost gave up on my dream many times. However, my husband, Chris, encouraged me to keep trying. Chris, thank you for believing in me even when my list of failures grew long. All the times I cried, you were there for me. And when I told you the Big Book News, you cried for me. Your support pushed me to type *The End*— and if it weren't for you making me watch *The First Wives Club* back when we were just boyfriends, none of this would have happened. I love you more than I can put in words.

Thank you to K.J. (Kelly) Brower for cheering me on, listening to me monologue about my characters, and keeping me supplied with emergency candy while I wrote. Thank you also to Anthony Nerada for sharing the pep talks as we both embarked on this journey. I appreciate you both, and notifications from our group chat BOOP always make me smile.

Thank you to my soul friends Callie + Chris (aka The Other Chris) Perry and Haley Jones. I'm so appreciative of the laughs, nearly unbelievable true stories, and wondrous trips around the world. Our friendship has worked its way into my fictional ones.

Thank you to Natalie Lloyd, my fellow Chattanooga author. You've been by my side since we met at Star Line Books and have offered me the best advice. I'm so grateful I get to call you a friend.

Thank you to my agent sibling and friend Ellen O'Clover. You have been there for me since this story was only a spark of an idea. I'm so happy our friendship has grown through our monthly phone chats, virtual hand-holding, and uplifting messages.

Thank you to Diana Urban and Elizabeth Eulberg for graciously guiding me through decisions with kindheartedness. Thank you also to Becky Albertalli, Rebekah Faubion, Emily Henry, Jason June, Brian D. Kennedy, Liz Lawson, Ryan La Sala, Steven Salvatore, Adam Sass, Phil Stamper, and Julian Winters for sharing wisdom on this journey and welcoming me with kindness. Additional thanks to Sydney Langford, Erin Baldwin, and Clare Edge from the 2024 Debut Group for your motivation and enthusiasm.

In no small measure, thank you to Caleb Finley, Caroline Mickey, Megan Emery Schadlich, Sarah Jackson + Blaes Green + Emily Lilley from my local indie bookstore The Book and Cover, and Star Lowe. Your friendship, words of encouragement, beta-reading feedback, and love for the story I've created make my heart happy.

Thank you to my parents, who taught me to read and spell before I even started school. You nurtured my love of books—even driving me an hour to the nearest store to get them—and raised me to stand up for myself. I love you both.

Thank you to Joan Reeves, my college English professor. You taught me to always seek to better myself, and I'm forever grateful that your assignment was the jumping-off point for me wanting to become a writer.

How could I write about hearts breaking and being put back together without Taylor Swift's music? Not because of tabloid nonsense but rather because of the dignity and grace she gives herself. Thank you, Taylor, for your heartfelt songwriting, helping me navigate tough emotions ever since your first album, and exhibiting the strength it takes to stand up for what you believe in.

Last but not least, thank you for reading *The Last Boyfriends Rules for Revenge.* I hope you continue to believe in yourself no matter the hate people spew, no matter how many times they tell you to sit down when you try to take a stand, no matter how hard the fight becomes. It is the best revenge, after all.

About the Author

Matthew Hubbard writes the kind of stories he wishes he had as a teen in rural Alabama. He grew up on a mountaintop farm and knows more than he is willing to admit about small towns. He studied English, marketing, and psychology in college and has spent a majority of his life speaking up to make a difference. When he isn't writing, Matthew can be found on a hike in search of breathtaking views, reading as many books as he can get his hands on, and cheering for his favorite hockey team. He currently lives in Chattanooga with his husband, their dogs, Layla and Phillip, and Jay Gatsby the cat. *The Last Boyfriends Rules for Revenge* is his debut novel.

MATTHEWHUBBARDWRITES.COM